I0716372

BEARDS

A Novel

CHEYENNE ISLES

PAGE 23 PRESS

ISBN 978-1-7380604-0-5 (paperback)
ISBN 978-1-7380604-2-9 (hardcover)
ISBN 978-1-7380604-1-2 (ebook)

Cover design and illustration by Samuel Perez

Published by Page 23 Press
www.page23press.ca

To my beautiful wife Karen, who's always there to love and support me.

&

*To my Grandparents — Albert and Ann — who always told me to
pursue my dreams.*

CHAPTER ONE

AUDRA

As hard as I tried, I couldn't seem to shake the nauseous feeling I had in the pit of my stomach. It had been a long time since I'd felt uncomfortable with what I was doing but, there I was, acting against my better judgment. Vivian had said I was just uneasy, that I "always had a discord with my parents." *Discord* was a delicate way to put it. I never got along with the idiotic ideals they had for me. In fact, I never agreed with anything that came out of their mouths. They were closed-minded and mean. I grew up in the south, in a small town outside of the city, to parents who were far too religious for my apparent "liberal thinking ways". Back home in Georgia the neighbors might've said otherwise. They considered my Ma and Pa to be the kindest folks they've ever crossed paths with. Perhaps that was true if they shared the same political view and were of a fairer nature. Anything past what might've been considered a good tan and they make some horrid remark and not think twice about it. It wasn't uncommon for our area – they were all prejudiced. That was just one of the reasons I couldn't wait to leave that God forsaken town.

Growing up, I'd never been popular. I might've looked and dressed like all the girls in my neighborhood, but our interests weren't anything alike. While all the other girls played with their dolls, I'd want to go exploring through the creek with the boys. While all the other girls were reading fashion magazines, I'd be reading *The Three Musketeers* for the third time that year. While all the other girls got ready for our high school dances, I'd be sitting on a park bench sketching. I was never one to have strong beliefs in something one minute and then change them the next just to impress someone or have them like me. If I believed in something I would outright say so.

When I was younger my classmates considered me a bit odd, so I guess I should've seen my cousin's foolish nickname for me catching on like a dang plague. *Audi the Odd Girl* – that's what they'd call me. For years I'd hear everyone in the halls giggle and mock me, but I did everything I could not to let it get to me... or at least... not let it show. At some point I thought that maybe if I had a few more friends everyone might've stopped joking about me, but that would require making friends with people I couldn't stand.

I rode the next few years out on my own, with only a select few people to pass the time with. I was never one to really care about my looks, but I couldn't help but notice the older I got, the prettier I became. It didn't take long before the boys at school started to notice me too – even flirt a little. I'd disregard them and their stupid little comments. Ignoring them wasn't any harder than ignoring my parents and my little sister, Faith, back home.

Between school and home there were just too many mindless social rules I couldn't wrap my head around. What? Just because a boy at school flirts with you, you have to flirt back? No thank you. I didn't find my folks' opinions any less ridiculous. I never found the rules at home applied to me because they never made any sense to me. For example: why I couldn't play with Taye and his sister, Nan, from down the road. They'd been so kind as to share their bubble gum with me one day and we got along, but because they were colored it was like our friendship was a sin to my folks. Their thoughts never seemed to form any sense of logic to me. They'd rather me hang out with a good for nothing bum than a smart intellectual because of something so ridiculous as the color of our skin. Growing up my folks were always showing an intolerance to anyone who didn't share the same views or values they did, they were also the most unwelcoming people to anyone who was "different" – so to speak. Then again, so was the entire town.

I remember vowing from the age of nine when my Pa, Clyde Lynch, banned me from seeing Taye and Nan again that I would get as far away from the state of Georgia as I possibly could.

However, I never let my Pa's threats stop me from sneaking down to the creek to spend time with them. Taye and Nan were the only true friends I ever had. We'd go on adventures and talk about things we read. Nan's folks couldn't afford to buy her any books to read so I always lent mine to her. Anytime she'd finished a tale, we'd sit for hours and talk about the grand adventures the characters had. Like me, Nan's favorite was also *The Three Musketeers.* She was so in love with the book that soon enough our trio had the same nickname: *The Musketeers.* Most of the time I felt like Nan was the only one I could truly relate to. She never once made me feel insignificant or small like all the kids at school did. Although our friendship was a secret, Nan was without a doubt my best friend.

I remember everything being as peachy as it could be until I was about sixteen. I was sitting in the cafeteria when Bobby Michaels, the boy all the girls considered to be the most dashing fella in school, came up to me. I was reading a book when he took a seat, and I could tell he was looking at me, but I didn't look up. At least, not a first. I just kept my book in front of my face. I didn't know what was going on, but I could feel the red-hot glares from my classmates. I wasn't sure if it was a prank or what he wanted but my gut said something was about to go very wrong. I pursed my lips together in annoyance as he slowly pushed my book down, forcing me to look at him. I had put my dark brown hair behind my ears and crossed my arms, just staring at him; ready for whatever he was going to say. I waited a minute while he stared back, but when the length of silence between us became long enough to make me uncomfortable I finally piped up.

"Unless you have somethin' to say, may I please

continue readin' my book?" I frowned as he smiled.

"You know, Audi-"

"Audra."

"Huh?"

"My name ain't Audi, it's Audra. If you're gonna address me, do it proper," I had stared at his dumbfounded face. For a moment, I thought he was finally going to get up and walk away but instead he laughed.

I remember looking at him, confused. What the heck was Bobby Michaels doing talking to me? As he finally began to speak, I felt my stomach twisting into a tiny knot. He began to tell me how pretty I was, and how I was different from all the other girls he'd met. How sometimes when I spoke in class, he got what I was saying. I had looked around, confused. It had to have been a joke, a trick someone wanted to play on me. However, as he continued talking, I realized what he was saying wasn't a joke. The problem was, the more he complimented me and the more beautiful he said I was, made the unease in my stomach worsen. The feeling was not mutual.

I knew what was coming, and I could do nothing but wait for it. Finally, it happened, he asked me out. He wanted to take me to the malt shop and a romantic walk in the park. I remember feeling as though everyone was leaning in listening, waiting for an answer, watching for my reaction. I just kept thinking – why me? I never ran in any social circles, I never dolled myself up, never wanted any attention from no boy, yet there he was. The most handsome boy in school was asking me on a romantic date, probably planning to kiss me under the moonlight – it was every girl's dream, yet I just felt disgusted by the whole idea.

"I'm sorry to say I'm gonna have to decline, but I do appreciate the gesture," I had said as gently as I could. I heard a gasp from some of the eavesdroppers and suddenly felt a deep sinking feeling in the pit of my stomach. Bobby looked as though he'd been given a pop quiz he didn't study for. He looked completely blindsided. It quickly occurred to me: he probably wasn't very used to being turned down.

It took me all of two seconds to realize Bobby Michaels did not take my response very well. And despite every girl's thankfulness that their prayers had been answered when I opened my mouth, they were very confused as to what sort of girl could say no to Bobby Michaels.

By the end of the day rumors had spread around the school that I was a queer girl that everyone should avoid at all costs. I did my best to ignore the rumors. As I had reached home, just when I finally thought I was done with all that nonsense, Faith came barreling into the room.

"Is it true?" Faith had yelled in shock. "Did Bobby Michaels really ask you out?"

"Yeah, he did."

"Well," Faith paused, "you didn't actually say no, did you?"

"Yup. I did."

"Great," Faith dramatically flung her back against the wall, slowly sliding down it to a seated position, her large yellow dress surrounding her like a blanket. "My sister's a lesbian."

"What?" I had snapped. "I ain't no lesbian, and don't be sayin' that in front of Pa. He'll have you over his knee."

"I ain't judgin', I'm just sayin' what kind of girl says no to Bobby Michaels?"

"This one."

"Well, does *this one* happen to be a lesbian? That's what ev'ryone's sayin' and we don't even go to the same school. I mean, I don't care if you're a lesbian I just care ev'ryone's gonna be mean to me 'cause you're one. I'm already dealin' with bein' the sister of an outcast, how's it gonna look for me to be the sister of a lesbian outcast?"

"You're so selfish."

"I ain't selfish, you're bein' the selfish one, puttin' your lil' sister through this whole nightmare."

"Oh please, you're the dramatic one of the family. I just keep gettin' roped into things," I rolled my eyes and began to walk away. I stopped. Faith, my younger sister by five years, the perfect daughter who always did what our parents instructed, had said something that caught my attention. I had slowly turned around, "you said you didn't care if I was a lesbian... did you mean it?"

"Well, are you?"

"Nah, I'm just wonderin'."

"Well... I don't really know if I care or not. I mean, all Ma's friends say it's a bad thing, and to be scared of them queers, but I ain't never met a lesbian so I don't really know," Faith finally pulled herself up into a standing position.

"But you care if someone's black."

"That's different."

"How's it any different? Bein' black, or white, or gay ain't somethin' you can just choose."

"I guess. I mean, I think that if I met a homosexual it'd be the same as if I met a negro, you know?"

"No, I don't."

"Well, when I see a negro I ain't never rude, but I don't associate myself with 'em. So, I guess it'd be the same. I don't care if they're a homosexual, but if they're a homosexual I just can't associate."

"You ain't makin' no damn sense to me."

"Don't go swearin' now, Pa will get mad."

"I don't give a *damn* what Pa does."

"Well, you ought to."

"Like hell I do. First you say you wouldn't care if I'm a lesbian, next you say you wouldn't be able to associate with me, which is it?"

"I don't know."

"What do you mean you don't know?"

"I don't know, I'd ask Pa, I don't know what I'm s'posed to do."

"You're s'posed to be thinkin' for yourself," I sighed in disappointment. "For a minute I thought you'd surprised me, but you didn't. You're just like the rest of 'em."

"Audi, that ain't fair!" Faith pouted, her eyes welling up.

"My name is *Audra*." I had stormed out of the room, leaving my sister in the front hallway, confused and unsure of what had happened.

That evening I had snuck out of the house, desperate to meet up with Nan to tell her everything that had happened, but that evening Nan never came. In fact, the next few days I hadn't seen either Nan or Taye, and slowly I had begun to feel very, very alone.

Every day after school I went down to the creek and sat hoping one of them would show up, but no one ever did. It wasn't until two months into my routine of sitting at the creek, waiting for my friends, that I actually saw someone. I would always remember the day clearly. I was sitting on the ground, leaning against a large tree, when I had heard a few branches snap, taking my attention away from the book I was reading.

"Nan?" I called out. "Nan? Is that you?"

I had placed the book down beside my bag and began walking around, "Nan? Taye?"

Suddenly I had heard a small yelp, sending my attention straight upward to the branches above me. I gasped and looked away as I found myself peering up a young girl's dress.

"Sorry!" I apologized as I took a few steps to my right to see the girl's face.

Before I had a chance to say another word, the girl had finally unhooked the piece of garment that had gotten her caught to the tree and jumped down. I remember smirking, impressed by this girl's climbing abilities, *and* in a bigger dress than even Faith wore daily.

"Nah, I'm the one who's sorry!" the girl exclaimed, realizing my embarrassment, "I didn't realize anyone else was out here."

"Me neither," I replied. "I'm Audra."

"I'm Irene," the strawberry blonde smiled at me as she shook my hand firmly. "So, what brings you out to this neck of the creek?"

"Oh, I, um," I had paused, "I used to meet some friends here, but um, one day they just stopped showin' up."

"Why? Did somethin' happen to 'em?"

"I don't really know. I came here one day after a real bad day at school, and they weren't here. I know it sounds stupid, but I just keep comin' here ev'ry day, hopin' maybe they'll show up."

I sighed, wishing we went to the same school so I could ask if anyone had seen them. I thought about going to their school and waiting, but the last time I got caught hanging outside the school for colored folk, I nearly got beaten by Pa.

"I'm awful sorry to hear that," Irene replied, "I hope they're all right."

"Me too," I had responded, unsure why I felt so at ease with the girl. I'd just met her, but her soft face made me feel comfortable. "They were my best, well... my only friends."

"Really?" Irene looked at me unsure of how serious I was, "you ain't got no other friends?"

"I really like to keep to myself," I answered, "and to be honest the last few years no one's really been interested in bein' friends."

"Why's that? You got some hideous secret?"

"Nah, there's a rumor 'round my school that I like girls."

"Oh," Irene took a seat on the ground, "and is it

true?"

"Nah! Of course not, I just... well, a couple months ago I turned down a real cute boy and I guess that's a crime now. I s'pose the rumor is my consequence."

"I don't think that's a real bad consequence."

"No? Ev'ryone else sure thinks so."

"Well, ev'ryone else seems to be a bit brainless these days, don't you think?"

I smiled; it was the first time I felt like I was having a real conversation with someone since Nan. As the weeks passed by, we became closer, much closer, close enough that I swiftly came to realize that those rumors that went around about me weren't rumors at all, and if there were any rumors about Irene... well... they'd be true too.

Irene was my first, but not my last.

I took a deep breath as I cleaned off the dining room table, feeling an unsettled sensation in my stomach as I pondered over the past and how unhappy I'd been. Things had been going well for me, I mean, for the most part. The thought of my folks arriving kept bringing up feelings of frustration, and I was doing everything in my power to push those emotions down. I had been so isolated and miserable for so many years. Until my move to New York, I swore the only good memories I had from Georgia were those secret meetings with Nan and Taye, and of course those evenings with Irene. I wished I knew what had become of those three important people from my past. Every once in a while, I wondered if Nan and Taye were okay, and what became of Irene after her family moved away before the end of the school year.

"It's almost four o'clock," I heard my fiancé, William McMahon's voice as he entered the living room. *Fiancé.* I still couldn't wrap my head around the word. There were many things I had wanted in my life, but a marriage was never one of them. Now, there I was, a few months away from the day I never thought would come, the day that I would get married… and to a man no less. William snapped me out of my thought as he spoke again, "Audra, are you okay?"

"Yeah, I'm just not lookin' forward to havin' my parents here that's all," I replied, "the idea of them bein' here just keeps bringin' on all these bad memories."

"I know, but we all have bad memories, they're what make us who we are," William said as he put his arm around me and kissed me on the head. I smiled, wrapping my arms around his tall, thin build. He had the sweetest heart, always trying to calm anyone down in a crisis. If I was going to go through this with anyone, I was glad it was with him. From the moment we'd met we just clicked.

I glanced up as he ran his fingers through his shaggy ash blonde hair and sighed. He was nervous, I could tell. I had done nothing the whole week except share horror stories about my parents, and now they were coming up early to meet the man I'm supposedly marrying. It was no wonder he'd changed his outfit more times than Vivian and I combined that morning. He wanted to come across sophisticated but not too uptight; the kind of guy that a traditional southern man would approve of for his daughter. I kept trying to remind him my Pa was a drunk and wouldn't notice nor care what he wore, but Will decided not to listen to me. I laughed at his panic; I couldn't help it. Once he'd met my folks, he'd understand.

My head snapped up, as a knock sounded on the door. I froze; they were here.

"Lord have mercy," I took a deep breath. I had to put a hand on my chest to make sure my heart didn't leap out since it was pounding so hard.

I could feel William staring at me, waiting for me to make a move. He caught my attention when he leaned his tall frame down to look me in the eyes, "it'll be okay."

I nodded as a second knock came. Before either of us had a chance to move, Nathan came down the staircase, adjusting his collar and let out a half laugh glancing at both of us, "I guess I'll get it."

CHAPTER TWO

As I saw Nathan head towards the door, I finally spoke up in a half-joking manner, "allow me, kind sir, I am Audra's *fiancé* after all."

No matter how many times I said it, it didn't feel real. It seemed like only yesterday that we had agreed to put on this charade. At first, we agreed that this was a great idea but, as each day passed, Audra's feelings began to waiver. I could tell she still wasn't completely sold on the idea and, truthfully, I had some reservations myself.

I remember the day I asked Audra out to grab a bite. Nathan and Vivian had left early to attend one of Nathan's work dinners. Despite her exhaustion that evening, Vivian fixed her hair, put on her best doating wife façade, and headed out with him. I watched how the two of them were together, how they supported each other and maintained their appearances in their respective worlds.

They had gotten married about seven years ago,

when they were in their early twenties. Nathan was working at a law firm, slowly inching his way up the ladder, and Vivian was struggling in the academic world. She had fought to teach at a local New York university, working twice as hard to prove herself to male colleagues who didn't think a woman could educate as well as they could. The way Nathan had described it to me was that they both knew at some point they would've hit a social wall being single and driven - especially Vivian. She had already been criticized multiple times for trying to put a career over her family life, and her uptight socialite parents were coming down on her hard. Vivian's parents hold an annual charity ball every year at their estate, and that year her parents were apparently a little more chipper than usual. She had just assumed they had a bit more to drink than they normally would, but it wasn't until the son of her father's business partner thought the event would be a perfect time to ask for her hand in marriage. Nathan told me she was so winded that he had to reach out to support her, thinking she was going to faint any moment from the shock of it all. She barely even knew him, which made Nathan inclined to think Vivian's parents had tried to arrange the marriage. Perhaps they thought if she got married that she'd settle down with kids, but being a housewife just wasn't in Vivian. As she gently declined, she became acutely aware that every guest in the room was staring at her, shocked at her response. Vivian panicked and before she knew it, announced that she was waiting until after the ball to share the good news - that she and Nathan were getting married. I couldn't help but laugh when

Nathan tried to describe to me his disbelief as the words came out of her mouth, but in the moment, it wasn't as though he could do anything except go along with it. However, it was that evening that they'd both experienced a whole new world. Vivian was not once talked down to, and for the first time in a long time, felt respected – almost empowered. A woman able to balance a relationship and her work life? How impressive. Nathan also found himself being spoken to with a great deal of admiration. The fact that he was attractive, smart, and prepared to settle down at young age seemed to portray a sense of maturity to his superiors.

They both carried a heavily burdened secret, and suddenly they found a way to lighten it. Nathan told me Vivian was by far more terrified about her future, but with good reason. If Vivian had never gotten married, she would've been isolated and shamed for being a spinster, yet if Nathan remained single – he'd be a happy bachelor. It wasn't fair, but that was the way things were, and frankly, still are. As I recall, Vivian first discovered she had an interest in women when she was nineteen, during a summer she spent in Toronto attending a few lectures with classmates from school. She had gotten into a deep discussion with a woman who was speaking at the conference. One thing led to another, and Vivian quickly realized that perhaps she wasn't waiting to meet the right man, because she didn't want the right *man* - she wanted the right *woman*.

Nathan, on the other hand, had known since he was

young that he had an interest in men. Oddly enough, it was his mother that had sat him down and asked him when he was a teenager. His mother noticed he wasn't chasing girls around the same way all his friends were, yet he seemed to have an interesting relationship with their paperboy. I'd always been a fan of Mrs. Porter; she was the perfect supportive mother anyone could ask for, especially in this day-and-age. If my parents were still around, I would've hoped they'd react the same way to finding out I was gay as Mrs. Porter did when Nathan came out.

Nathan and Vivian decided to get married to hide their secret. To the outside world they were the perfect, doting couple – when in reality they were able to go out and date other people. No one would ever know.

I thought about it for a long time, whether Audra would be open to the idea of us following in the same footsteps. We weren't necessarily faced with the same pressures that Nathan and Vivian had been, but sometimes I thought it might be a bit easier. I'd been dating Nathan for nearly five years. Audra and Vivian had basically been joined at the hip as often as they could for nearly three years now. We all lived in the same three-story townhouse. We had our routines and our lives sorted out; not that we shared the details of our living arrangements with anyone, but it made a lot more sense that two married couples were sharing the rent on such a large space than a married couple and some friends. Plus, even the way they supported each other at work functions or family gatherings was admirable. Any time Vivian's family has a socialite event, Nathan is right by her side to take off any of that pressure. Not that I had any family I needed to impress, but for work or even tax reasons I thought it might be worth exploring. Plus, Audra couldn't deny it'd be nice to stop being harassed. They'd see her shiny little ring, and no one would ever question when she's planning on getting married, or who she's with, or any of those silly little things they push on women - especially one in her late twenties. Not that we're old but, from what I've noticed, if a girl isn't settled down by then people seem to think they have permission to be rude, particularly other women. Weren't women supposed to support each other, not knock each other down? Apparently not.

When I proposed the idea to Audra, so to speak, she just stared at me blankly. But, in her defense, I probably should've opened with something other than, "will you marry me?" I may have jumped the gun a bit and blindsided her with that. Once I explained more along the lines of what I meant, she was less shocked but still didn't come across as open to the idea as I thought she might've been. For someone that was so suppressed in every aspect of her life for so long and fought to just be free, it was understandable that she wasn't too thrilled about the idea of becoming my beard. However, she didn't say no. She thought about it, for longer than I'd anticipated. Truthfully, I think Vivian might've had a hand in her decision - to this day Audra still seems unnerved about the idea.

I glanced back at Audra who stood waiting for me to greet her parents. I couldn't tell who was more anxious between the two of us. I took a deep breath and composed myself before I opened the door, revealing the couple standing on the other side. On the right stood a tall, broad, and overweight man in his sixties with dark grey hair and a moustache. Next to him stood a woman who looked like an older, much more feminine Audra. She was about five foot seven or so in her heels, but she still looked petite next to her husband. Her pitch-black hair was large and done up with so much hairspray that it looked stiff as a board. However, I couldn't smell the faintest whiff of it as the stench of her perfume took over the room. It was so strong I wouldn't have been surprised if she had bathed in it. Her bright ruby red lips popped against her fair skin, and she flashed me a kind smile.

"Hello, welcome," I finally said. "You must be Mr. and Mrs. Lynch."

"We sure as heck are. Willie, is it?" Clyde grabbed my hand before I had a chance to offer it myself.

"William," I corrected him.

"That's what I said, ain't it?"

"Not quite."

"Hi, Pa," Audra said from behind me. I felt myself get pushed as Clyde's large frame barreled past me to greet his daughter. I shifted to the side so that her mother could enter afterwards. She was kind enough to actually *wait* for me to move. I closed the door after she made her way in.

"Well, look who it is," Clyde roared, "I almost didn't recognize my little Audi all grown up... and gettin' married... to a man! Guess 'em awful little rumors weren't true, huh, Audi?"

I watched as Audra winced at the sound of *Audi*. Apparently, I was not the only one blessed with a bad nickname.

"It would appear so, wouldn't it?" she replied.

"Well, now, don't be rude. Introduce me to your little friends here. I already know your future husband, Willie, here-"

"William," I corrected again. "Or just... Will... even," I trailed off. Maybe I shouldn't have said anything. Then again, did I really want every Christmas card sent to say, "To Audi and Willie"?

"Like I was sayin', Audi, introduce me to your little friends."

"Sure, this is, uh, my dear friend Vivian," Audra said gesturing to Vivian who had just come in from the kitchen with a tray of cheese and crackers. Vivian placed the tray on the table and reached out to shake Clyde's hand. She glanced at Audra as he grabbed hers and turned her palm down, kissing the top of her hand.

"How'd you do?"

"Very well, thank you," she took her hand back and smoothed out her flared beige skirt and smiled sweetly at him, trying to be polite.

"You talk real good, darlin', anyone ever tell you that?"

"Yes, they have, but I appreciate the compliment."

"And this is her husband, Nathan," Audra said, uncomfortably. I watched her lips purse tightly together as she tried to smile. I wasn't sure if she knew that she made a weird face anytime she referred to Nathan as Vivian's husband. They'd been together long enough now that I'd thought she'd gotten over the jealousy that she felt. It wasn't like they were husband and wife in a traditional sense… just… legally. Audra then gestured to her mother, "and ev'ryone, this is my Ma, Francine."

"It's a pleasure," Nathan spoke up, "can I offer you anything to drink?"

"Whiskey, if you got it," Clyde replied.

"Pa, it's four in the afternoon," I could hear the annoyance in Audra's tone.

"Right, it's practically night," he chuckled back.

"Leave your Pa alone, a glass of whiskey ain't never hurt no one," her mother came to his defense, much to Audra's apparent dismay. She told us several times that his drinking was out of hand.

"Scotch then," Clyde requested after Nathan told him we had run out. We weren't big whiskey drinkers but usually had a bottle for company. However, Nathan had recently hosted a dinner for his boss who was a lover of fine whiskey and cigars. He had practically licked the bottle clean. "No real man lives in a house without scotch. Am I right, or am I right?"

"Couldn't have said it better myself," Nathan replied. I could tell he was agreeing to get on her father's good side. He was good at that, pinpointing what to say and how to come across, getting others to like him. He was so charming; it was no wonder I fell for him. Well, his charms and his good looks.

When I first met Nathan, I wasn't sure what to make of him. He seemed like the dream man. He was tall, broad, and manly, but with a soft face. His black hair was smoothed back, and his short, well-maintained facial hair showed off a chiseled jaw. His eyes were dark and mysterious, yet kind. He carried himself with a confident demeanor and appeared to be the definition of class. I had seen him a few times at the local market. He'd come down near the dock first thing on Saturday mornings and purchased his groceries. At the time, I was helping a friend with his fruit stand. It wasn't anything special, but it was nice to make some pocket change on the weekend since I didn't have anything better to do. I noticed Nathan right away; he was hard to miss, especially since it felt like every woman there turned to fawn over him. I used to laugh at this pair of sisters that worked at a stand a couple down from us who would get all dolled up, anticipating his arrival. Anytime he came they'd become completely speechless. Honestly, I don't remember how we started talking but it was casual and light, something about apples maybe? He was incredibly charming, even with small talk. Despite his attractive nature, I tried not to get too infatuated, the way everyone else did when he came. After all, I had two things working against me. The first being the fact that he was clearly straight, and the second was the wedding ring that was situated on his left hand. Perhaps the girls kept praying it'd be like a novel - that he'd leave his wife for them and whisk them away. He did look like the physical embodiment of every lead man in a romance novel. For a while I thought maybe his wife had passed away, as I never saw her with him. Weeks went by and every Saturday he showed up alone, maybe that's what kept the hope alive in his admirers. Maybe he was widowed, or divorced, but why would he continue to wear his ring?

Finally, the dreams of the girls had been crushed when Vivian had actually shown up one sunny, hot Saturday in July. Much to everyone's dismay, she was beautiful. She looked different than I had pictured. I had imagined his wife as some tall, very slender, dark-haired woman. One that had her hair pulled back tightly in a bun and scowled a bit, acting like she was above everyone. I'm not sure why I had pictured such a kind man with someone so cold, but I just saw it happen so often. They'd get so blind-sided by a woman's beauty that they didn't realize the bitter beneath. That being said, I've seen it the other way around too, women were just as capable of marrying an egotistical cad. However, Vivian was anything but what I had imagined. The first time I saw her, she wore her golden blonde hair down and loosely curled. Her makeup was soft and natural, giving off a gentle glow. She wore a bouncy navy dress and a large white belt that showed off her curved hourglass figure. She walked in stylish white shoes with a strap on the front of them, with just enough of a heel to give her a bit of height but short enough that her feet wouldn't get too sore walking through the market. She wasn't tall by any means, with her two-inch heels she stood at maybe five-foot-five, which looked short in comparison to Nathan's five-foot-eleven stature. I don't think she realized the bitter and jealous eyes that stalked her while she made her way through the market, but I found the glares hard to miss. When she first spoke to me and introduced herself, I couldn't help but think how incredibly sweet and genuine she was, and how even though he was married and unobtainable – at least Nathan had someone deserving of him. It didn't completely take away my jealousy of her at the time, but it helped.

"Appreciate it," Clyde replied as Nathan handed him his glass.

"I'm sure you do," Audra couldn't help but remark.

"Leave your Pa alone," her mother responded.

"I'm sorry, I'm tryin' to stop him from bein' a drunk."

"I ain't no drunk. Nathan, my boy, am I a drunk?" Clyde asked.

"I'm afraid I don't know you well enough to say," Nathan replied, trying not to get involved. He just wanted to be a good host.

"What about the missus? Think I'm a drunk?"

"Me, sir?" Vivian asked him, uncertain if he had spoken to her or not. She shook her head, "you know, I'd rather not get involved in family affairs."

"Who said we'd need to have an affair? Not that I'd object," he joked. I saw Vivian shift in her seat uncomfortably, which also did not go unnoticed by Audra. "I'm just pullin' your leg. I was just askin' if you thought I'm a drunk."

"She means she don't want to answer on account of it bringin' out family drama she don't want to be involved in."

"Maybe she just don't want to offend you by sayin' she disagrees, Audi."

"She don't disagree, you smell like a damn brewery," Audra shot. Her mother gasped, as her father stood angrily.

"That's a damn dirty lie!" he yelled back.

I felt like I needed to say something, to intervene. Audra wasn't wrong. When I had greeted them at the door, I couldn't smell anything over Francine's perfume but now that they stood apart, it was clear he reeked. I tried to open my mouth to speak but nothing came out. Damn it. What was wrong with me? I sighed as Nathan spoke.

"How about we drop it, and we talk about something else?" he started as Clyde took a seat back down, agreeing to change the subject. He turned to Audra's mother, "Francine, I saw you looking around when you came in, what do you think of our place?"

"I have to admit, it ain't quite my taste."

"New York ain't like home, Ma. We ain't huge fans of bright floral wallpaper and lace draped over ev'rythin'," Audra laughed.

"But Audi, lace is so pretty," Francine replied. "You know, I have to say you have quite a little set up here, it's just not how I thought you'd still be livin'."

"Ma..."

"Just let me get this through my head one more time. Now, I know you explained it to me on the phone but, you and William are together, but you two live in this house with those two?"

"Yes."

"Vivian, dear, how long have you been married?"

"Seven years," she replied.

"Then what in tarnation are you two doin' livin' in a house with another couple? Don't you want to get started on a family or a life of your own?"

I watched as Vivian tensed up, she was once incredibly sly at dodging people's remarks about child rearing and could explain her way through any questions about her life decisions. However, since she and Nathan had hit the five-year anniversary mark, she found it much more difficult to get around the inquires the way she once could. She told me she could see the confusion and judgment in people's eyes when she announced they'd been married for so long.

"Oh, yes, yes of course," she muttered, "um, well, you see-"

"What my wife is trying to say is that with the cost of living nowadays and our rising careers, we're not in any sudden rush to be having children. Since our home is big enough to accommodate the four of us, we decided it would be a good idea to live together for a short while," Nathan explained, coming to her rescue. As he sat on the arm of the couch, he reached for Vivian to comfort her. "With Will and Audra saving up for their wedding and future home, we figured we'd help our friends and save some money ourselves."

I glanced at Audra's mother who looked

disapproving of his answer but seemed to decide to let it go.

"Fine," she dragged the *i* out in a long Southern drawl. "I'll change the subject. Let's talk about your weddin' plans."

I nearly choked while taking a sip of my drink. I glanced at Audra as she responded, confused, "what'd you mean by *plans*?"

"Who are you invitin'? Like Mamaw and Papaw, oh, and Auntie Sharon, and Phil-"

"Ma, I'm gonna have to stop you there. I'm sorry to say I ain't invitin' 'em."

"What're you talkin' about? They're your family."

"And see, that's the thing... I want a very tiny weddin'... only a couple people. Not a big-"

"What? Celebration? Is that not what a weddin' is? Between two people who love each other so?"

"Yeah, but-"

"But what, Audi?"

The women were stopped by a knock at the door. I don't think I have ever been so relieved for an interruption before in my life. We watched as Nathan welcomed in a young woman. She looked just like Audra, only younger and much more feminine. Her hair was perfectly curled, and her lips were bright shade of pink that matched the ruffled knee length dress she wore. She stood silently for a moment and smiled sweetly as she held onto the bouquet of flowers she'd brought. Before she had the chance to try and say anything, Francine spoke up again, directing her attention to who I was certain was Audra's younger sister.

"Faith, honey, listen to this: your sister here don't want herself a nice big ole white weddin'. Now, ain't that the most peculiar thing you ever did hear?"

"Well, if she don't want a big ole white weddin', she ain't gotta have one," Faith responded. It was clear her answer took Audra off guard.

"Faith, not you too," Francine rolled her eyes, looking defeated, "I had high hopes on you bein' the normal one but lately you've seemed off your rocker."

"I guess I'm just feelin' a bit more democratic these days."

"Now don't be startin' with that nonsense," Clyde spoke up as he took the liberty of pouring himself another glass.

"Yes, Pa."

I could tell she wanted to say something else but found herself unable to. Faith had spent most of her life with a sister who consistently went against the grain, always standing on the other side of the fence than her parents. From what Audra told me, Faith remained the good girl who always did as their father said and always defended them in arguments. However, watching her reaction, I had to wonder if she truly believed what she said or if it was an act for her parents. If it was, she clearly wasn't finding it so easy to break free of the role she played.

"Shall I grab a vase for those flowers?" Vivian asked the young girl, breaking the moment of silence. I think Vivian got the same feeling I did and couldn't help but go to

Faith's rescue. "Come on, I think I have one in the kitchen."

"I ain't got the slightest clue what's goin' on with that girl," Clyde spoke after Vivian had led his youngest daughter out of earshot. "She was always my little Southern Belle. Now all of a sudden she's comin' up with all sorts of mad ideas. Sayin' whatever pops into her little head."

"Maybe that's a good thing," Audra replied. "Maybe she's finally learnin' to think for herself."

"It's true," Nathan decided to speak up to lend support to Audra. "Far too many people just say what they're told these days, but our most forward intellects are the ones that think outside the box."

"Well, I liked her better inside the box," Clyde huffed. "Some opinions are best not expressed. She's at a fragile age."

"Pa, she's twenty-one!"

"But your Pa's been swattin' at boys for years now," her mother replied. "They're always whistlin', except when he's 'round. They heard he got himself bullets for his shotgun all stocked up. Ain't no boy gettin' close to her any time soon, not until he says so. I mean, if she'd been a little more conservative like yourself, not leadin' 'em on... I've always worried she loves the attention unlike you. You ain't never paid any attention to no boy, always starin' right past 'em."

I held back a snicker; Francine's comment didn't surprise any of us.

"At first, I loved Audi's innocence, never had to worry about her until she got a little older," Francine continued, now directing her attention to Nathan and myself. "We were gettin' worried when she didn't notice no fella, no one caught her eye. No one good enough, I s'pose. We started panickin' when all those other girls Audi's age started gettin' hitched. She was still uninterested in findin' someone, and then she decided to come up here to the big city out of the blue-"

"Ma, stop," Audra begged. I couldn't tell if she was becoming angry or embarrassed. Perhaps a bit of both.

"Well, it don't matter now darlin', now that you've got this handsome gent. Her daddy and me started to panic the devil had been in her mind."

"The devil?" Nathan asked before I had the chance to, just as confused as to where this story was going as I was.

"Yeah, you know, the one that gets the queers," Clyde piped up, sinking lower in his seat as he continued to drink.

"So…" I said, unsure where to go from there. I felt a sickness in my stomach and tried to keep my cool. I was becoming exhausted with the swiftly changing conversation and the heavy weight of the content. I wanted to change the topic, the last thing I wanted to do was allow Clyde or Francine to rant about their disdain towards the very people they were unknowingly surrounded by. "You were saying about *Faith*. What has she been doing that's been upsetting you both?"

"She keeps buyin' things from the convenience store two blocks away from us."

"What's wrong with that?"

"A negro owns it," Clyde answered in an aggravated tone.

"I'm sorry, but I don't see the problem with that."

"I don't want my daughter associatin' with no colored folk."

"Pa, enough!" Audra shot, her voice rising. "No colored folk ever done anythin' wrong to you!"

"Audi, I don't know where you got this attitude from but-"

"I've always had one. I ain't never agreed with your views. I even got colored friends here in New York I play cards with on the regular."

"I think I'm gonna have a heart attack," Francine said.

"Oh Ma, don't be so dramatic, it ain't like we're associatin' ourselves with criminals."

"I'd rather you be."

"I'm sorry?" Vivian said as she stood at the kitchen doorway next to Faith, with a vase of flowers in her hand, having heard the tail end of the conversation. She placed the vase on the table before turning to Francine, "you'd rather us associate with a white criminal than a hard-working black man?"

"Yes."

"Well, that's just-"

"Look Ma," Audra said, cutting Vivian off. Traditionally, Vivian could hold her tongue even in the most trying of situations, but we all knew she was about to tell

Francine off. Audra was quick to speak up, she didn't want her involved or fighting a battle she'd spent her whole life losing. "You can't just come into our home, say those things here, and think it's okay. Just because a person is darker than me, I'm s'posed to treat them bad? No. It ain't gonna happen. Colored folks ain't ever been anything but kind to me my whole life. They have a hard enough time as it is. I ain't gonna be one to make it harder."

"Audra-" Francine said with a warning tone.

"What if he was gay?" Audra snapped.

"I'd beat the bastard," Clyde shot.

"What if you didn't know he was gay?"

"I think I'd know if a person was a homosexual or not."

"How?"

"They'd do... well, they'd be doin' homosexual things..."

"See! You don't even know," Audra snapped. "The only difference is that you can physically see if a man is black, but you can't see if he's gay. Heck, what if Will was gay?"

I shot a look at Audra, why would she do that? Why would she drag me into the fire like that? I know she was pretending to speak with hypotheticals, but she was hitting too close for comfort. I tried to get control of the knot twisting in my gut. I was already uncomfortable and that just made everything a lot worse. I don't think I've ever been surrounded by such ignorant people, and more importantly, people who had no problem openly expressing violence.

"Considerin' you're engaged, I should hope that's not the case," Clyde replied. I don't know if he looked at me or not because I did everything in my power to avoid eye contact.

"Well, I mean, *obviously* he's not, but s'pose he was... you'd never be able to tell. You like him now but if he said he was gay you'd have a completely different opinion of him."

"Audra, enough. You're givin' us both a headache," her mother groaned. I think that was the first time I was thankful to hear Francine's voice.

"Your mother's right, Audra, *honey*," I looked at her, trying to give her a clue that I wanted this conversation to move on. It was just as awkward and uncomfortable for me as it was for Vivian and Nathan who were showing the same pinched lips and creased brows as I felt on my own face. We were all visibly tense. "Let's leave this topic alone. Your parents just got here. Let's wait a few more days before we let family matters upset everyone."

"Will's right, Audra, *please*," Vivian said, trying to get her to acknowledge that we'd all had enough. In the short period of time that they'd been in our house, they'd already managed to put us each on edge.

"How about you head to your motel and freshen up, perhaps relax a little?" Nathan said to her parents and sister. "Then, later tonight, the five of you can go for dinner."

"The five us?" Audra looked at him.

"You, Faith, your parents, and Will. They just got here, and it should really just be your time to reconnect and have them get to know Will. Vivi and I will have dinner here. We can join you another day."

"Yes, besides, I have a lot of work to do before my meeting on Wednesday," Vivian smiled sweetly. I couldn't help but feel jealous they had so swiftly come up with excuses not to join.

"All right, it's settled. We'll see you at seven," Francine said. She helped Clyde out of his chair and retrieved Faith's hat for her before the three of them headed out. As soon as they left and Nathan closed the door behind them, we were all suddenly overcome with a sense of relief.

There was a moment of silence before Audra finally spoke, "this was a terrible idea."

I sighed. I could not agree more.

CHAPTER THREE

NATHAN

After Will and Audra left, I changed into something a bit more comfortable, attempting to relax. Will was so worked up about dinner his stress was becoming infectious. I could feel myself getting overwhelmed, and I wasn't even going. I felt the need to decompress. I knew without a doubt, that when they returned, Vivian and I would hear all about it. I wanted to be there for Will, I always want to be there for him, and to do so I had to be in a kind of peaceful mindset that would allow me to comfort him as best as I could. He was so flustered over the short interaction we'd had that I couldn't imagine the mood he'd be in after dinner. He looked like he was going to lose it every time Clyde called him Willie. I had to give it to Audra; she had truly described them down to the pin.

I sighed as I tugged on the belt of my navy robe that Vivian had given me last Christmas. I walked downstairs towards the kitchen but before I got there I stopped and stared at her as she sat under a blanket of papers.

"Are you all right?" I asked her as she let out a heavy sigh. She looked at me with tired eyes and a sad smile. I shook my head as I walked over to her and began to pile the papers up that she had across her lap.

"What are you doing?"

"You're exhausted, Vivi. You need sleep."

"You sound like Audra."

"Then that should indicate some truth," I shook my head as she took the papers back.

"It's not as though I can go to bed now anyways, it's too early, and besides," she yawned, "I need to be up by the time she gets home. She's going to need to let off some steam and complain about the evening... and I *really* do need to finish grading these papers."

"I don't understand how that man belittles you every day. He insists that he is more intelligent than you are, and yet he has no problem getting you to do all his work," I tried my best not to raise my voice, but I couldn't control my frustration. For months now that so-called *Professor* she works for had sent her home with stacks of paper nearly every night. If it wasn't essays to grade, it was lessons to plan. I was also certain she has been taking on work for his history class even though she was only employed by the English department. He worked her like a mule. I wanted to support her like I always have, but I also couldn't help but feel the deepest desire to grab every piece of paper she had and use it as kindling for our fireplace. I just wanted to shake her and say enough was enough. I sighed as I took a deep breath and tried to suppress the resentment I felt. She'd heard enough from Audra who had explicitly expressed her dismay on multiple occasions. I smiled softly at her, hiding my feelings, "would you care for a cup of tea?"

"Yes, please," she replied, holding back another yawn. I could see her exhausted eyes attempting to focus on the page in front of her. I was truly surprised she could see anything.

I left to make her a pot of black tea and a snack. We both had such a small meal after Audra and Will had left, that I was getting hungry again, and although Vivian would say she was fine, I knew she wasn't. She always declined my offers, and yet, ate whatever I put in front of her. More often than not, she was too tired to realize she was hungry. Unless her stomach growled to remind her, she would just go about her day. I swore, if the woman didn't have a scheduled lunch break at work and the three of us at home to remind her, she'd simply forget to eat. She hadn't changed in the ten years I'd known her.

My thoughts drifted off as the kettle began to boil. I didn't feel like anything too heavy so decided to cut up some fruit for the two of us. I put the plate of apple and pear slices on the tray next to two teacups before filling the remaining space with the teapot. I carried the tray out through the swinging door and couldn't hold back a smirk when I saw Vivian passed out on the couch. I put the tray on the table before I went and collected the papers I had previously tried to pile up.

As I stared at her, peacefully asleep, I contemplated on leaving her there to nap until Audra came home but my protective side told me that she needed to sleep more than Audra needed to complain. I would be the support for the two of them instead. I knew once Audra saw how exhausted she was, she'd agree I made the right call.

Once all the papers were stacked neatly on the coffee

table, I turned to the woman I called my wife and slipped one arm under her legs and another around her back. She groaned as I lifted her and rested her head against my chest before making my way up the staircase. I walked past Will and my room to the one she shared with Audra. I placed her on the left side of the bed and pulled the cover over her. Luckily, she had the same desire to relax as I did and had already changed into her evening gown before starting on her paperwork. She let out a faint but relaxed sigh as her head rested comfortably on the pillow. I kissed her forehead before turning the light off and closing the door behind me.

I shook my head, wishing Vivian would take a break or slow down for her own sake, but I knew she was too scared to. She had worked too hard to get her foot in the door and if she gave any indication that it was too much work, they'd use it as an excuse to push her right back out. She was stuck working with incredibly bigoted men, but she was determined not to back down. She kept telling me it was only temporary, but how long was temporary? I didn't want to get too strong-willed, as that was Audra's territory. I had heard them bickering recently that Audra was tired of going to bed by herself and how Vivian was drowning too far into her work. The argument went on for nearly forty-five minutes before they finally reached a state in which they could be a bit more level-headed.

Audra and Vivian didn't fight often but when they did it could get heated. They were both stubborn in their own ways. Audra was very opinionated, and her heart was so big that sometimes she could come across as controlling. The fights would usually start with some kind of remark such as her asking Vivian to go to bed, but she'd more so instruct than ask. Sometimes her bluntness would set Vivian off if she was tired or stressed, no matter how kindly Audra may've meant it - if it sounded like an order, there was a risk of a fire starting. During their last tiff, Audra made an agreeable argument about how negative Vivian's work had been to her health. Vivian may love what she does, but if she kept going at the pace she was, she'd start to crash and resent her work. Vivian denied it, but from the sound of her voice she couldn't hide that she knew Audra's words were true.

Vivian had always taken pride in what she did. When it came to work, her school, social events, or even general activities, she put her whole heart into it all. She cared about what she did and more importantly, her reputation. I'd never once brought her to a work event and not had her impress everyone. I also never once asked her to make me look good, but somehow, with her friendly and admirable personality, she did it naturally. However, by putting so much energy into her work and reputation, she lacked the ability - I'd even say care - to *actually* maintain her health. For years, if I didn't make a meal, she'd grab something to go or prepare herself simple meals of no real substance. When company would come over she was always happy to refill drinks or bring the food out, but it was all an act. She hated cooking, and she hated cleaning. Truthfully, she hated anything that resembled housework, but God forbid people learnt she wasn't a good housewife on top of the million other things she did.

I blamed her parents. I'm not saying that one's parents are the root to all their issues, but Vivian's definitely contributed to hers. There was a weird sense of pride in that family. They never wanted anyone to know anything could possibly be flawed, despite the fact that there were persistent issues. Her father, who I admired for all he'd done for us – especially getting me into a fairly prestigious law firm - was the worst for his pride. Which, I admit, I'd always found that interesting because he had the complete ability to embarrass himself with his temper yet never noticed. He'd been caught multiple times bantering in public at others. He also didn't seem to be aware that everyone knew he had been cheating on Vivian's mother long before the divorce. I think he stayed in the marriage for so long for Vivian and her brother, Timothy's, sake although it seemed to do more damage than good. Her uptight and cold mother would continuously complain that her husband was the reason she began drinking. She couldn't deal with his aggression. As for Vivian's brother, he couldn't seem to help but stir up trouble. A privileged boy with nothing better to do than get into trouble and spend his parent's money. Yet, somehow, no matter how many times he got picked up by the police, his record would magically disappear thanks to his dear old dad. We had tried to explain that they were just enabling Timothy, but it fell on deaf ears. I felt angry over the way they took advantage of Vivian's good nature as she'd drop everything for them, especially her mother who was still complaining that she didn't have a grandchild.

I think she resented Vivian for trying to make something of herself. After all, her mother married young and to a man who easily replaced her, leaving her spending years bitter and spiteful. It seemed old habits die hard. I couldn't help but roll my eyes when they'd invite us to their charity balls and Vivian's parents would show up as if they weren't plagued by their deep rooted and entirely vocal spite for each other.

Audra had met them only a handful of times in passing. She had never spent a concentrated period of time with them as I had, but she'd heard and witnessed enough to lose it. If I thought I was protective, I was nothing compared to Audra. I once heard her yell at Vivian, almost in tears, asking why she let herself be taken advantage of repeatedly.

"They treat you like crap," Audra tried to reason.

"Your parents are awful to you, yet I hear you calling them every week."

"My folks are awful to ev'ryone else, but they ain't never treated me bad like that," Audra responded, "there's a difference."

It was true, Audra's relationship with her parents was strained on account of their views being different and their inability to listen to reason. Vivian's parents were in a league of their own.

For the next hour I sat on the couch and read. I kept the radio on in the background as I was never fond of complete silence. I glanced up at the clock a few times. It wasn't as though it were late, but William and Audra had been out for nearly two hours, and I'd figured they'd be eager to get home as quickly as possible.

As if on cue, I heard the front door open. I closed my book and headed towards them, "how'd it go?"

"How do you think?" Audra replied expressionless. I could tell she was tired. I couldn't image sitting through an entire dinner where your only options were to ignore everyone the entire evening or argue yourself to death. "Where's Vivi?"

"She fell asleep," I answered her.

"Vivi? The night owl I have to drag to bed?" she said

glancing at the clock, confused when she saw it was only half past nine. As she went to speak again, I saw her eyes fall on the pile of papers that laid half marked. She shook her head and sighed, there was nothing left to say that we hadn't already heard. She'd been expecting Vivian to crash at some point, but I could see she was upset it had been today of all days.

"Audra, I'm here if you need to talk about anything," I started to offer. I saw her think about it for a moment before shaking her head, gently declining my offer, and stating she was tired. I don't know why I had expected her to let me be there for her. She had been a bit on edge lately, and I couldn't help but worry I'd done something to upset her.

Vivian had told me I was being ridiculous when I voiced my concerns one day that I felt Audra was avoiding me. I couldn't help but think that Vivian had said something to her as she was making a conscious effort to be nice, but I still felt an underlying awkwardness.

I'd never mention it to Vivian but there was always a weird sense of tension between Audra and me. Over the years our relationship had gotten better but it was never as great as I'd hoped. Vivian and Will would go out all the time and enjoy each other's company, but whenever Audra and I spent time alone it was okay, but felt a bit forced from her end. I know she tried, that was clear, but I always wished there was a way that she didn't have to try – that we could naturally get along. I don't think she ever really got over her feelings about my relationship with Vivian. Despite being told on multiple occasions that there wasn't anything more than friendship and a well-constructed façade, I think she was still a bit on edge about the whole thing. I just prayed maybe she'd understand after she married Will and saw for herself that it was nothing more than an arrangement.

I wished her goodnight before she headed for the stairs and went up to bed. I waited until she was out of earshot before turning to Will, "so?"

"So, what?"

"How'd it go?"

"It was interesting."

"That's it? That's all you've got to say?" I watched as he plopped down on the couch and rubbed his face.

"It was stressful," he shrugged, "but honestly, I don't know if it was stressful because *they* happen to be a lot of work or because I don't have a lot of experience with parents."

I could sense the uncertain tone in his voice. I understood where he was coming from. He had a dual meaning to his statement; he didn't have a lot of experience with parents in any area of his life. Will lost his own parents at a young age, and he had never needed to impress anyone else's parents, as most of the men he had dated lived in secret from their families, much like Audra and Vivian did. He hadn't met Audra's family before today and had only met Vivian's father once in passing. The only parent he'd truly met before was my mom, and I hate to say it, but we have a unique relationship. I didn't even have to tell her I was gay – she just knew.

When I was fifteen, I was really upset one day coming home from school. I didn't really know why I was flustered and on edge; I just was. I always had an easy time in school. I was a good-looking kid, I got good grades, and I made friends easily. I had even made it onto the football team in my freshman year. I remember that day so clearly, I was coming out of science class and had just reached my locker when one of my closest friends – Alice – approached me. I specifically recall thinking it was an odd time to see her since her next two classes were located on the other side of the building and I generally only saw her when we walked to school together in the morning, and then not again until lunchtime. At first, I thought maybe she left her math book in her locker, but when she stood next to me just staring, I got a weird feeling.

"You okay, Alice?" I had asked, feeling uncomfortable as she gazed at me wide-eyed and unsure. She looked as nervous as I did but for completely different reasons. Before I could utter another word, she leaped forward and kissed me. I was so shocked; I didn't know what to do. I just froze, standing there with her lips pressed against mine. Before I knew it, I felt myself push her. I didn't push her hard, just enough to get some space between us. I looked at her as she stood there mortified with wide eyes. I didn't know who was more embarrassed. We both stood in silence, not knowing what to say. "Alice-"

"No, it's okay, I just thought-" she shook her head, trying to make sense of the situation. "I just thought that you felt the same way."

"The same way?" I had questioned, realizing what she meant. "Oh."

"I don't get it, every guy in school has asked me to the dance except you."

"Yeah, but Alice... I thought we were just friends," I replied, not knowing what else to say. I could see the confusion in her face. She was popular and beautiful, and she knew it too. I had heard almost every guy on the football team say at least once that they'd give anything to go out with her, and knowing she was one of my best friends they'd always ask me to put in a good word for them. Alice was without a doubt smart, clever, and stunning, but I just didn't feel anything more than friendship for her. She could have anyone in the entire school, so why like me?

"We can go to a dance, *and* be friends, Nathan," she said with a bit more edge than I had expected, tossing her long dark locks over her shoulder.

"I didn't mean to hurt your feelings," I had replied, reaching for her arm but she pulled away.

"I know," she answered before she walked away.

I had just stared as she walked down the hallway. I sighed without another word as the third member of our little group, Leo, approached me and put a reassuring hand on my shoulder. I felt an overwhelming wave of relief and comfort as I looked at him. Leo and I had grown up together and had been best friends since the third grade. I felt like I could confide in him, and always rely on him to have my back.

"Did you know she liked me as more than a friend?" I asked him.

"Are you kidding? She's always looked at you with big puppy dog eyes," he replied.

"I didn't know," I began to fumble over my words. "I feel awful that I... I mean... did I ever make it seem like I liked her... like that?"

"A little. I mean, we're all close, but you treat Alice way nicer than any other guy does. Actually, you treat all the girls at school so nicely I wouldn't be surprised if more thought you liked them the way Alice does."

"What do you mean?"

"You know, like how always holding the door open for them and stuff," Leo answered.

"I'm just being polite."

"Yeah, but see, you think about those things. You're a really good guy, Nathan. It's what makes you different, special. Most of the other guys only think about doing that kind of stuff if they want to impress a girl, but you just do it for everyone regardless of who they are or what they look like," Leo said. I watched as he bit his lip before continuing, "hey look, um, would you mind if I asked Alice to the dance?"

"What?"

"Well, I always sort of thought maybe there was something between you two so I never said anything, but I kind of always had a thing for Alice and since you don't like her like that... would you mind if I asked her out?"

I said no, not knowing what else to say. I felt jealous and uneasy, but I didn't know why. I had turned Alice down and didn't really want to go with her, so why did I care if Leo did?

When I first arrived home, I was trying to make sense of my feelings. I thought maybe I had been upset about what happened between Alice and myself, but the more I thought about it, the more I realized that wasn't what had me on edge. I felt bad about how her feelings had been hurt, but it wasn't what made my insides ache. I had sat in my room for hours before my mom finally came up with a cup of cocoa. She handed it to me before sitting down on the edge of my bed, and asked me what all mothers ask, "do you want to talk about it?"

I did and I didn't. After my dad died, I told my mom everything. We were so close, and she was my best friend, but I didn't know how to talk about something that I couldn't comprehend - luckily for me, she did.

As it turned out, I wasn't upset about Alice - I was upset about Leo. I realized that what Alice felt for me, was what I felt for Leo. I felt bad for Leo, but also relieved, when he told me that Alice declined his offer to take her to the dance. It turned out we all got our hearts broken that day.

I asked my mom how she knew I was gay, and she simply smiled and said she always knew, that it was mother's intuition. I sighed, feeling out of sorts. I had felt so overwhelmed with emotions and couldn't understand how it was so obvious to her, yet my eyes were just opened only hours ago. She placed a hand on my cheek to comfort me before taking my hands in hers and said that one day I would look back and realize that I always knew too. Sometimes we don't notice things until they smack us in the face, and when we realize the truth, we wonder how it wasn't obvious the entire time. My mom loved and supported me my entire life through everything I did, whether she agreed with it or not, as it was my life to live. I'd always lived my life in secret for I didn't want to risk the career or future I desired. When I would discreetly go to bars to meet new partners or friends, I would often hear stories about their family and friends and how they'd been quick to kick them out or disown them upon discovering the truth. I always wondered how I ended up with a mother who was so open to love and equality in a world so quick to judge and hate. I remember when I first introduced Will to my mom. He was so nervous and the first thing she did was wrap him in a hug and ask him if he wanted anything to eat.

I think the only time my mother ever voiced her dismay for a decision in my life was when Vivian and I told her we were getting married. She had and would always love

Vivian, but she did not agree with what we decided to do. We tried to explain to her the benefits of marriage, but she was scared that such a lie would get out of hand, and that in the end we would both get hurt. Nevertheless, when we told her we were doing it anyways, there she was at our wedding – right by our side, always there if we needed her.

We understood where she was coming from. How would we explain this to potential lovers? What if we fought? Would we be expected to have children? These were all things we had thought through and things we knew we'd have to face in time, but we'd tackle the challenges together.

"I think I'm going to follow Audra's lead and head to bed," Will replied, "this whole evening took everything out of me."

"All right, I'm going to put my dishes away and I'll be right up," I gave him a kiss before taking the tray into the kitchen. I sighed as I looked at the clock, noticing it had only been twenty minutes since Audra and Will returned home. I yawned, feeling fatigued myself. It looked like it was going to be an early evening for all of us.

I turned the lights out before heading upstairs. I'd only taken about ten minutes to clean up, but it was just long enough for Will to have been able to get changed and crawl into bed. When I reached our bedroom, I leaned against the doorframe and smiled. I stood there for a moment watching him while he sat in bed reading his novel. It took him a page to notice I was standing there, staring.

"What?" he smirked at me.

"Nothing," I replied as I closed the door and walked closer to him, "I just missed you, that's all."

CHAPTER FOUR

VIVIAN

When I was a little girl, I was often asked why I was so insistent on carrying a notebook around with me. I would tell those who inquired that it was to document things – the things I saw, feelings I had, people I'd meet. I would also, on occasion, write novellas about the heroines I'd dream up. The written word had always called to me, even at a young age. Perhaps I used it as an escape; it was much easier to run away into a haven of romantic adventure than to face the reality of an uncomfortable life. People always said they envied me – how lucky I was to be blessed with such opportunity and wealth; things others could only dream of. I knew I was fortunate in many ways; I never disregarded the fact, but there were plenty of cracks beneath the surface of my seemingly perfect, painted, life. It had come as no surprise to me that just about everyone I knew expressed their utter shock when I insisted on going off to school. I suppose I was expected to shine as a socialite rather than get the education I so desperately desired. I wanted more out of life. People think when you have money all your problems are solved, but all it does is create a new set of problems. I grew up in a world of constant duplicity where everyone fought behind closed doors and wore masks in the presence of company. Their fake smiles and white lies made the air so tense and stale you'd feel as though you were suffocating. It was no life to live. There were weeks I'd just carry on aimlessly and empty. Sometimes it just felt like too much. The only salvation I had was to escape and live vicariously through the characters that spoke to me.

After I married Nathan, I felt as though he'd saved me from a pit of endless despair. He helped me see literature as a pleasurable past time rather than a survival tool. I had never stopped carrying around my notebook though. I found I still had too many thoughts crossing my mind not to take notes. I guess it was my version of a diary – only lacking mindless doodles, such as the names of people I fancied. I recall being in school next to a group of girls that couldn't help but scribble *Alan* across the pages with little hearts. I couldn't help but think that surely something ran through their brains, other than our classmate, who wasn't even good-looking. He was by all accounts even less attractive when he opened his mouth. If you didn't read the course material, you ought to duck your head and avoid being picked by the teacher, not raise your hand, and quote whatever nonsense you'd read from your adult magazine that morning. I swear my jaw had dropped when he asked if I'd help him with his paper for the end of term. A part of me wanted to laugh and ask if he was serious, but the other part of me wondered if anyone was actually home in his seemingly displayed pea-sized brain. So, curiosity got the best of me, and I agreed to help him. Alan didn't get a perfect mark by any means, but he did get a grade good enough to help him pass the class. When I had originally agreed to tutor Alan, I admit I was fairly cynical. I thought it would be a lot of work, and I would hate it. It turned out I was only half correct. It was a lot of work, but I didn't hate a moment of it, I found I was enjoying it. Something in me felt a surge of satisfaction every time he understood a concept. I quickly realized that perhaps teaching was my calling. I began to tutor more and more classmates to ensure I really did like educating others – and I did. In fact, it didn't seem there was much I enjoyed more.

I sighed as I sat on the same bench I had almost every day for years, provided the weather was pleasant, and stared out onto the greenery. The bench was perfectly positioned under a large Norway maple tree that provided some shade against the bright sun. It was on that very same bench where I had first met Audra five years ago.

When I first began working at the university, I found it hard to fit in. Honestly, it was still hard to fit in. At first, I'd eat my lunch outside because it was nice to get some fresh air, and I enjoyed watching people play whatever sport called to them each day. There was always something different happening in the area people referred to as "the courtyard". Eventually, I began eating there alone because I had trouble fitting into the "boys' club". I was smart, even when I first started, but none of them wanted to give me the time of day. It wasn't necessarily uncommon for women to be teachers, but it seemed uncommon for them to strive for the heights I wanted to. It seemed it was not a problem if I wanted to teach elementary school, but God forbid I prove myself worthy of such a prestigious university.

It was a brisk day in September at the start of my second year when a soccer ball rolled towards me. I looked up from the book I was reading when it tapped my ankle. I placed the book down as I reached for the ball. I stood up and handed it to a beautiful dark-haired woman who had come to retrieve it. She tossed her curly hair over her shoulder and graced me with a large, stunning smile.

"Thanks," she said in a strong Southern accent, which had taken me off guard, extending her hand to me. "I'm Audra."

"Vivian," I replied. There was a moment of silence between us. Our hands were still together, and our eyes still locked. I wasn't sure what came over me, but I suddenly felt my legs go weak and I did everything I could to keep myself grounded. I finally broke eye contact from her and retracted my hand. I put the strand of hair that had fallen loose from my bun behind my ear and gestured to her friends. "I guess I should let you get back to your game."

"Sure," Audra smirked, "you should join us sometime."

I watched as she headed back towards her friends and tossed the ball to one of the players on her team. As I took a seat back down on the bench, I picked up my book. I had tried my best to stay focused on the words in front of me, but my eyes were constantly drawn up towards her. I felt my heart skip a beat when I noticed the woman standing next to Audra take her hand and entwine their fingers with hers. It was at that moment that Audra looked over her shoulder towards me and happened to make eye contact. It caught me so off guard that I fumbled my book and dropped it. I swiftly collected my belongings and headed back into the school.

I hadn't seen Audra before that day, but since we'd met it seemed she was in the courtyard every day. At the time, I didn't know if she could tell I kept looking at her, but I could tell she was looking at me. Finally, she acknowledged my presence and softly gestured a hello when I sat down for lunch one Friday. I smiled back before I opened my book and began to read. I became so deeply engrossed in the chapter that I hadn't noticed she'd approached me until she sat down on my right. I lowered my book and looked at her when she spoke.

"You a student here?" she had asked.

"No, I'm a teaching assistant," I replied.

"So, why do you sit out here alone ev'ry day when your colleagues are right over there?" she asked, gesturing across the courtyard where three of the professors and one teaching assistant stood together smoking and chatting.

"I, uh-"

"Don't really fit in with the boys club?" she said. I looked at her; it was as if she had taken the words right out of my mouth. "You probably just intimidate 'em."

"Thanks," I smirked, I appreciated her efforts at making me feel better about the situation.

"Vivian, right?"

"Yes."

"Wanna have lunch together tomorrow?"

"Pardon?"

"Lunch. There's a café 'round the corner from here, I could meet you and we could walk together. Grab a bite to eat?"

Audra and I ended up going together for lunch every

day for the next two weeks, and had she not started her new job we probably would've kept going. One thing led to another and before we knew it, we began seeing each other, but in the evening rather than mid-day. I preferred it that way, it felt like we really were seeing each other rather than two friends trying to squeeze in as much time together as possible in a such a short lunch period.

"I didn't think I'd ever get out of there," I looked up as I heard a familiar voice speak, breaking me out of my thoughts. I moved my bag, so my friend Elaine had room to sit. She heaved a heavy sigh as she pulled a handkerchief out of her pocket and cleaned the lenses of her glasses before putting them back on and reaching for the pocket mirror in her purse. I watched as she stared at herself in the mirror, adjusting her dark black bangs and reapplying her lipstick, attempting to look less frazzled before finally leaning back into the bench to relax for a moment. "I am exhausted and it's only noon. I swear they're just bringing useless files into that office to make us work harder."

"They have the budget; I don't see why they don't hire more staff."

"Are you kidding? The only thing that budget is going towards is making those idiots richer," she pointed to the professors who were exiting the building for the lunch break. "Why would they hire more staff when they can just work us to death? They refuse to hire anyone or increase our salary. They know we can't afford to quit so they're just going to pile on the work because they can."

I shook my head, I wish I had some words of encouragement for her, but she spoke the truth. Shortly after Audra had gotten her job working as a cashier at a bank, and

I began to eat my lunch alone again, I met Elaine who'd recently gotten hired to work in the university's administration office. To be honest, I don't completely remember what we had bonded over, but our friendship had just clicked.

"What's going on with you? You seem quiet today," Elaine said. I didn't think my unease was so obvious. "Did something happen with Audra last night?"

"No, well yes, but no."

"Spill it."

"Nothing in particular. Her family is in town so she's on edge, and she's upset I've been taking home so much work."

"She's always mad that you take home too much work. Nathan's mad you take home too much work. Heck, I'm mad you-"

"I get it," I smirked. I truly did. I was upset about it too, but Elaine knew just as well as I did that I didn't have much of a choice. She, herself, had the unfortunate experiences of crossing paths with many of the professors the university chose to employ. Several of whom were the ones responsible for making her job harder.

"Are you sure that's everything?" she pressed, sensing I was holding something back. "I've heard and seen enough of your spats with Audra to know there's more to the story."

It was true. She did know everything; next to Audra and Nathan she was the person I went to for everything. It was different expressing my troubles or thoughts with Elaine over Nathan and Audra – it was nice to be able to have a friend who was just that, a friend. We had no romantic ties, nor were we bound by secrets and relationships. We were just good friends and nothing more. I didn't have a lot of friends, so I cherished the ones I had. I found myself at ease having a confidant who knew my complicated home life and passed no judgment. I had initially been hesitant to tell Elaine, but her open and free-spirited demeanor implied to me she was someone I could trust.

"I, uh, I got a letter," I confessed.

"A letter?"

"From my mother."

"That doesn't sound good," she replied. "What did it say?"

"Oh, it starts off with the usual rambling about the current drama circulating the country club," I answered her, before reaching into my purse and passing her the letter so she could read it herself. She took it from me and began to read. I watched as her eyebrow went up as she reached the bottom.

"And I thought *my* mother was on my case about having kids," she shook her head, "this is just mean."

"Well, I suppose when you've been married for as long as we have, in her world, it looks a bit disgraceful," I sighed. "This is the fourth letter in three weeks."

"Have you told Nathan or Audra?"

"God no," I shook my head. I had less of an issue telling Nathan for he was used to my mother's overbearing and obnoxious ways. He had already been subjected to her badgering about children in the past so this wouldn't come at much of a surprise. We hadn't heard much from her in a long enough while that we had assumed she'd just given up. Audra, on the other hand, I wasn't sure I wanted to bring it to her attention. She was under a lot of stress and although I owed her the truth, I felt nervous and didn't want to deal with her reaction. I knew she'd be upset and start to ask a thousand questions that I just didn't want to answer. She was my girlfriend, and I should tell her the truth but a part of me wanted to be selfish. I was already trying to process things myself and struggled with the idea of adding her emotions into the mix. She was already on edge with her parents visiting and the wedding quickly approaching, that bringing this up was just asking for a full-blown debacle.

"Can I ask a question?"

"Of course."

"Do you want children?"

I looked at Elaine and tilted my head before I shrugged, gazing out onto the field. Truthfully, I wasn't sure how to answer the question. It wasn't a matter of wanting children, but a matter of what I was willing to sacrifice to have them. I wouldn't only be looking at sacrificing my career, but I was potentially putting Nathan and myself in an awkward position. I had never been with a man, nor wanted to. Truthfully, the idea gave me an overwhelming sense of nausea. I also knew Nathan hadn't slept with a woman before and I wasn't sure if he possessed the same ill feelings I did or not. I trusted him with every fiber of my being, but I was scared if we decided to try for a child and it didn't work out that it could potentially damage our friendship. I didn't know if I could even will myself to get that close. Besides, I didn't know if Nathan even wanted children.

"Look, I don't want to tell you what to do but I want you to be careful. Don't do anything that's going to get you hurt," she started. I nodded to her; I understood what she meant. "I also think you should tell Nathan or Audra if this is upsetting you this much. You said Nathan knew she had previously bothered you, so maybe mention it to him. He might have a cooler head than Audra."

"Yes," I replied, accepting that I would have to deal with Audra's wrath if she ever found out I talked to him before speaking with her. I sighed as I looked at my watch; it was probably best to head in. I had always cut my lunch break short to ensure I was in the classroom before Professor McKay arrived. I took the letter back from Elaine and put it in my bag before packing up. "Thanks for listening."

"I'm always here if you need me," Elaine replied, embracing me in a hug. "It will all work out."

"Thank you," I said before we parted ways.

I sighed, praying she was right.

CHAPTER FIVE

NATHAN

I yawned as I made my way down the hallway towards the stairs. I had been reading up in my room for the last several hours, catching up on a book I was recommended by a colleague at work, when I decided I needed a drink. As I walked down the stairs, I raised an eyebrow at the light still on in the living room. I sighed as I saw Vivian sitting on the couch with a glass of wine in hand, staring aimlessly at the pile of papers in front of her. I stared at her for a moment and shook my head before I continued down the stairs.

"Vivi?" I called, stopping as she jumped, nearly spilling her wine.

"Oh Nathan, you startled me," she took a deep breath with a hand on her chest as she looked over at me.

"I'm sorry," I apologized. "What are you doing down here? I thought you'd already gone to bed."

"I couldn't sleep. Besides, I figured there was no use in trying. We both know Audra and Will are going to make a ruckus when they get home."

"Yeah, they've been out a while," I noted, looking at the clock. It was nearly eleven and we had expected them back hours ago. This was their third outing with Audra's parents, much to their dismay.

"Probably trying to pull Clyde away from the bar. I wish we had gone; Audra's going to be such a mess when she gets home. I'm sure William will be as well."

"If Clyde calls him Willie one more time-"

She laughed, "it's a pretty awful nickname."

"We're lucky. Nate and Vivi are quite nice," I smirked as I sat next to her. She finished off her glass of wine before she poured herself another one. Based on her slight slur, I assumed she was on her third. She was still balanced in her movements, but her eyes were beginning to gloss over. As I watched her put the bottle down before she took another sip from her glass, I noticed a letter sitting on top of her work. If the letter was from who I thought it was, it would explain the wine. Vivian was a social drinker, and it was unlike her to be sitting alone on her third glass without reason. "Is that a letter from your mother?"

"Who else?"

"May I?" I asked, waiting for her approval before I took it and began to read. I didn't have to read it to know what it was going to say, but I figured I'd better be certain before saying anything else. "How many of these has she sent?"

"A few," I could tell she was holding back. I shook my head; this was getting out of hand. Vivian's mother had always tried to meddle in her affairs, but it seemed as the years went by the worse she became. When we were first married, her mother would only make the occasional remark when we saw her at events. She would passive aggressively hint to Vivian that she should retire her teaching *hobby* and focus her attention on being a good wife and mother. At first, she was easy to brush off and ignore, until her commentary became more frequent. She began writing letters and calling her every few weeks, even going so far as to speak to me on the phone and apologize for her daughter's choices. She praised my patience as a husband, having to deal with a wife so headstrong, and that she hoped her daughter would come to her senses. I would always relay the conversation back to Vivian so that she was aware of what her mother was saying. I will never forget the look on her face a few months ago when her mother told me that it was within my right as a husband to force Vivian to quit and so that she could take proper care of me.

"No wonder you broke out the wine," I stood and went to the cabinet to grab myself a glass. After I walked back over to the table, I poured myself half a glass to join her. As I was about to take a sip, she spoke.

"Do you want children?" she asked.

"Vivi, pay no mind to those letters. You know what your mother is like."

"I'm asking *you*, Nathan. Do you want children?"

"I thought we talked about this."

I watched as she took a few large gulps from her glass before lowering it from her lips and looking at me, "I really need to know."

"To know what?"

"The truth."

I reached out and put my hand on her wrist, preventing her from taking another sip. I took the glass of wine from her and put it on the end of the table out of reach.

I understood she was upset, but I wasn't going to stand there and let her drink like that.

"You want the truth?"

"Yes," she shook her head. "I really do."

I sighed as I sat next to her. "I do want kids. The fact is, Vivi, I think I *need* kids. I mean, I can imagine us taking our little girl to dance class or watching our son at his first baseball game. I can picture coming home early one day from work and seeing you poorly attempt to teach them how to bake cookies and getting completely covered in flour. I do want children. I know having a child was never a dire need for you, but I think somewhere deep down it is for me."

"Nathan..."

"Despite what your mother says about adoption, love is what makes a family – nothing more, nothing less. I mean, it doesn't need to be anytime soon, but at some point, I guess I hoped..." I sighed as I looked into her eyes. I took her hand in mine, realizing maybe I had said too much. We had gone so long saying we were never going to have kids but recently things had changed. I started feeling the need to have kids, but I was also sure my expression of that need in addition to the stress of her mother may have been a bit too much for her. "Vivi? I'm sorry, I just, I mean..."

"No, it's all right," she replied, looking at me. "I've been thinking about it recently."

"Kids?" I continued once she nodded, "have you been thinking about it because you might *want* kids, or because you want to please your pestering mother?"

"I don't know. I mean, I want kids," she looked as shocked at what came out of her mouth as I did. She paused for a moment, as if she was thinking about what she wanted to say next. She heaved a heavy sigh, as she looked up at me, "I do. I would love the chance to raise strong willed thinkers and be able to support and love them unconditionally. I'll admit I can see everything you said, but at the same time I had this dream of a big career and really making my way, proving a woman can conquer the educational world like a man... but my mother's right, I'm not getting any younger, and I just feel rushed for time."

"We can wait, there's no rush."

"Nathan..."

"There's no age limit on adopting," I half laughed, biting my lip afterwards, sensing her unease. I put my hand under her chin and tilted her head to look back at me when she looked away, trying to avoid eye contact. "Vivian, what is it?"

"I don't know. I've been thinking and talking to people, and I don't know, I'm... I guess I'm just confused."

"Confused about what?"

"Maybe it's just hitting me now."

"What is? Vivian, you're not making any sense," I tried to direct her attention.

"I think I want to be a mother," she spat out. I wasn't sure why, but her cheeks became bright red in embarrassment. She motioned for me with begging eyes to give her back her glass of wine, and I found myself unable to say no. She took a sip and a deep breath before she spoke again. "I don't know what to feel or do. I mean, on the one hand I didn't want to be a mother, I didn't want all that, and then on the other hand I'm thinking, do I want that now? Am I holding on to old feelings? Have I changed my mind or am I just conflicted because of all the pressure? I guess I just knew

I had to choose between career or motherhood and so career was the obvious choice, I mean, I'm not like you Nathan, I can't just have both so easily."

"Vivian, you're rambling," I said. With hesitation, I topped up her glass. She was speaking so rapidly it was difficult to keep up. The effect of the alcohol wasn't helping her focus. "What are you trying to say?"

"I think... that maybe, I *do* want to be a mother," she finally got out.

"That's wonderful, Vivi. It is," I said with less enthusiasm than I thought I'd have. I could sense she was holding something back and couldn't help but notice the sense of sadness and dread in her voice as she spoke. I didn't get it. I mean, maybe she had spent so long trying to convince herself she didn't want children that to change her mind made her feel she was giving in. I couldn't help but worry that deep down she didn't truly want children and was just doing it to please those around her. She always struggled putting her own needs and desires first. Truthfully, I was proud she was still teaching and moving forward to achieve her dreams despite the pressure she as under. I sighed as I looked at her. Her green eyes glossed over as she glanced from me down to her lap, avoiding eye contact. I couldn't tell what was going on in that mind of hers, but I wished she'd tell me. "What is it, Vivi? Please."

"I think... I think that maybe a part of me..."

"A part of you, what?"

"Might want to actually... *have*... a child."

"You mean... you want to get... *pregnant?*" I asked cautiously, unsure if I understood her correctly. When she retracted her hand and pulled away, I realized that was exactly what she meant. I tried to reach for her, but she stood too quickly. I rose to meet her, as the swift moment seemed to cast a dizzy spell over her. I put my hand under her arm to steady her and looked at her. "Vivian..."

"Oh God, this is embarrassing," she pulled away from me, mortified, and raised her arms defensively, "I'm so stupid, I shouldn't have said anything."

"Come here," I begged her in the calmest voice I had. She stared at me for a moment before she took a step closer. I placed her wine glass on the table before I took her hands in mine and pulled her closer. "You're not stupid, and you shouldn't be embarrassed. What you're feeling, it's completely natural."

"Maybe, if we were in a normal relationship," she replied with tears in her eyes, "but we aren't Nathan. I don't know when these feelings started, and I don't know how to get rid of them. It makes me sick because I know it's something that'll never happen. I wish I could just go back to when I never wanted kids because it made more sense to me."

"I know," I took her in my arms and held her in a tight embrace. I rubbed my hand up and down her back as she rested her head on my shoulder. I could only imagine what she was feeling.

Before I could utter another word, the door slammed open, and Vivian and I split from our moment of comfort to turn our attention to our partners who had just come barreling through.

"What happened?" Vivian asked, breaking away from me as she watched Audra storm into the living room. Will trailed behind after he gently closed the door.

"I don't know," he said, confused. "We were having a

surprisingly good time. Her parents were being well behaved, then this!"

"She's killin' me!" Audra exclaimed.

"Who is?" I asked, unsure who she was referring to.

"Faith."

"Why? She was wonderful," William replied.

Audra shook her head pacing back and forth, "she's up to somethin'. She ain't never been that agreeable. She's Ma and Pa's little angel. Their *darlin' little Faith.*"

"So?"

"So? All she's been doin' this evenin' is disagreein' with my folks and agreein' with us, on *ev'rythin'*. I'm the rogue one; I'm *Audi*, so why is little Miss Faith being all... *opinionated?*"

"Didn't you say you wanted your sister to be opinionated?"

"Yeah, but this is different. Somethin's goin' on."

"Maybe she's just grown up now?" Vivian slurred a bit, suddenly holding onto my arm.

"Is she drunk?" Audra questioned.

Before we could respond, Will cut in, "maybe Faith has finally realized you've been right about your parents all along, or maybe she's met someone?"

"What?"

"It's possible," I agreed, Will made an excellent point. "Your parents did say she's been... different. Perhaps she's met a handsome young lad who's more of a forward thinker, maybe it rubbed off on her."

"She didn't mention a particular crush."

"Would she have though? In front of your parents? From what I've gathered, it's highly unlikely," I said. I swore

I could see the wheels turning in Audra's head as she contemplated the possibility. "Your parents already made their opinions clear about her new attitude."

"Maybe they're scared she'll turn into you," Will said, taking a step back, "no offense."

"What's that s'posed to mean?"

"I just mean, you left home as fast as you could," he continued, explaining himself. "You felt you had a bright new future and although they weren't thrilled about it, you left anyways. Now maybe they're scared she's following in your footsteps, and Faith recognizes that so she's treading cautiously."

"Will has a point, sweetie," Vivian spoke up again, squeezing onto my arm. "Some people have a very hard time not living up to the expec- expec-"

"Expectations?" I helped her out.

"Yes," she nodded. "The expectations of their parents."

"From the sounds of it, what Vivian is trying to say, is that your parents have a strong grip on Faith and now they might be afraid of losing her. Your sister is probably struggling to be who she wants to be without making them react the way they did to you," I added. I sighed as I continued. "Might make them feel like they're losing everything."

"Maybe that's not such a bad thing."

"Audra, really? Can't you have a bit of empathy?" Vivian shot, much to all our surprise. I held her back as she tried to take a weak step forward, keeping her at bay. I tried to keep her from saying more but it was no use. "You want them to understand your views and get all angry when they don't, yet you never act like you're trying to see their side of things."

"Well, I'm sorry that I have a different view than my folks and that I choose to it make known. You know very well I ain't one to disagree and then go along with the insanity, like *some people*," Audra snapped back. I could see the instant remorse on her face when the words slipped from her lips. She would never intentionally take a shot at Vivian like that, it just happened. We stood in silence as Audra sighed, walking over towards us. She put her hands on Vivian's flushed cheeks and offered a soft apology. Vivian let go of me and held onto Audra for support.

"How much has she had to drink?" Audra asked softly.

"I think most of the bottle at this point," I replied. I'd only drank about half a glass by the time I had finished refilling Vivian's during our conversation.

"I'm ready for bed," Vivian said to no one in particular, her eyes a bit vacant.

"Do you need help taking her up?" I offered.

"Nah, we're fine," she shook her head. "Goodnight."

I watched as Audra held onto Vivian's arm and guided her towards the stairs. Vivian slowly made her way up the staircase using the railing and Audra as support for her shaky legs. Once they were out of sight, I shook my head and sighed as Will made his way over to me. He took my hand and squeezed it, offering his silent comfort.

CHAPTER SIX

AUDRA

I placed a cup of tea on Vivian's side table, next to the glass of water I had gotten for her last night. I looked down at her as she stirred. I'd woken up early and decided to let her sleep until she came to herself, hoping the more sleep she got the less nauseated she would feel from the aftermath of the wine. It was nearly noon, so I assumed she'd be waking at any moment. Vivian loved to sleep, but even she found it difficult to stay in bed past lunch. I sat at the edge of the bed and ran my hand through her messy blonde hair. I smiled as she shifted, slowly opening her eyes. I placed my hand on her rosy, pink cheek, stroking her soft fair skin. She sighed as she leaned into my hand, slowly waking and yawning. She pulled herself into a seated position and took the glass of water I handed her, taking several large gulps to quench her thirst. She placed the glass back down on the table and smiled as she saw the tea, picking it up almost immediately.

"Mmm," she sighed, as she took a sip. "I needed this."

"What you need is water, but I figured you wouldn't mind a tea to go along," I replied as Vivian nodded before taking another sip. "You feelin' all right?"

"A bit of a headache, but it'll pass," she answered, putting her tea down in her lap and reaching for my hand as she saw my head tilt down. "What is it?"

"I'm sorry for what I said last night, it wasn't fair," I apologized. She shook her head confused; I sighed realizing she didn't remember what came out of my big mouth. "I made a remark about you and your folks, and it was uncalled for."

"I'm sure it wasn't as bad as you think, and besides, I understand. You're under a lot of pressure right now-"

"But it's no excuse," I said. I watched as she put the tea back down on the table to her right and opened her arms. I offered a small smile as I climbed over her and laid on her left, wrapped in her arms. I took a deep breath, inhaling the smell of her perfume that still lingered on her body from the night before and felt the comfort of her embrace as she ran her hand up and down my back. I looked up as she leaned forward and pressed her lips to mine.

"You don't owe me any apologizes," she said softly. "I love you."

"I love you more," I responded back as I entwined my fingers in hers. "Is everythin' all right, Vivi?"

"What do you mean?"

"Last night, you were drinkin'."

"What? I can't just enjoy some wine if I want?"

"I just mean, it's not like you to drink alone like that unless somethin's the matter."

"I'm fine, Audra," she replied in an unconvincing tone. I sat up and stared at her, worried. "What?"

"I wish you'd talk to me," I said, my eyes pleading with hers to tell me what was going on. I sighed in defeat as she responded once again that she was fine before grabbing her tea. It drove me crazy when she did that. Anytime she became worried or upset by something she seemed to shut down. She would become anxious and isolate herself, letting her stress fester. Sometimes it'd take hours, sometimes days, before she was ready to talk about whatever had her unnerved. When we first started going out and I noticed she did that, I became worried and eventually asked if Nathan could figure out what was going on with her, but she'd keep him in the dark too. He said it was just something she did. It was almost as though she needed to make sense of whatever situation or emotions she was feeling upset by before she was able to talk about it. I hated it. I couldn't bear to see her upset by something and not do anything to help. I understood she needed time, but she'd get these sad eyes that I'd struggle to look past. Nathan would just let her be, and she'd ring herself out until she was willing to talk to him or anyone for that fact. I couldn't do that. When we first started seeing each other, Nathan told me to stop pushing her and that she'd come to me when she was ready. I was so furious, and just couldn't do it. Perhaps I was being pushy, but I wanted Vivian to know I was there for her no matter what and hopefully in time she'd be able to just talk to me about whatever was on her mind. As the years passed, that was exactly what happened. As soon as she was upset or feeling on edge, she'd tell me about it. It was rare she'd keep something bottled up, which was what had me worried now. Something had really gotten to her, and I wish she'd just tell me what it was.

"What happened at dinner last night?" she tried to change the topic. I debated on saying something but decided to let it go. I'd bring it up later, for all I knew it was just the pressure she was feeling at the university, as usual.

"My sister."

"What about her?"

"I don't know what to think 'bout the whole ordeal," I replied honestly, and I really didn't. Everyone kept telling me how lovely my sister seemed, but I couldn't help but feel something was going on. It seemed as though every time I opened my mouth my sister was right there, agreeing with everything. I found it hard to believe a girl who spent her entire life pleasing my folks, all of a sudden supported whatever comes out of my mouth. People just don't change their views like that. I couldn't help but think about what Will had said last night, about the possibility that she met someone. I mean, if she did meet someone with views similar to my own, it'd explain why she hadn't told my folks. Then again, one had to go through great lengths in that town to keep a secret. I knew that better than anyone.

"I think maybe you should give her a chance," Vivian said to me with a shrug. "Why don't you call the motel, or better yet, go down there and personally invite her for lunch? Perhaps you could have some alone time away from your parents? That way you could see if she really is *up to something* as you suspect, or maybe you'll see she really has changed."

"People don't change."

"That's one opinion."

"Vivi-"

"Audra, really," she said. "Give her a chance. I mean, think about it. You told me she was quick to go along with *Audi*, but since she's been here, I've not heard her call you anything except Audra."

I frowned, realizing she was right. I couldn't remember her calling me Audi once, which was out of the usual for her, especially since our folks constantly called me that. I sighed.

"If you really think it's a good idea to invite her, I trust your judgment," I said. "Just don't be shocked when she shows you her narrow-minded and obnoxious self."

"As long as you aren't shocked when she doesn't," Vivi replied.

"We'll see."

It took nearly two hours before I decided to take Vivian's advice, regretting it as soon as I made my way over to the motel.

I stood at the entrance of the courtyard, contemplating whether to go in. I had decided to walk to the motel my family was staying at rather than drive although the walk was a bit long. I knew it'd give me some time to think about whether I actually wanted to invite my sister out to lunch. I was feeling hesitant about the whole thing. Vivian's voice kept replaying in my head, telling me to give her a chance. Maybe she had changed, maybe she was different. The issue was that I had another other voice in my head saying she was still the stubborn and selfish girl I'd grown up with. She was still the girl that tattled on me any chance she got, she was still the girl who pretended we weren't related in school for nearly two years, and she was still the girl who burned my diary when I turned sixteen. Maybe my grudge was petty, and maybe I was overthinking things, after all there was a bit of an age gap between us – but did that take away the years of anger and confusion I had? I'd always wanted a sister I could confide in, that I could be proud of, that I could be friends with, but every memory I had of Faith sparked negative feeling in me.

I felt shivers down my spine as I heard the church bells ring in the distance. My mind flashed back to sitting in church back home. I never paid much attention in church; I was always focused on not falling asleep. I hated the pastor - he was an ignorant man. There was always something phony about him. Almost every word of wisdom or kindness he attempted to preach had a sarcastic tone or was followed by a snarky remark. I vowed back in Georgia that I'd never step foot into a church when I came to New York, but I was convinced by a friend here to give it a try. She kept saying the pastor here was different, and I had to admit she was right. He preached what I always thought should be shared in church: compassion and respect. Of course, he shared the usual wisdom of God, but when you stepped into Pastor Christopher's church you felt safe. It wasn't like back home where I used to go.

I remember when I was no more than fifteen, I was seated next to my sister on the bench. I couldn't recall what Pastor Dan had said at the time, but after he spoke, we had bowed our heads to pray as we usually did. I'd tilted my head down but kept one eye open, I'd only lowered my head for show in case someone noticed me. I glanced at Faith who seemed real focused; I leaned towards her and tapped her shoulder to make sure she was okay. What could she have been concentrating so hard on?

"What're you prayin' for?" I whispered.

She tilted her head up and looked me square in the eyes, "you."

I shifted back in my seat, just staring at her. She kept her eye contact for a moment before turning her head back down and continuing to pray. I was silent the rest of the hour until we were free to go. As our folks headed towards the car, I pulled Faith aside and out of earshot.

"What was that?"

"What was what?" she asked with her chin tilted up, and a slight smirk.

"You know what," I replied. "Why'd you say you were prayin' for me?"

"'Cause I was."

"What? Why?"

"Is it wrong I want a normal sister, Audi?" Faith replied, putting her hands on her hips, and shaking her head. "Pastor Dan says if we pray hard enough that God will answer us."

"Faith, what're you talkin' 'bout?"

"You ain't got no friends, you're the laughin' stock of the school, and people are *always* askin' me why my sister's so *odd*," she snipped. "The girls at school say you're just linin' yourself up to be a spinster."

"I'm not-" I cut myself off, it was no use arguing with her. I watched as she stood there tapping her foot on the ground.

"Well?" she said, waiting for a reply. "Am I wrong?"

"Yes."

"I am not!" she whined. "You don't even make an effort, Audi!"

"An effort to what?" I asked her. "To make friends with people who talk behind my back and don't even like me?"

"Maybe they wouldn't talk behind your back if you just acted normal for once."

"What is normal, Faith?" I snapped, grabbing her shoulders, trying to talk some sense into her. "Ev'rybody in this town acts the exact same. They all do the same thing. They're mean to the same people, they like the same things, they live the same lives. Why? Because everyone else is doin' it; there's no other reason. Ev'ry woman in this town finishes high school and gets married and pregnant, and ev'ry man works for own pa's business. People only look at me different because I don't want the same life ev'ryone else has, I want my own, and you should want your own too. If you opened your eyes, you'd realize there's a world out there full of people who are so different and free."

"I wish you weren't my sister," Faith had pulled away from me with tears in her eyes.

"Faith, please," I begged her to stay but she shook her head and left. I remember leaning against the side of the church and sighing in defeat.

My attention snapped up when two of the girls from my school laughed as they walked up, clearly having only heard the tail end of our conversation.

"See, even her own family don't like her," they laughed, motioning to me before they left.

By fifteen, my mind was already set on leaving Georgia. I couldn't remember how young I was when I realized I wanted something more in life, but by that age, I was doing everything in my power to keep to myself. I just had to make it through until I was old enough to hop on a train and head as far away from home as I could. I wasn't sure where I wanted to go, or what I planned to do, but I knew I would never be happy or free until I left for good.

As the church bells stopped ringing, I finally decided to head towards the motel. As much as I wasn't in the mood to talk to Faith, nor did I necessarily want to reconcile things with her, I decided to listen to Vivian and invite her to go out to lunch with us. I bit my lip as I headed up, staring at room number forty-three, until I finally had the courage to knock. I waited a moment, feeling a wave of relief when no one answered the door. I squeezed my eyes shut as I heard it open just as I was about to leave. I turned to see Faith standing in the doorway, dressed in a little pale blue dress.

"Audra?"

"Hi," I replied, turning back to her. "Where's-"

"They went to the market," she replied. "The one William works at on Saturday mornings. Ma was in the mood to shop, apparently there's some nice handmade items there."

"Yeah, there are."

A moment of awkward silence passed before she finally spoke, "I'm sure they'll be back soon if you wanted to wait."

"Well, actually, I was here to speak to you," I replied. I couldn't help but notice the surprised, yet almost happy, expression that appeared on her face.

"You are?"

"Yeah, um, Vivi thought that maybe the three of us could go out for lunch tomorrow. We could catch up and spend some quality time," I said. Originally, Vivian had suggested we go today but I used her headache as an excuse to push the date to tomorrow. Truthfully, I felt I needed a day to emotionally prepare myself.

"I would really love that," Faith responded. "What time should I be ready?"

"We'll come pick you up at half past noon. Would that work?"

"That'd be perfect."

"Great," I said. I wasn't sure what else to say so I just nodded and turned to leave. As I began walking down the steps, I stopped as she said my name.

"Audra?" I looked over my shoulder at her as she smiled and nod to me, "thank you."

I offered a soft smile in return and turned back to leave, suddenly feeling the need to leave as quickly as possible. I wasn't sure what just happened or what I was feeling, but I found my eyes were beginning to gloss over. As I exited the courtyard I leaned against a wall around the corner. I took a few deep breaths and wiped the single tear that ran down my cheek as I contemplated the woman claiming to be my sister. Who was she?

CHAPTER SEVEN

Nathan!" I smiled as I saw my partner head towards the booth I was working at. I took the bag he handed me and gratefully sighed, realizing I had forgotten my lunch at home. Of course, it wasn't the worst-case scenario as I could've just bought something there. I tilted my head, noticing the odd expression on his face. He'd seemed off since last night and I couldn't help but shake the feeling something was wrong. I told Hank, the guy I was working with, that I was going on an early lunch and luckily, he didn't seem to mind.

"What's going on?" I asked him as we walked past the neighboring booths, towards the pier, "is everything okay?"

"Yeah, everything's fine," he said unconvincingly as he put his hands in his jacket pockets and shrugged.

"Don't do that," I begged.

"Do what?"

"Act like nothing's wrong when something's obviously on your mind. We deal with enough of that at home with the girls," I offered some light humor, happy to see him smirk at my remark. It was true. Nathan and I had always been pretty good at getting off whatever was on our chests right away, compared to Vivian and Audra who we had to drag the information out of. "What's going on?"

"You have to promise not to repeat this to anyone," he stopped, catching my eye seriously. "Promise me, you won't breathe a word to the girls."

"Okay..." I replied hesitantly, it wasn't keeping the secret I was concerned about; I was worried about what he was about to say. Nathan was always so composed, even when it was just the two of us. He always had a sense of togetherness and now he just seemed a bit lost. I suddenly began to panic, fearing the worst, "are you okay? Are you sick? Did-"

"No, no, it's nothing like that. I'm fine," he answered quickly. "I just, um, it's about Vivian."

"Vivian?" I asked, confused. Her name caught me off guard.

"Yeah, I, um..." I watched as he struggled put what he was thinking into words. He awkwardly looked around, hesitant to speak in front of so many passing people. I motioned for him to follow me, as I led us to a bench towards the side of the pier that was more secluded. He visibly relaxed as we reached the quieter, more isolated spot.

"Nathan, whatever you say, it stays between us," I

said, looking at him.

"She was drinking yesterday, and she told me something in confidence… at least, I think it was in confidence."

"All right… Is she okay? Is something going on between her and Audra?"

"Oh, no. They're… they're fine. Um, I think she's having second thoughts on wanting to have a baby."

"She is?" I shook my head in disbelief. Vivian? Were we talking about the same woman who swore up and down she didn't want children from the day I met her? I leaned back on the bench and took a second to digest the information. I sighed, a part of me was surprised and the other part of me wasn't. I had always pictured Vivian becoming a mother, she'd make a wonderful one, but after her years of protest I guess at some point I just stopped imagining her having kids. Maybe, deep down, she did want them, but didn't consider it a possibility. Instead of getting upset by the idea of not being able to have any, it was easier to just try and convince herself that she had no desire. "What did she say?"

"Well, at first she just talked about kids and how she realized she wanted them," Nathan said, "which, I was really excited about. I mean, I'd always wanted kids. I mentioned adoption and she told me she wanted to get pregnant."

"How'd you respond?"

"I didn't, really," Nathan let out a long sigh, "you and Audra came home."

"I knew something seemed off," I responded. "So, where does this leave you?"

"What do you mean?"

"Are you thinking about having a baby?"

"What? With Vivian?" Nathan ran his hand through his dark hair and leaned forward, resting his forearms on his knees, looking out to the pier, as he got lost in space. "I guess I never really thought about it."

"You haven't?"

"You have?" he asked me, shocked. He shook his head in disbelief and shrugged.

What was I supposed to say? I had never said it out loud, but was I going to lie and just tell him the thought never crossed my mind? I went into our relationship knowing it was a possibility that he and Vivian might consider having a kid one day. If they wanted to adopt, then it was fantastic and it worked out for everyone, but if Vivian really did want to have a child one day, there weren't a lot of options for her. It was something I knew I'd have to wrap my head around, but as I looked at Nathan's face, I realized he'd never actually thought about it.

The first time I had met Nathan, and not just a casual and far hello when he and Vivian passed by the market, but actually spoke to him was in a bar not far from the pier. I was surprised to see him enter alone, as it was unofficially known as a club for gay men. I took a double take when I saw him head towards the bar and order a drink, awkwardly sitting down. He kept his head down and glanced around, clearly nervous. I shook my head, thinking he was lost. I finally walked over and took a seat next to him on the stool to his right.

"Nathan, right?" I asked as he looked at me, seemingly surprised that I knew his name.

"Yeah," he said, "you work at the market, don't you?"

"Will," I shook his hand as he smiled. "Look, don't take this the wrong way, but I think you made a mistake."

"What do you mean?"

"This bar, it's sort of for a particular group of men," I tried not to embarrass him as I gestured towards the two men in the corner who were standing incredibly close and flirting. I turned back to Nathan and shrugged.

"I know," he replied to my surprise.

We were drawn to each other in a way I couldn't describe. Truthfully, I didn't know much about him for the first two months after I'd met him that evening. We'd agreed to meet each other for drinks a few times a week, but we usually didn't make it past the first beer before we'd find ourselves in a secluded location getting to know each other in a more physical way. For weeks, I thought he was just a closeted gay man cheating on his wife. He'd offer a kind hello on the Saturdays he came to the market but didn't stop to chat much.

One Saturday, I saw Vivian walking alone down the street with a basket in hand. I did my best to avoid eye contact, cursing myself when I glanced up and caught her eye. I felt a sense of dread as she walked towards me.

"You're William, right?" she had asked. I nodded

before she asked if I minded stepping away with her. I was terrified, I wasn't one to be in the middle of an affair and I knew it was only a matter of time before his wife started noticing something was wrong. I just didn't think it'd be that quick. "My name is Vivian."

"Nice to meet you," I had said as I shook the hand she'd extended to me, confused by her kind voice. I kept waiting for the aggression to show, but it never did.

"I just wanted to meet the man that Nathan's been talking so much about," she smiled.

"Wait, what?"

"I know I shouldn't say anything, but he really likes you," she said. When I started looking around, puzzled, she raised an eyebrow. "Is everything all right?"

"I'm just confused," I'd answered honestly.

"About what?"

"Why you're... I mean, you *know*?" I shook my head. Clearly, she already knew he was gay, she just said her husband liked me. I rephrased my thought, "I guess I'm wondering why you're not biting my head off."

"I don't understand," she shook her head.

"Usually when a woman finds out her husband is cheating on her, with a *man* no less, friendly greetings are not what's exchanged."

"Nathan didn't tell you?" she asked slightly stunned. "I'm surprised given how much time you've spent together."

"Well, honestly we haven't been doing too much talking," I smirked sheepishly. She raised her eyebrows, and nodded understanding.

"I'm sorry, had I known I wouldn't have-"

"Tell me what?" I interrupted her; suddenly curious what Nathan had neglected to tell me.

"Um, well um," Vivian glanced around to make sure no one was within hearing distance before continuing. "We have a bit of a *unique* marriage."

"Yeah, a wife who doesn't mind her husband sleeping with men... definitely one for the books."

"Well, it's a bit more than that. Nathan and I are married, but we aren't together in the traditional sense," she hesitated a moment before continuing. "We're only married for political reasons."

"Political reasons?"

"So that we could feel free to see and date who we wish without anyone suspecting anything... you've seen it yourself, we look like the perfect married couple."

"You purposefully married a gay man to meet other..." I stopped midway through my question, nodding as a grin flashed on my lips finally understanding where she was going. I glanced around to make sure we were still out of range from eavesdroppers, "are you a lesbian?"

"Well, it wouldn't make a lot of sense to marry a gay man if I wasn't," her cheeks flushed as she smirked. "I'm sorry to have thrown this on you. I really did think Nathan had told you."

"I'm sure if we actually made time to talk it would've come up eventually," I'd responded.

"Would you like to come to dinner tonight?" she

had asked suddenly; I think it surprised her that the offer had come out of her mouth. "I mean, it seems Nathan likes you and it's been a while since he's met someone, and you seem really kind and... I'm sorry, that must sound so-"

"No, it sounds great," I replied, "what time works for you?"

Nathan told me that he was incredibly embarrassed that Vivian had invited me for dinner like that but was also thankful for it. It pushed him to really get to know me, and it was the start of the longest and best relationship either of us had experienced. It felt natural, Nathan and I just clicked. I couldn't help but deny the slight jealousy I felt when Nathan and Vivian went out together for fancy dinners at work events or charity balls, but I knew it was all an act, and that envy quickly faded. Their "marriage" wasn't anything to be envious of. It was two close friends putting in a lot of work to protect their appearance, that was all. Everything they did as a *couple* was an act, it was made up. What Nathan and I shared, or what Audra and Vivian shared was something real, concrete. I tried to convey that to Audra for a long time, but she seemed to have a bit more of an envious side than I did. I think there was something in her that was worried and felt like she couldn't have Vivian fully to herself while she was still married to Nathan, but whether they were married or not made no difference. From day one they'd never slept in the same bed, they had different routines, they dated other people; they were just a rouse for each other. As I thought back, it occurred to me that it was possible Vivian had also suppressed her desire to have a baby in fear of Audra's reaction. I could only imagine what Audra would say if she caught wind of what was running through everyone's minds.

"So, let me ask you this," I started, "did she just generally say she wanted to have a baby, or did she talk about actually *having* a baby?"

"I don't get the difference."

"Well, I mean, was she just confiding in you that she wished she could get pregnant, or did she say she wanted to get pregnant?" I asked. It was one thing if she was just expressing her emotions and wishing it were a possibility versus saying she actively wanted to get pregnant. I sighed as I watched him try to recall the conversation they'd had. "I think you need to talk to her before you get worked up. For all you know she was just drunkenly sharing her emotions, but if she is thinking she might want to get pregnant you need to think about whether that's something you're comfortable doing, and I think she needs to think about that too. You should also talk about whether it'd affect your relationship as well."

"What about ours?" he looked at me.

"Whatever you decide, you and I, we're okay. I get it. I mean, I'd rather my partner not sleep with someone else but if this is something you two seriously want there's not much of a choice. You can't just wish upon a star and like the Virgin Mary she'll get pregnant. I told myself a long time ago that if this was a decision you two made, then I would have to be okay with it," I told him. It was true. They didn't give much thought to it ahead of time, but I did - I had to.

A part of me wanted to tell Nathan it was a bad idea. I didn't see the state Vivian was in, but if she looked anything like Nathan, and I figured she did, then the whole idea was going to be a train wreck. He looked panicked and pale, unsure about the whole situation. He seemed to have no idea what he thought or what he'd do if Vivian did say she wanted a child. I wasn't sure he'd even go along with the idea. Heck, maybe it was just the alcohol talking and Vivian would back out. Nathan had never slept with a woman, and Vivian had never been with a man. They were fully and completely uninterested in the opposite sex, so they'd be in for bit of a surprise. I slept around a lot when I was younger. After my parents died, I didn't feel the need do anything other than drink and socialize. I had always had an attraction to men, but when I was younger, I didn't know any better. I slept with many women before my first drunken encounter with a man who had been just as curious as I was. I realized there was no sex like sex with a man, at least for me. I found I was generally more attracted to men, however, that didn't stop me from still sleeping with a few women from time to time. Nathan and Vivian were different, they knew a long time ago the type of person that caught their attention. They didn't need to experiment; they didn't need to try something new. Vivian was always modest when it came to sex, she didn't talk about it much and considered it to be a private manner. Nathan was a bit more relaxed about it but still quite intimate. I, on the other hand, didn't think the topic should be taboo. Maybe it was because I'd slept with my fair share of people and had more experience, but I found it liberating to speak freely. It felt weird to be in a household where everyone was a bit more reserved. When she joined the conversation, Audra was a bit more willing to share her stories, but she wouldn't naturally bring up the topic herself. I never asked, but from my knowledge she too had known from a young age that she had a different sexual preference. I hadn't met too many people that knew the truth so young, and somehow, I ended up in a household with three of them.

I sighed as Audra popped into my head, I couldn't even imagine how she'd react if they did decide to test their boundaries and try to get pregnant. I did not want to be there for that conversation. It would just confirm her worries about their relationship. She'd never see it just as sex; she'd see it as so much more. I think for the most part it's easier for men to see sex as sex, for women it tends to be a lot more intimate, and Audra would be no exception.

"Nate," I put my hand on his, snapping him out of his thoughts. "Just talk to her. You two don't need to decide anytime soon. Besides, she'll want to talk to Audra and you know how that'll go. She might change her mind by the time Audra's through with her."

"Yeah, that's true," he seemed to calm a bit with my comment. After all, he knew I wasn't wrong. "Thanks."

"Walk me back to my booth? My lunch is pretty much finished," I said, glancing at my wristwatch. He nodded as he stood, and I patted him on the back. I wanted nothing more than to pull him into a tight embrace and assure him everything was going to be all right, but I held my composure as I always did in public. I'd wait until I saw him at home.

Maybe by then he'll have spoken to Vivian and things will have sorted themselves out. I could only hope they'd make the right decision.

CHAPTER EIGHT

AUDRA

I stood at the top of the stairs, just around the corner and out of sight. I took my time getting ready, trying to postpone leaving. Usually, I would be set to go, urging Vivian to hurry up as she casually took her time debating on what to wear – but this time I moved at such a glacial pace, even Vivian took notice. What I didn't anticipate was my sister deciding to show up early. I knew as soon as I heard a knock on the door that it was her, who else would be showing up on a Saturday? I heard Faith apologize for arriving early when Vivian greeted her at the door. She wanted to get some fresh air and figured it'd be a nice walk over to our place rather than us going out of our way to pick her up. I shook my head, what she didn't say was that our parents were probably bickering again. Faith couldn't deal with their arguing any more than I could. I took a seat on the top step, listening as they spoke.

"Audra should be down any moment, I think she's

just putting on her face," Vivian said, offering her something to drink.

"It's all right. You know, before this visit, I'd never seen her all done up with makeup," Faith said. "Well, I guess she's still not done up like ev'ryone use to expect her to be, but her hair is real nice and she's wearin' makeup for the first time in her life. She used to swear she'd never use the darn stuff."

"Really?"

"Oh yeah. When I was little, I used to offer to help her do her hair all nice and teach her how to put her shadows on, but she always got mad at me and would walk away," she said a little sadly.

"I take it from the stories you weren't very close."

"Yeah, but I never took it personally."

"No?"

"Nah, she was never real close to anyone. She wasn't real friendly with no one either, people didn't really talk much to her," Faith said. I debated on going down and breaking up the conversation. I wasn't a fan of her talking about me while I wasn't in the room, I wasn't sure what was going to come out of her mouth. I decided to give it another moment, to see where she was headed.

"She didn't have any friends?"

"Well, people tried, but she wasn't too interested in being theirs. She'd call 'em simple-minded and ignorant. I think she was bein' a bit simple-minded and ignorant not givin' 'em a chance," Faith answered. "That's why ev'ryone was so shocked when Bobby Michaels asked her to the prom."

I decided to take that as my cue to disrupt the

conversation. I didn't need her going into details of my past. I'd already told Vivian all about the Bobby Michaels disaster, and I didn't need my sister retelling the tale from a third-party perspective. I stopped as I heard Vivian speak up.

"I heard all about it. I find it odd they started those rumors just because she said no. She had the right to not want to go out with him," she replied, pausing for a moment before asking a question that caught my attention. "Can I ask a personal question?"

"Sure."

"Did you ever encourage the rumors?"

"Oh! No! No, I didn't," Faith was quick to respond. I sat back down, continuing to eavesdrop on their conversation to see where it was headed. "In fact, I tried to stop 'em. I felt bad 'cause although we weren't close, she was still my sister. I got teased for defendin' her, but I still denied 'em. You know, even after all the mean things she said to me, I still put up a fight for her."

"Mean things?"

"She'd call me simple-minded too, and she'd yell at me. I don't think it was real fair 'cause I was little. I mean, I'm six years younger than her. I guess now that I'm older I see why she'd do that."

"I'm not sure that there's a real excuse for someone treating their sister poorly," Vivian responded kindly. I couldn't help but roll my eyes; she was being a bit hypocritical. She said some pretty choice words about her brother, granted he was in a league of his own, but there's always a reason and often it's a good enough one.

"She was upset and, between us, I can see why she

was so mad, why she didn't act like the rest of us. She had open eyes, and we were just goin' 'bout our little sheltered lives. She was always standin' up for people or fightin' for the right to spend time with someone who was different. Always put her in a lot of hot water, but she ain't never cared. She always had gumption. But," she paused, her voice lowering, "I figured out her secret."

"You did?" Vivian said in an insecure tone.

Although I couldn't see her, I could picture Vivian's face going pale. I felt my stomach turn. She knew? Was that why she was being so nice? To hold something over my head? For a moment I felt sick, and I didn't know why. I thought I would be overcome with relief. Would it really be so bad if she knew? I tried to shake off my panic and continued to listen. I prayed that Vivian urged her to explain, what was it she knew exactly? I wanted to go down there and intervene myself, but I knew I should stay.

"I did, and I never told a soul. That's why I was so insistent on comin' up here with our folks."

"Oh?"

"Yeah, and I'm proud of her for stickin' to her beliefs."

"You are?" Vivian sounded as confused as I felt.

"Yeah, I know all about her creek friends, and I really needed to talk to her 'bout-"

"Wait, what?" Vivian tried to get her to backpedal. I could almost feel the relief rushing through Vivian's body as she realized the secret she thought Faith had known was not her own. "What creek friends?"

"The friends Pa scorned her for playin' with 'cause

they were black. She used to go see 'em in secret but she don't know I know, and somethin' real important came up that I need to talk to her 'bout."

"Oh, um-"

"Am I interruptin'?" I said as I finally walked down the stairs, breaking up their conversation. I glanced at Vivian who looked at me with obvious relief, before looking at my sister who was startled by my sudden appearance.

"No, not at all," Vivian replied. A moment of silence passed by before she spoke again, cutting the tension. "Shall we go?"

We were originally going to drive to the restaurant but decided to make our way to a local café instead after Vivian raved about how delicious the soup was. It was a couple blocks away, so we chose to wear our more comfortable dress shoes before heading out. The walk was quiet. No one knew what to say. I could tell Faith really wanted to talk to me, but her silence made me feel the topic was meant for a private conversation. I was dying to know what it was she had on her mind, and my chest felt tight just thinking about it. She said it had something to do with Taye and Nan, but what could she possibly have to say to me about them? I hadn't seen them in years. They were my best friends and they vanished into thin air without a clue as to where or why, so what could my sister, who'd never met them, have to say? I could tell Vivian felt the tension and was unsure of what to do. She looked like she kept trying to find topics to talk about but fell short. I was probably overthinking things. For all I knew she just wanted to brag that she'd uncovered my secret and had known all this time.

Once we reached the café and found our seats, Faith finally spoke, breaking the silence.

"It's real nice of you to invite me here, especially without Ma and Pa. They're so controllin' I feel like I'm back home except for the taller buildin's."

"Well, that's a shame. At least they were more than happy to bring you with them. I think maybe they also needed alone time," Vivian responded.

"You're tellin' me."

"So, how have you been enjoying your trip so far?" Vivian asked. "Anything you were hoping to see but haven't yet?"

"I really wanna go see a play; I hear the theater here in New York is amazin'."

"We do have some wonderful entertainment."

"Do you think you'd be willin' to take me?"

"Faith," I shot with a hushed tone, but it was strong enough to catch her attention. "Don't be rude, she ain't gonna take you."

"Audra!" Vivian objected.

"What? She shouldn't be askin' you that."

"She can ask whatever she'd like," she said firmly. She shook her head and raised an eyebrow as she stared at me with dismay. I couldn't believe she was upset with *me*. All I was saying was that my sister shouldn't be asking someone she barely knew to take her out for an expensive outing. Who was going to pay for the tickets? It wasn't as if Faith had any money and my folks sure as hell weren't going to pay for the tickets.

"Fine," I grumbled, turning back to my sister,

"sorry Faith. Ask whatever you'd like, but she's not takin' you."

"Audra, really?" Vivian snipped at me before turning back to my sister. "I'd love to Faith. How's tomorrow? I'm sure we can find tickets for something exciting."

"Really?" Faith asked excitedly, almost jumping out of her chair.

"Are you kiddin' me?" I asked her, furious.

"Audra, can I speak to you in private?" Vivian motioned for me to get up, but Faith stood before either of us had a chance to move. She said she needed to use the restroom, but we both knew it was to give us a minute to speak alone. Vivian waited until she was out of sight before she turned her attention to me. "Why are you being so rude to her?"

"Why are you bein' so nice to her?"

"Because I'd like to think we're becoming friends."

"Friends? You just met her! This is the most you've talked since she's arrived."

"Fine. At the very least she's your sister and your behavior is unacceptable. Audra, what's gotten into you? This is completely out of character," Vivian shook her head. I tried to hide the fact that I knew she was right. I wasn't usually so spiteful, but I couldn't help it. When I was around Faith it just came out. Vivian didn't understand. This wasn't Faith. No one changes so quickly. I don't care what she told her about defending me against any rumors she heard or sticking up for me, I knew for a fact that she didn't. If she had been on my side, she wouldn't have ignored me in the school hallways, and wouldn't have cracked jokes about me to the popular kids when I walked by just to earn a laugh. I hadn't forgotten, she was just as much a part of what made my life in Georgia miserable as anyone else was, perhaps more. As I listened to Vivian, I knew the reasonable side of me should give her a chance. Maybe she was really turning over a new leaf, but I just couldn't move past my stubborn feelings. "Look at her, Audra. She's not the little girl you disliked as a teenager, she's a lovely young lady who is here to visit *you*. She wants to see you, her *sister*. So, stop whatever *this* is and treat her like a sister, *kindly*."

I bit my lip as I looked into Vivian's eyes. She didn't say another word but the look on her face pleaded to me to do my best. I nodded; I'd at least try.

I took a deep breath as Faith cautiously made her way back to the table. As she sat down, I smiled and apologized, though I wasn't sure I really meant it. No matter what Faith said, I promised myself I wouldn't get upset and that I'd keep a calm and cool head. I could do that for one meal... I hoped.

CHAPTER NINE

Through my sunglasses I watched as Nathan made his way across the courtyard towards me. Over the last few days our conversation had been minimal as we found ourselves unsure of what to say when we were left alone without the buffer of Audra or William. On my way out the door this morning he had asked if I wanted to grab a bite to eat on our lunch hour, and that he'd take an extended break and meet me at the school. I told him I'd love to but deep down I couldn't help but feel unsettled. I felt embarrassed ever since I'd drunkenly shared the thoughts that had been running through my head. Truthfully, I wasn't quite sure what I wanted or what I thought, but clearly what I said put him on edge. He tried to act normal, but his attempt came off a bit strained.

I walked towards him as he waved. I embraced him in a hug before we headed off towards the restaurant we had decided on. It was a new bistro around the corner from the school; I'd been there a few times before and had enjoyed my last few meals. We had reserved a table so were seated right away, and we were fortune to be seated in the corner by the window, creating a bit of privacy.

"What's good here?" he asked, looking at the menu.

"The butternut squash soup, or the salad is nice," I told him, glancing over the menu debating if I wanted to try something new or stick to a safe and familiar choice. By the time the waitress came around I had decided to play it safe with a pasta salad I had ordered once before, whilst Nathan went for a grilled chicken plate. Once the waitress left, we both sat in silence for a few minutes, unsure who was going to break the quiet first.

"I wanted to talk to you about the other day," Nathan finally said, it seemed it was easier to get to the point than to beat around the bush. I shifted in my chair uncomfortably, which did not go unnoticed.

"Nathan, I had a bit too much to drink and let myself ramble. I don't even really remember what I said," I was only half lying. I did have too much to drink but I recalled exactly what I had blurted out. "We don't have to talk about it."

"We do though," he replied, catching himself on his quick words. "I mean, we should, or we can-"

"Nathan..."

"I guess, I guess I just need to know if you were serious."

"Serious about what?"

"Wanting a baby," he said as he searched my eyes for an answer. I wasn't sure he'd find one. I didn't know what I wanted for sure, and I certainly hadn't figured it out in the last few days. I broke eye contact with him while I took a sip of water. As I put the glass down, I saw he had not looked away from me, holding out for an answer.

"I don't know. I don't know what I'm feeling," I replied. "I'm telling the truth."

"So, what you said-"

"I don't know. I suppose a part of it was true. I do want children, but I don't know if I can have kids," I answered him, shaking my head, and looking out the window. "There's just been so many factors that have pushed me from that vision. Between my career and our, well, our relationship it just wasn't really in the cards. I guess I just started thinking about kids and adopting, and I was really excited about the prospect of adopting, but out of nowhere I started getting these visions of what it would be like if I got pregnant."

I had started looking into adoption after Elaine mentioned her experience working as a volunteer at a local orphanage. There were so many children who needed homes, but not enough people wanting or able to take them in. I could just imagine bringing a little one into the house and showering them with so much love. I even thought about the idea of convincing Nathan to adopt a child a little older in age. I know he loved babies, but babies found homes so much easier than some of the children. The child would also be old enough to go to school, so it'd be perfect with my work schedule. They are demanding in a completely different way than a baby, but perhaps we were better suited for those challenges. I also had Audra and William to factor in, because although Nathan and I would legally be adopting the child together, Audra and William would be viewed as parental figures as well. I know Audra would be a wonderful parent no matter the age of the child, and for all we knew she and William might've considered following suit and working together to adopt a child themselves. It was a lot to think about and a lot to discuss with everyone, but it just seemed like a perfect way to create a family.

For a moment, I had felt confident, ready to talk to Nathan and hear his opinion on the idea. I thought perhaps we could even go to the orphanage to see how we felt once we were there, but then the moment of certainty faded, and I found myself overwhelmed. Instead of going home and speaking to him, I chose to go dress shopping. I was by myself, and I picked a pink one off the hanger and decided to try it on. It looked beautiful hanging there but didn't fit my shape at all. It hung loosely around my hourglass figure and made me look wider in the hips than I actually was. I turned to the side, shaking my head at how terrible the dress was and paused. I couldn't stop staring as I stood to the side, focused on how the dress flared out midway through my stomach, creating a slight bump. I looked around to make sure no one saw me as I slowly placed my hand on my stomach, feeling my hand tremble. As I left my hand lightly pressed on my abdomen, I exhaled a long breath as feelings of sadness and horror took over. I had not once thought about getting pregnant before that moment, but out of nowhere, by chance, I had a momentary glance of what it might feel like, and I hadn't been able to shake the image since. I quickly changed back into my own clothing before I left the store in a haste. I hadn't told a soul about that moment, not even Audra or Elaine. I knew it was normal for women to experience those feelings, but I still felt embarrassed. I couldn't look in the mirror for days without unconsciously looking at my stomach. When I was alone, I found my hand gradually move over my abdomen, resting there before I noticed what I'd done. I had experienced vivid dreams that left me so happy while I slept but would leave me emotionally drained and upset when I woke. I didn't want to experience those feelings, but I did. I was so angry; I was set on adopting - it was the only thing that made sense. Perhaps the inability to carry a child was making my subconscious want it more.

I shouldn't have said what I said to Nathan, they were thoughts I hadn't been ready to share. They just sort of slipped out, and then I couldn't stop myself. It was different when I was casually and theoretically talking to Elaine, but to admit to anyone how deep those feelings truly were made my insides twist in knots. I had barely touched on exactly what I was feeling, I had just said that it was something I think I might want, and already Nathan seemed to spiral into a world of confusion and stress.

"I've just been thinking about what you said."

"What did I say exactly?" I inquired, raising an eyebrow. We paused our conversation as the waitress brought our food over and waited until she was out of earshot before continuing.

"I just want to be there for you, no matter what you're feeling. If you decide you don't want kids, if you decide you do, if you – the point is, I want you to be able to come to talk to me and feel comfortable."

"It's not the most comfortable of conversations, Nate."

"Have you spoken to Audra?" he sighed as I shook my head and looked down. I didn't know what I'd say to her. It was a conversation with no good outcome. I'd only lightly chatted with Elaine about the options, and she was impartial. She didn't have any emotional ties besides friendship, and I felt she might be better to offer some insight. I already knew what Audra would say, that I was crazy to even entertain the thought. I guess deep down I knew it would never be a reality, so why start an argument?

"Like I said, it's a difficult conversation."

"When did you start feeling this way?"

"I don't know," I answered truthfully.

"Well, I guess it doesn't really matter, the fact is you feel this way now," Nathan replied. "I'm here for you and whatever you decide I will support you no matter what."

"I know."

"I just want you to know you have some options, and we'll figure it out," he answered, taking my hand from across the table and giving it a tight squeeze. I slowly pulled my hand away from him, which caught him off guard. I took a second to run his words through my mind; I was a tad confused. What did he mean by *some* options? As far as I was aware I had two: have no children or adopt. His use of the word *some* indicated more than two. I felt my heart pound as my anxiety began to increase, I wasn't sure if I understood him correctly.

"Nathan…"

"I'm just saying, if it's what you truly want, it's not out of the question," he said, his words and eyes confirmed what I thought he was saying.

I took another large sip of water and fiddled with the napkin on my lap. I wasn't sure how to respond. I suddenly felt overwhelmed. I realized how easy I had things only moments ago. I just had to struggle with the fact that I wanted to have a baby but couldn't. Nathan was now proposing that the possibility of carrying a child was an actual option and I felt the weight of the world crushing down on my shoulders. I looked down at our untouched plates. We both seemed to have lost our appetites.

"I don't know, Nathan," was all I could manage to get out.

"If having a baby is something you really want, there's not much of a choice. I just want to let you know I understand how you feel. Maybe not to the same degree but I get it," he said. "I've felt those same feelings. You know, when you're young you have these dreams of having a perfect little family one day and for a lot of people, that dream comes true. I think for us, as we've grown, that vision has gotten lost along the way. It didn't seem like it could be real, so we buried our feelings, and we were okay with it. That is, until our friends started having kids. We watched their dreams become a reality. We watched the joy a baby brought them, and the life they were able to build. For some, having kids may not be a priority and that's okay. But for the others who do want kids, when faced with the reality that it just might not ever happen, it creates a bit of a void that nothing can quite fill. It's okay if you're one of those people, Vivi. I know I am."

I tried to hold back my tears as my eyes glossed over while he spoke. I was thankful to be sitting with my back to the rest of the restaurant. I wiped the one tear that managed to escape and bit my lip. I didn't know what to say. I didn't think that Nathan could possibly understand, I never even thought to consider it a possibility. As I sat there in front of my best friend, I felt so vulnerable but so comforted knowing that I didn't need to explain what was going through my mind. I think he had pinpointed exactly what I couldn't find a way to say to him.

"I'm scared it would ruin us," I finally spoke honestly. "We've always had this perfect relationship. It was never complicated. We just worked because we were a team, but we lived our separate lives. We made our own rules."

"That wouldn't change."

"Sex complicates things, Nate. Plus, we wouldn't even know what we were doing – and Audra and Will… how would we explain that to them? I can't even imagine my own reaction, let alone theirs," I said in a hushed tone, not wanting anyone to overhear us. I stopped as Nathan sat back in his seat and avoided eye contact. I leaned forward, we had lived under the same roof long enough that I knew when he was holding something back. My tone changed unexpectedly, as though I could sense I wasn't going to like what he was about to say, "what?"

"Will knows."

"Will knows *what* exactly?"

"I might have told him," he replied awkwardly.

"Nathan!" I snapped, unable to keep my voice quiet. I halted and bit my lip as I realized a few people had glanced over when I had responded a bit louder than I intended. I lowered my voice, feeling my cheeks flush in anger. How could he? "That was meant to stay between us."

"I didn't know."

"Yes, you did," I shook my head. He knew very well what kind of conversation was meant to stay between us and which he could share with William. I understood he talked to William about almost everything, just as I talked to Audra, but there were things Nathan told me that I had never told Audra out of respect for him. He knew this was something I did not want anyone knowing, I didn't even really want Nathan to know. I was so furious I found myself unable to speak. I put the napkin on the table and pulled my chair out to stand.

"Where are you going?" Nathan asked concerned as he got to his feet.

"I can't do this right now," was all I could say as I turned around and left the restaurant. Nathan could take our untouched meals with him and settle the bill; I couldn't stay there another moment. My blood was boiling, and my nerves were shot. I felt as though I was being thrown back and forth. One minute I felt comforted and secure, and the next, I was open and exposed. I had been rattled over discussing the situation with Nathan, and to learn he had shared the whole thing with William mortified me. God, what if Will had let something slip and Audra found out before I spoke to her? What if Will suddenly resented me over nothing more than a thought? I wiped the tears that streamed down my face as I walked back towards the campus. I tried to keep them at bay to prevent my makeup from running, but it was no use.

I gasped as I suddenly felt someone grab my arm tightly and pull me back, swinging me around. It happened so fast; my heart skipped a beat as I was taken into a tight embrace. I knew right away as soon as I was drawn into his arms that it was Nathan. He must've run after me when I left the restaurant. I tried to push him away, I wanted to be left on my own, but he wouldn't let me go. It was no use, I couldn't struggle, and he was too broad and strong. In defeat, I rested my head against his chest and continued to cry. He loosened his grip and stroked his hand over my hair, soothing me as I tried to catch my breath.

"Vivi, I'm so sorry," I could hear the pain in his voice. I cried as I nodded and put my arms around him, reciprocating the hug. I knew he was, and I couldn't help but feel like, for some reason, I was too.

CHAPTER TEN

I don't think so," I shook my head as I stared into my reflection, I felt like I'd tried on a dozen dresses and I hadn't liked any of them, whilst my Ma gushed over each and every one. I could've put a white sheet on, and I was sure she'd love it. It wasn't like I looked bad in them; I just didn't like them. Plus, they were real expensive, and I just felt sick about spending the money on something so ridiculous. Maybe if this was a real wedding and I was walking down the aisle to Vivian I'd feel different, but that wasn't the case. I felt bad because, to my Ma and sister, this was a real wedding. They never thought I'd get married, heck, I never thought I'd get married - but there I was trying on satins and lace. I asked if I could just wear Vivian's and get it tailored, which she said would be fine with her. She had a beautiful ivory A-line dress, with soft lace trim and dainty long sleeves. It looked like it could be altered easily and then we could use the money on something else. Although Vivian didn't mind my family sure did, they kept saying I needed my own style. Whatever that meant. I think they just wanted to watch me try on a bunch of dresses.

"Oh, but Audi, you look so nice in that one," my Ma said, disappointed I had turned down another one of her choices. I shook my head; it was too heavy, and the sleeves were itchy.

I watched as Faith came towards me with a dress that looked a bit too fluffy for my taste. She begged me to try it and since it was her first pick, I decided to give it a chance. When I came out, I was surprised. It wasn't as big as I thought. It was a tee length dress that flared at the hip. It had little cap sleeves, but an open front with a slight v-neck that showed off my chest just enough to still be tasteful. I looked at Vivian to see whether she liked it or not. I raised an eyebrow as she offered a slight smile, but I could tell it wasn't genuine. Her eyes looked sad, and her smile was just a slight curve of her lips. I watched as she glanced down at the ground. She had been real quiet the whole time, which had made me suspicious something was up, but now I was certain.

"Would y'all mind lookin' for some more options? I ain't quite sure if I found the *one* yet," I said to my sister and Ma, giving them an excuse to leave the room that wouldn't be too obvious. They didn't even bat an eyelash; they were up and out of the room before I could say another word. Once I knew they were out of sight I stepped off the pedestal and walked towards Vivian, who finally looked up as she saw me coming towards her.

"Is everything all right?" she asked me.

"I was 'bout to ask you the same thing," I replied as I crouched in front of her. I placed my hands on her knees for support as I leaned on the balls of my feet. I rubbed her thighs as I looked at her. "You seem off."

"I'm fine, really," she answered unconvincingly.

"You don't seem fine," I said as I reached my hand up and placed it gently on her cheek and stroked her skin. She leaned into my hand and sighed before she looked at me, insisting everything was all right, claiming she was just tired. I knew the difference between when she was tired and when something was troubling her. I felt uneasy as I looked into her glossy eyes. It was not like Vivian to be keeping secrets, I thought we had moved past her need to keep everything bottled up, but it was like old habits were resurfacing. "Vivi…"

"I'm okay, really. I suppose there's a lot on my mind."

"You look so sad," I commented on her expression. I watched as she glanced up and saw herself in the mirror, letting out an embarrassed sigh. "What is it?"

"That dress is beautiful on you."

"Thanks," I was confused. She didn't exactly give me an answer.

"How are you doing?" she changed the subject again. "You don't look very impressed up there."

"Well, tryin' on dresses for a weddin' that's not real ain't my idea of a good time."

"To them it's real."

"What'd you mean?" I shook my head, raising an eyebrow.

"I mean that the wedding is more for them than it is for you. When Nathan and I decided to get married, it was to be able to blend into society and live our lives with as little judgment as possible. I could be fifty and dating someone new every night if I wanted to, but to my family and everyone else, I was married, settled, and... *normal.* We had a wedding bigger than we wanted, but the wedding wasn't for us, it was for my parents and for the people who had dreamed of my wedding day. It was a fun day of dancing and drinking, but Nathan and I didn't want or need a wedding. You don't care about trying on dresses but from the moment you were little, your mother pictured this moment. It's for her."

"Don't mean I have to like it," I replied.

"No, I suppose it doesn't."

"Can we talk tonight, please?" I begged her, staring at her with concern in my eyes. She nodded and glanced around to make sure no one was there before leaning towards me and kissing my lips. I sighed; I missed her lips. Although I was right there with her, she felt so far away from me. It had felt that way for days.

I stood just in time for Faith and my Ma to come back through the door with a few more gowns. As they brought them to the dressing room, I glanced at Vivian and nodded before throwing a smile on my face and bearing through it. She was right, this was for Ma. This whole ordeal was for them, and they would be heading back to Georgia in a day so I might as well grin and bear it the best I could.

Before we had left to go to the Bridal store Vivian told me she didn't expect to be so emotional about the idea of watching me try on wedding dresses, and I knew she didn't mean in an excited way. She seemed to dread the idea as much as I did. As I tried on dresses, I couldn't help but wonder if maybe she finally understood what I've been feeling for years.

I think I knew I loved Vivian from the moment I saw her, or maybe just after that. I used to look down on people who said things like that. I didn't understand how you could fall for someone so quickly. How could you possibly know that you would have something other than a physical attraction? Sex was one thing, but to truly connect with someone was completely different. I always rolled my eyes when people would go on a date with someone they'd just met and come home saying they knew they were the one. The number of times the relationship broke apart a month later was too many to count. Meeting Vivian changed my views. I hadn't had an attraction to someone so quickly before in my life. From the moment she opened her mouth something just caught my attention. Maybe it was the way she looked, maybe the way she carried herself, maybe her manner. I couldn't really say. After our first encounter, I just thought maybe it was a crush but every day for nearly a week I couldn't stop staring at her and I noticed she couldn't stop staring at me either. I'd catch her watching me as she sat under the big tree in the courtyard at the same time almost every day. I kept showing up more just to see her. I finally got the courage to ask her to lunch, and we just clicked. I had noticed the wedding ring she wore, but she was so quick to give me her answer to lunch that I thought maybe she just wore it for show.

Keep the guys off her back. I knew lots of women that did the same thing, especially when they got asked out a lot. It wasn't uncommon so I let it go. I didn't bring it up for the next few lunch dates we had because I really liked where things were headed, and I figured she'd tell me if she was really married. It had taken nearly two weeks before she was able to summon up the courage and broach the subject. I had sat back in my seat and shook my head.

"What's his name?" I knew this story, I'd seen this story, I'd dated this story. Woman marries man, realizes she has a thing for women, starts to secretly date outside the marriage, but never actually wants to leave him. I couldn't be in a relationship like that. I couldn't fall for someone and give her everything I had, but then have her go home to someone she didn't love. I couldn't be in a relationship with someone and know the intimacy we shared, both emotionally and physically, was also being shared with the man they were married to.

"Nathan," she said honestly but was quick to continue. "But it's not what you think."

"I bet it's exactly what I think," I replied, shaking my head. She had begged me to meet her after she was finished work, and promised she'd explain but the restaurant we were at wasn't a great place to talk. I hesitantly agreed, finding it hard to say no as she pleaded with me to hear her out.

I kept my promise and met her after school in the courtyard. We had walked together to an isolated area where she told me everything just like she promised. It was a damn shame that I didn't believe her. I had a hard time wrapping my head around the fact that someone who had seemed to be so accepting of who she was could get herself into such a web of lies like that. She explained everything to me and answered every question I had. She let herself be an open book.

"Please Audra, you have to believe me," Vivian replied.

"Okay, let's say I *did* believe you; I don't know how this whole thing would work," I answered her honestly. "It just seems a bit awkward and complicated."

"It might appear that way from how I'm explaining it, but it's really not. We live in the same house, and we attend each other's work functions for show, but other than that we're just friends."

"So, you're tellin' me there's not *once* been anythin' more than friendship?"

"Never. We've always had separate bedrooms. I've never been with a man, and I don't intend to ever be with one."

"He feel the same 'bout you?" I couldn't help but ask the question. For all I knew she felt that way, but maybe he was secretly in love with her and hoping she'd fall for him some day.

"Nathan is in a very healthy relationship with his boyfriend," Vivian replied as she shook her head. "Trust me, please."

I didn't know how to feel. I had heard whispers of people doing such things but never met anyone who'd actually done it. It just didn't make sense to me. Vivian told me that her family and the world she was from was difficult, but it couldn't have been any more difficult than my life was back in Georgia. I had insisted on meeting Nathan before we kept seeing each other because I was still unconvinced. I just did not get it. Even if I were still stuck back in Georgia, I wouldn't have scarified my morals just to appease others like she did.

Except that I did... or was going to. I sighed as I thought back to how strongly I'd felt that the idea was absurd, and now there I was, standing in a wedding dress to make everyone else around me happy. What had happened to me?

I felt more secure about what Vivian had told me after meeting Nathan. She had arranged a double date that Friday night so that I could see there was nothing to hide. At that point, Nathan and William had been together for nearly two years and they seemed very devoted to each other. I was shocked when she had told me that William lived under the same roof with her and Nathan. It threw me off to imagine her living with two men but, for what it was worth, she was right; they did seem be very happy together and I sensed everything that was said was truthful. They actually made me more comfortable than I had anticipated, and I was more convinced about the arrangement than I had been previously.

What I had not foreseen was the jealousy that I quickly developed towards Nathan. I knew I didn't really have anything to be envious of but, over the years, even after I had moved in as well, I couldn't shake the feeling in my stomach. Every time he and Vivian went to a work event together, or a charity ball, or a wedding, or whatever came up, I felt overcome with resentment.

Everyone thought they were just the sweetest couple and even I couldn't deny they looked good together. I wished I were able to take Vivian out to places like that without the fear of something happening. I wished I could whisk her away on the dance floor or put my arm around her like Nathan did for show. I knew it was just friendship, and I was confident he would never do anything, but it still rubbed me the wrong way. It was a feeling that, even to this day, I couldn't shake.

As I came out in another gown, I looked in the mirror and stared at Vivian's reflection. She had a small smile on her face, but I could tell it was forced. I couldn't help but wonder if she felt uncomfortable watching me try on wedding dresses – I know I certainly would have if the roles were reversed. I sighed; it was easier for her when she got married. Neither she nor Nathan were in a relationship, so they didn't have anyone to be concerned about - unlike Will and I did. I often questioned if she got as upset when Will and I went out, as I did when I saw her with Nathan. I wasn't sure she did. Will and I were friends, but we weren't close like Nathan and Vivian were... granted, they had years of friendship on us. Still, I had to wonder.

"Oh, Audi, you look pretty as a peach," my Ma said gasping, catching my attention through the mirror. I glanced from her to my sister who looked equally excited about the dress I was in. To me it looked exactly like all the others, but they seemed attached to this one in particular. "What'd you think?"

I turned and looked at myself in the mirror. The dress didn't make me feel anything, but when I watched

Faith and my Ma through the reflection, I could tell how excited they were.

"I think this is the one," I responded to them, watching the delight spread across their faces. I kept reminding myself that this was for them. I just had to stay focused on that for the next couple of months until we got through the wedding, and then it'd all be over, and things could get back to normal.

CHAPTER ELEVEN

I jinxed myself. I had believed the evening was going to go smoothly. It was our last dinner with Audra's family before they left for their long drive home in the morning. We had finally reached a point where I didn't feel awkward around them, and they had stopped calling me Willie. That alone was progress. Her father had quit his quips at me, her mother always included me in the conversation and, much to Audra's dismay, I was getting along incredibly well with Faith. I was amazed at how well we bonded, though I was careful not to agree too much with her if she had a disagreement with Audra, even if I thought she was right. I knew Audra was sensitive about it and I didn't want her to think she was being ganged up on.

Things were going really well at the beginning. We went to a restaurant that wasn't far from the house. We all sat down, ordered food and drinks, and everyone was behaving. That was, until Faith opened her mouth.

"Y'all should come back to Georgia with us," she had said. I was so caught off guard by her suggestion that I embarrassed myself by choking on air when I silently gasped. I had a hard time understanding what I had just heard because it came from left field and at first, Audra seemed to be in disbelief as well.

"What?" Audra asked, confused.

"It's just, Mamaw can't travel all the way up here for the weddin' and I'm sure she'd really like to meet Will before he's part of the family," Faith said with wide eyes as she batted her eyelashes, as if that tactic would work on Audra.

I didn't think I had ever seen Audra so angry. I could almost see the steam coming out of her ears as she sat there, furious. Just as she was about to object, Francine decided to put her two cents in.

"Oh Audi, that'd be such a lovely idea!" she exclaimed. "You haven't seen Mamaw since you left, and she ain't gettin' any younger. Wouldn't it be nice if y'all took a drive down? You could show William where you grew up."

"Ma, I don't think that's a good idea. I doubt Will can get the time off work and of course I-" Audra tried to argue her, but her mother was persistent. It was clear where Audra got her stubbornness.

"Audi, really. Even if Will can't take time off, you still ought to come down to see Mamaw. She's always askin' about you."

"Your Ma's right, Audi. Ah, common, it'd be fun," Clyde chimed in, before taking a sip of his drink. "You don't wanna disappoint Mamaw."

Audra's eyes were glossed over as she held back tears, her cheeks flushed with fury, but her facial expression showed only horror. I could tell she was having an internal debate; I would be too if I were her. Just when I thought that maybe Audra was starting to give Faith a chance, her little sister decided to go and pull something so risky and set her off again. How could Faith really expect her to just pick up and leave like that? Their parents were due to leave tomorrow morning, and Audra couldn't have been more thrilled to have them heading out at dawn. She wouldn't have to see them until the wedding, and she could relax for the first time since they'd arrived. I could see Audra shift uncomfortably, privately debating the proposition. She'd told us many times how close she was to her grandmother, and that she called her all the time. Her grandmother had encouraged her to pursue her big city dreams and had always supported her in everything she did. However, I was fairly certain her grandmother was also in the dark about Audra's relationship history. I couldn't say I blamed Audra for keeping her mouth shut, she was probably too scared to take the risk of telling her and losing the closest relative she had. Although she called her grandmother all the time, it wasn't the same as seeing her. I got a sense that a part of her wanted to visit since it'd been so long since they'd seen each other, but the other part of her didn't want to go back to the place she had run away from. Not to mention, she didn't like that Faith had sprung something like that on her.

"William, you think you could get time off?"

Francine asked, putting a hand on my shoulder.

"I guess I can ask," I replied, not knowing how else to respond. I shrugged when Audra shot me a nasty glare. What else was I supposed to say? I understood she wanted me to be her scapegoat, but I was not the best at lying on a whim.

"No, no, we ain't droppin' ev'rythin' and drivin' all the way there. We've got too much to do here and-"

"Audi, quit bein' so stubborn," Clyde replied.

"Stubborn? Are you really gonna sit there and-"

"Audra, can I talk to you a moment?" I interrupted her. She snapped her attention to me, caught off guard. She also seemed a bit frustrated that she kept getting cut off. She heaved a heavy sigh before she agreed to follow me. We excused ourselves as we walked out of the dining area. We decided to step outside to get some fresh air and have a moment to ourselves. As soon as we walked out the door, she turned to face me.

"What?"

"Audra, you don't need to get angry with me. I'm not the enemy."

"You're right, I'm sorry," she sighed. I didn't take it personally. She was overwhelmed. She had anticipated the evening going a bit smoother than this, but then again, should we really be that surprised? I wanted to get her away from the table to take a moment to collect herself. Audra could be hotheaded and say things rashly and I just wanted her to think about how she really wanted to proceed. Her parents were leaving tomorrow. She only had to make it through dinner. All it would take is a "no" and a well fashioned excuse to Faith's suggestion. We could make it through dinner, and they'd be gone by the morning. The problem was, based on how Audra looked, I could tell she wasn't completely sold on a "no" to the proposition.

"Do you want to go?" I asked. "Honestly?"

"Are you crazy? I ain't drivin' all the way back down there."

"So, you don't want to go see your grandmother?" I searched her eyes. If there was one reason that Audra was even considering the idea, it was for her.

"Well, yeah, I mean, of course I do but it's not a good time. I can't decide to just get up and leave," she rubbed her forehead and put her hands on her hips as she began to pace back and forth. "And this ain't fair of Faith. She knew Ma would hop on board with the idea, and it was somethin' that she should've asked me in private."

"You're right."

"And the nerve of askin' you to drop ev'rythin' to go down there-"

"Audra," I reached out to grab her arm. She stopped dead in her tracks and turned to look at me, confused. I released the hold I had on her forearm and sighed, "it's okay."

"What is?"

"If you want to go down there," I answered her. "I get it. There are a hundred reasons to not go back, but there's also one very good reason to go."

"Faith just made the suggestion to bug me."

"Maybe she did," I responded, "but it doesn't take away from it being a good point, about your grandmother."

"I'll go down eventually."

I took a seat on a nearby bench and motioned for her to sit next to me. She hesitated before she gave in and took a seat to my right; she fiddled her thumbs as she sat with her hands in her lap.

"My uncle practically raised me. I lost both my parents when I was seven. I was young, but I still remember every little thing about them. I remember how my father would throw a ball around with me, or how my mother's hair smelt. We were incredibly close, and I didn't have any siblings, so they gave me all their attention. They died in an automobile accident. They were driving home after a night out, and some drunken sailor hit them and the car flipped. Nobody could have foreseen it, and it was hard on me, but my Uncle Dave really stepped up. He was like a second father to me. Taught me everything he could, and we got close. My grandparents had already passed away, and with my parents gone it was just the two of us. He never married. I think he was too busy trying to be everything for everyone else," I told her, glancing at her as she looked up at me. I sighed as I continued. "When I was twenty or so, I moved here from Boston. I used to call my uncle here or there; just to tell him what I was up to. I was busy, going out drinking, having sex, enjoying life. I kept thinking I should go visit him, it wasn't that far, but I was young, and I was too busy figuring out who I was. I called him one night and we talked about the usual, and he asked me when I'd come see him. I promised him I'd take a train the following weekend. I got a call the next day that he had a heart attack."

"Will, I'm so sorry."

"I just," I took a second to collect myself, every time I spoke of him it made me tear up. "I was always saying next week, but every week I'd have an excuse. It wasn't that I didn't want to see him; I just got too busy with life. I think he understood because he always said I was just like him. Before he took me in, he was always out socializing and doing his own thing - unlike my father who settled down young. The point I'm trying to make is that you can't gain back time. I'd do anything to go back in time and have hopped on that train a few weeks earlier. You're always talking about how close you feel to your grandmother, and I just don't want you to make the same mistake I did. I'm not saying you have to go now, but don't let yourself get too wrapped up to remember you need to take advantage of those little moments."

"I never thought of it that way."

"No one ever does. It is possible Faith said that to bug you, but for all you know, she really meant it. She would know as well as anyone how close you were, and for all you know your grandmother said something to her about wishing she could be at the wedding," I reasoned, watching as she looked at the ground, sadly. I put my arm around her as she leaned into my side and rested her head against my chest, sighing. I rubbed her arm, comforting her.

"*If* I decide I want to go, would you-"

"Of course," I said, she didn't need to finish her

question. She needed someone to lean on and that someone was me. She couldn't very well go back home by herself. Besides, it might give her closure to show up to her hometown and brag to the people that had made her miserable. She looked beautiful, had a good job in the big city, and a new fiancé. Sure, she'd have a fake fiancé, but they'd didn't need to know that. "We could leave in a couple of days, and just meet your family there. That way we don't have to spend all that time travelling with them."

"What about Nathan and Vivian?" she sat up concerned.

"They'll understand. Besides, Nathan is busy with a big case right now and Vivian has exams coming up so they'll both be working late for days."

"I don't know…"

"I'm just saying if we go down for five days they won't even really notice, they'll be too preoccupied. We'll be home by the time they're wrapping up their hectic week, and back to their normal routines. If anything, the timing works out perfectly."

I watched as she ran through the facts in her head, she knew I was right. They both had jobs that often left them with weeks of demanding hours. With Nathan approaching a hearing and Vivian prepping for exams we were barely seeing them as it was and had already been heading to bed alone for the last week. It wouldn't be until the end of next week before they wrapped up their work.

"Thank you," she said as she took my hand and squeezed it. "I mean it, Will."

"In our own weird way, we're family, and I'd do anything for you."

She laughed as she leaned back on my shoulder and nodded, "same goes for me."

CHAPTER TWELVE

NATHAN

"**P**ut down the paperwork and step away from the table," I announced as I walked in the front door, startling Vivian. She put her pen down and took her reading glasses off before turning around to look at me, confused, "second degree murder."

"The case?"

"They tried to make a plea to lower the sentence to manslaughter in the first, and it was risky proceeding to trial on the evidence we had but the fool served himself on a platter once he got up on the stand. As soon as he opened his mouth, we knew we had him. So," I raised the bottle of wine I had in one hand and the food in the other, "we celebrate."

"Nathan, I'd love to but-"

"You can take the rest of the evening off. I know those papers aren't due for two more days and you're almost finished," I tried to convince her. She bit her lip as she contemplated. She watched as I did a little dance with the alcohol and food, trying to get her to lighten up. She finally gave in; I knew she'd be starving. She probably hadn't left her desk from the moment she got home. She went to the kitchen to grab some plates and cutlery as I went to get some glasses for the wine. I uncorked the bottle and filled each of our glasses halfway as she returned. She took the takeaway meals out of their containers and made us each a plate. I was fortunate enough to be friends with a chef, who didn't mind preparing me extra meals to pick up and bring home as long as I made the request ahead of time. He knew our schedules were hectic, so on weeks like these, he was more than happy to help me out. I smiled as I watched Vivian. I could see her eyes roll to the back of her head as she inhaled the scent of freshly made pasta, and I could practically hear her stomach rumble from across the table.

"Did you hear from Audra today?" I asked as I took a seat.

"No, but she told me yesterday that there was some kind of family dinner or something so it might be difficult to call. I assume you haven't heard from Will?"

"Actually, he called me early this morning," I said, as I took a sip of the merlot. "He mentioned the dinner thing too."

"I can't believe he agreed to go down there with her," she shook her head in disbelief, as she took a sip of wine herself. "I know it meant a lot to her."

"I think he felt she needed the support, and he *was* invited," I replied. It wasn't much different than what I'd done for Vivian at her family dinners and events. Then again, I'd never driven that sort of distance and had to spend five consecutive days with Vivian's family. I wouldn't be surprised if I lost my mind; Vivian could hardly spend more than a day or so with them herself.

I watched as she nodded before taking a bite of her food. I saw her glance up at me as I took a large gulp of my wine and immediately refilled my glass. She wiped her lips with her napkin and swallowed before she spoke, watching as I proceeded to top off her glass although she had only had a few sips, "is everything all right?"

"I'm fine. Just celebrating our hard work," I said as I raised my glass and waited for her to do the same before we clinked them and took a drink. "So, how was your day?"

"The usual. Professor McKay must be the oldest, most rigid man I've ever met. He is also completely unreasonable. I'm reviewing the pre-exam preparation and doing the paperwork for the actual test. Whilst I am already drowning, he's now asked me to start designing the new lesson plan for next semester. He already has me buried in paperwork, and yet can't help but pile on more," she sighed as she shook her head before continuing. "To make matters worse, his lessons plans are almost as ancient as he is, and he wants me to make new ones but not deviate from the ones he's always used. I don't understand why he asks me to design them when what he really wants is for me to reorganize and rework the same material each semester."

"Why don't you just say no?"

"I can't," she sighed as she shook her head. "I'm scared they're waiting for an excuse to replace me."

"You've worked there for years, and with the number of hours and dedication you've put in, they can't."

"But they can," she shrugged as I took the liberty of topping off her glass again. "They are misogynistic jerks, and there's nothing I can do."

I watched as she sighed, leaning back in her chair, slowly drinking her wine. Any time Vivian spoke about work she always seemed to need a drink. I took a few sips of my own, watching her. When we finished eating, I put the plates away and came back into the living room to see she had migrated to the sofa to get more comfortable. After hours of sitting on a wooden chair, her back must've welcomed the soft cushioning. I brought the wine to the table and took a seat next to her on the couch. Pouring the last of the bottle into her glass. I watched as she raised an eye at me suspiciously. She didn't say anything, but I think she had caught on that I kept refilling her glass anytime it seemed to fall below the halfway mark, not that she objected. In my defense, I kept mine quite full as well.

I urged Vivian to continue to discuss the difficulties she was having at school, as I always found she felt better after getting her frustrations off her chest. As she continued talking, I noticed the wine was taking effect when she tripped over a few of her words. She wasn't quite drunk, but she was definitely cloudy.

"Nathan, are you okay?" she asked as she finished her drink, staring at me as she placed a hand on my shoulder. I sighed as I looked back at her, her eyes were getting glossy, and her cheeks started to flush a bright red. "Nate?"

"I'm fine," I answered poorly. She stared at me for a minute, unconvinced from my tone of voice. I suddenly got up and headed towards the liquor cabinet. "Would you, uh, would you like another drink?"

"Nathan Philip Porter, are you trying to get me drunk?" she laughed jokingly, and shook her head. When I didn't return the smile, her expression went from playful to serious. I thought she would be angry, but she just seemed confused. "I was joking but you are... aren't you?"

"I'm sorry, Vivi," I replied. It wasn't what she thought, it wasn't my intention.

"I don't understand," she said as she tried to stand up, fumbling a bit. Having drank so quickly, the alcohol was hitting her suddenly all at once. I reached out to take her hand to steady her, but she retracted it.

"I... let me explain."

"Yes, I think you should," she said firmly.

"I just, I just wanted to talk," I said. I sighed as she took a step backwards shaking her head furiously. "I just thought it'd be easier if we had a few drinks."

"Then you *tell* me that!"

"I wasn't thinking," I replied as I plopped down on the couch, defeated. I felt awful. It wasn't my plan to finish a bottle that quickly, I honestly had just brought it home to celebrate our hard work, but once I had a glass, I started thinking about the elephant that seemed to be in the room every time we were together. I wanted to see if she had thought about what she wanted to do, and I started to panic. Last time we'd talked she ended up in tears. I just thought if we had a couple glasses it'd loosen us up and we'd be more willing to have a truthful and open conversation. I should've just told her, but at first, I didn't think about it – I just refilled her glass. Suddenly though, the thought had crossed my mind and I ... it was poor judgment. I shook my head; I wasn't that guy. I felt embarrassed and ashamed. I thought what I was doing was innocent, but as I saw Vivian's wary and unnerved reaction, I realized it wasn't. My actions were deceitful no matter how well intended I had thought them to be.

"No, you weren't," she sighed as she came closer and sat back on the couch next to me. "You know how I feel about tricks like this."

I did. Too many times during her family's functions did young men persistently get her drinks in hopes of her letting down her guard. For the most part, she'd been very perceptive, but it didn't take away the fear and frustration when someone tried. I'd always had a hatred for those men and suddenly I felt like one of them.

"I'm so sorry, Vivi. I wasn't- I didn't- I just-"

"It's okay," she took my hand and leaned her head against my shoulder. "I jumped to conclusions."

"I shouldn't have given you a reason to have to jump to conclusions. I just wanted to have an easy conversation."

"Drunk or sober, it'll never been an easy conversation," she sighed as she glanced at me before looking down to her lap and shaking her head. "Besides, I think it's a conversation I need to have with Audra before you and I even consider it an option anymore. After all, if she's not okay with it, then I can't be either."

"That sounds good," I released a heavy sigh of relief. She raised an eyebrow at me, confused. I think she really misunderstood. I wanted to be there for her and ultimately whatever she decided I would go along with just as I had said. The thing was, I couldn't help but let my mind wander. As each day passed, I became more uncomfortable and awkward. I thought talking to Will about it would help, and at first it did, until I was left on my own. I didn't want to admit it, but I dreaded the idea. I loved Vivian, I really did, but the idea of us being together in that way made me uncomfortable. She seemed to have an easier time getting over the idea than

I did. I kept running the situation through my mind and I kept getting nervous. What if I couldn't – I didn't want to think about it. I hadn't slept with many people, and I knew Vivian had been with even less. Not only was I nervous that Vivian was right, and it would complicate things, but I feared the actual situation. It was as if my deepest fears could become a reality, fears I didn't even know I had. I knew it was stupid, but I was worried I wouldn't be able to get in the mood and it would make everything worse. I kept telling myself I'd just have to picture someone else, that it'd be quick, and we could just move on like it never happened. The thing was, deep down, a part of me knew I wouldn't be able to do it. I knew Vivian wasn't set on the idea and had reservations herself, but I didn't want my nerves and my feelings to set her back from something like this if it was what she really wanted.

"Why did you answer like that?" she watched as I got up and headed to the liquor cabinet. I needed a drink. I reached for the scotch, needing something stronger than wine. I motioned to see if she'd like one as well, knowing very well she'd decline, as she hated the taste. As I went to close the door, I heard her continue, much to my surprise. "I will take gin though."

I poured her a glass and brought it over to her before I sat in the chair across from the sofa, placing the bottles on the table in front of us.

"I just meant that it makes the decision for us."

"What does?"

"You talking to Audra about it," I replied, unsure why she was so confused. "Do you honestly expect her to react the same way Will did?"

"No, but-"

"It's fine, it's perfect really. We've been so stressed over whether this was a good idea or not, and that will make our decision easy," I took a sip of the scotch as she took a surprisingly large gulp of her gin, catching me off guard. "Vivi, take it easy. What's wrong?"

"I know she'll be furious at the very idea, so there's no point even bringing it up to her. I'd just be asking for a fight," she sighed before she continued. "I suppose a part of me had the smallest bit of hope that she'd consider it, at the very least to just have an educated discussion."

"Why?" I leaned forward in my chair, trying to read her expression. "Are you telling me you really and truly think it's a good idea?"

"No, I think it's a terrible idea," she sighed. "But it doesn't change the fact that it's really the only option if I want to carry a child. I've realized I'm having trouble letting go of the idea. I knew it was never really an option, but still."

"Vivi..."

"From what you told me, Will at least looked at it from a perspective other than his own and I guess that's what I want from Audra. I want to know what she would do if she were me, I don't want to know her opinion as my partner because I already know what that is," she replied, finishing her drink. I contemplated taking the bottle away as she poured herself another drink, but she looked like she needed it. "She'll never be able to look at it from a different perspective, will she?"

"Probably not. It's not in her nature. She loves you and she's only ever going to look out for your best interest," I answered as Vivian sat back into the couch, resting her head on the cushion behind her. She knew I was right. Audra was passionate and forceful. She had no problem expressing her feelings and emotions. She wouldn't even give the idea a second thought and she'd be very vocal about it. That was the difference between Audra and Will. Audra would tell Vivian exactly how she felt and exactly what she wanted, but Will was more laid back and open to things. He would lay the facts out and let me guide my own way there. On the one hand, I was thankful for the freedom, but on the other hand sometimes I wished he'd just tell me how he really felt about things. I wondered if he was as upset about the idea as Audra would be, or if he was truly all right with it. He'd told me he had thought about it, that he always knew it was a possibility. He made it sound as though he made peace with the idea long before Vivian and I had even considered it, whereas Audra had tried to suppress even the thought. She'd already gotten over her jealousy towards the relationship Vivian and I shared, and I worried if the idea was even suggested, it could bring all those feelings back up again and, in a way, validate her fears.

"I know, I'm really lucky," she replied as she poured herself more gin. "We both are."

"I can drink to that," I smiled as we clinked our glasses together. I raised an eyebrow as she stared at me with a smirk, "what?"

"I don't think we can do it. I was being really selfish, and I am sorry I dragged you into my crazy idea."

"It wasn't crazy."

"But it wasn't good, for any of us," she said. "It could've ruined our relationship, and our relationships with the people we love. Besides, neither of us have any idea what we're doing."

"That's for sure."

"So, when they get back, how would you feel about filling out an application to adopt?"

"Really?" I looked at her, shocked to hear what came out of her mouth. I searched her eyes for certainty and smiled.

"Really. And no, it's not the gin talking. I think maybe we're ready. We all are," she replied, her slurring becoming noticeable. "I can't count the number of times I have detoured past the orphanage and just stopped, watching the kids play – they are so cute, and we can give them a home. I want to adopt, and I know you want to. I feel like maybe I got to a point where I was ready and then I panicked. Maybe I just second guessed the whole pregnancy thing. Could you imagine though? You and me?"

"Uh-"

"Because I cannot. You make a dashing husband Mr. Porter, but I think you're much cuter with your clothes on," she laughed before she reached for the bottle of gin. I extended my hand to help but she shooed me away and told me to drink my disgusting scotch. I chuckled and did as she said, refilling my own glass, feeling myself getting fuzzier with each sip.

"I agree with you, *Mrs.* Porter," I joked back with her.

"You know, we could just get a set of them."

"Of what?"

"Kids. You know, they're good in groups. They can play with each other and help each other with homework," she replied, leaning on the edge of the couch as if she found it harder with each moment to sit up straight. "And we can pick, like go there and meet them. There's so many."

"Yeah, you can decide if you want a boy or girl."

"Oh, I never thought of that!" she exclaimed excitedly. "It's so much better. Besides, I hear having a baby really hurts."

"I've heard that."

"And what if we had a kid and I turned out like my *mother*," she dragged the word out horrified.

"Well, we do not want that," I said as I finished the rest of my glass off like a shot. I wasn't as drunk as Vivian, but I sure was getting there. I had a lot of weight on her, and it'd take me a few more drinks to reach her level but she was so happy that I intended on meeting her there. I was quick to have a few more drinks, feeling the world shift in front of me as I found myself dizzy but blissfully content.

"I want to make a toast!" I proclaimed, raising my glass. She spilt a bit of her drink as she moved her hand up too quickly to join mine. "To decision making."

"We are good decision makers, aren't we?"

"Yeah, and I'm proud of us because it was *hard*."

"I don't like when things are hard," she whined, pointing to the pile of papers on the table, "like those stupid tests. They're too hard because he doesn't teach the students properly. They're all trick questions. It's not fair."

"He's a bad teacher."

"He is... I should tell him."

"Definitely."

"...I won't do it, but I want to, but I won't," she sighed, "he'll be done teaching soon, and maybe I'll finally get my wish and get to teach his class."

"You should teach his class. You're smarter."

"I am smarter."

"Okay, okay. Cheers to decision making, and

intelligence, and here's wishing that old, bad teachers quit!" I laughed, feeling my mind in a complete fog as I tried to focus on what I was saying.

"I will drink to that!"

CHAPTER THIRTEEN

VIVIAN

I felt sick. So sick, in fact, even the simple act of opening my eyes was a daunting task. I wanted to move but my head felt full of rocks and every minor move I made sent waves of nausea through me. I slowly brought my knees to my chest and wrapped my arms around my waist, trying to steady my breathing and keep my nausea at bay. I didn't think I'd ever felt so ill before in my life. My mouth felt dry, and I was parched. I reached for the glass of water I always kept on my nightstand but was confused when I couldn't immediately grab it as I usually did. Through blurred vision and painfully swollen eyes, I tried to see where it was. As I opened my eyes the best I could, I placed a hand to my head to try and cease the pounding. I laid there for a moment, unsure why I was staring at a picture of Nathan and William on my bedside table. I closed my eyes for a minute; trying to preserve what little strength I had, before opening them again. I pulled my sheets up to my chin as I felt chills. It took me a minute before I realized the sheets in my hands were navy. I slowly pulled them away confused; Audra and I didn't own a set of navy sheets. I glanced from the bedding to the picture on the side table. I didn't want to turn around; I didn't want to see what I feared I would. Please God, let him have slept on the couch. Finally, I looked over my shoulder to see Nathan laying on my left. I tried to recall the evening, but my mind was completely blank. The last thing I remember was talking about adoption and drinking far too much gin. I put my fingers to my lips, if I was drinking gin why did my mouth taste like scotch? I hated scotch.

Using every bit of energy that I had left, I scrambled from the bed and ran out of the room and into the bathroom, slamming the door behind me. I held onto the edge of the toilet as I felt all the contents of my stomach being thrown up. As soon as I was finished, I reached for a cloth and wiped my mouth. Leaning against the cold wall, I could vaguely hear Nathan's voice from down the hall, and I found myself queasy again. I glanced down, noticing I was wearing my nightgown. I must've changed at some point in the night. I tried to force my memory back, but it was no use. Oh God, I kept thinking. It mortified me that I couldn't recall a thing. Finally, I rose to my feet, holding onto the wall for dear life as I opened the door and walked out of the bathroom on unsteady legs.

"Vivian? Are you all right?"

"No," I responded honestly. "What happened last night?"

"What?"

"What happened last night?" I repeated.

"I, uh," I watched as he tried to rerun last night's events through his head, but from the confusion on his face, he too was drawing a blank.

"It appears I slept in your room last night," I replied, as I rubbed my forehead with my free hand while using the other to hold onto the doorframe. "What did we do, Nathan?"

"Nothing, I'm sure it's a misunderstanding. We probably just had another late night chat and passed out," he said, referring to the evenings we spent together years ago. We'd never slept in the same bed, but when we first moved in with each other there were several evenings when one of us wanted to talk after we'd headed to bed for the night, and we would sit and talk for hours in the other's room. The thing was, we never once fell asleep and we hadn't had one of those conversations in nearly four years, so what changed last night?

As I stood with him staring at me, I suddenly realized I felt very exposed. I grabbed Nathan's robe that hung on the inside of the door and wrapped it around myself, feeling more secure as soon as I pulled the tie tightly together.

"I think we'd better not get upset until we know what actually happened."

"Can you tell me with complete certainty that nothing happened?"

"No," he replied honestly. I looked at the ground and shook my head, this couldn't be happening. It was a nightmare - it had to be. I tried to run the evening through my mind but kept hitting a wall. I wanted to remember to ensure we hadn't done anything we'd regret, but I was terrified to get my memory back in case it confirmed my fears. I looked up as he continued, "I mean, it doesn't make sense. We've never crossed the line before, and we've never wanted to because even the thought alone deters us both.

Besides, I recall us talking about adoption."

That, I remembered. I recalled toasting our decision to adopt. We'd settled on it, and I was content with the verdict. I could vividly remember being at peace with the choice. For a moment I felt better, that is, until the thought of waking up in Nathan's bed flooded back into my mind and I felt sick again. Something had happened, I was sure of it. I placed a hand on my lower stomach and groaned, feeling my muscles cramp. Everything hurt. I knew the pressure I had in my abdomen wasn't from throwing up, and it was different than the cramps I experienced during my time of the month, which I'd finished just over a week ago. No, this was a not a feeling I'd had before, and it was not a good one.

I felt the need to throw up again and turned as I walked into the bathroom, closing the door behind me. I leaned against the wall, needing a moment to myself. I took a few deep breaths, trying to suppress the sickening wave I had. As it passed, I leaned my head back against the wall.

When I opened the door, Nathan looked at me warily, searching my expression, "are you all right?"

"No," I answered him. I wasn't. I felt horrid. I was confused and embarrassed, and entirely sick to my stomach. Not only did I feel like I was drenched in sweat and alcohol, but I also felt pain radiating from every bone in my body. My legs felt like they were going to give out, my hips hurt, and my muscles felt weak, as if I hadn't slept in weeks. I also felt emotionally drained, the stress alone was enough to make me shake and clench my aching body.

"Okay, um," he rubbed his face. Nathan didn't look much better. His hair was in disarray, and he had bags under his eyes. He stood in front of me without a shirt on, which I wasn't even sure he'd noticed. From the way he was squinting when he was looking at me, it was clear he was also fighting off a splitting headache. "Why don't you take a bath and fresh up whilst I make us tea. We'll figure this out. All right?"

I nodded, hoping a warm bath would make me feel better. If not, it'd at least wash away the sickening scotch scent.

"I'll meet you downstairs when you're done," he said.

I nodded as he headed towards the stairs. I held onto the wall as I turned and went back into the bathroom. I closed the door and took off Nathan's robe. I reached for the handle and began to run the water to warm it up while I used the toilet. As I went to pull my knickers down, my eyes suddenly went wide. I wasn't wearing any. How had I not noticed that I didn't have any on? I always wore my undergarment, even in the evening. I felt uncomfortable without them. I took a deep breath, trying not to panic any further. Perhaps I had been so drunk I forgot. Maybe, I had thought I put them on and never did. I hadn't noticed when I woke up, why would I notice during the height of my inebriation?

I sat on the toilet for a moment and placed my hands on my lap. As soon as I did, I froze. Gasping, I looked down. Why were my thighs sticky?

I flushed the toilet as quickly as I could and ripped my nightgown off, wanting to burn it. I felt tears streaming down my face as I stepped into the bath, wanting nothing more than to scrub myself clean. I couldn't deny what had happened anymore. I couldn't remember anything, but all the evidence pointed towards one thing. I was drunk, I woke up in his bed, I was in pain, I felt different, and now I had… something… on my thighs. I shivered, I couldn't bring myself to say or even think the word. Everything that had happened could've had an explanation, except what I had touched on my leg. Granted, I was speculating, but when I pieced together the rest of the puzzle, it all pointed to one thing.

I stopped scrubbing as I felt my skin becoming raw and sensitive. I slowly pulled my knees close to my chest, burying my face in them, and I began to cry. I felt myself shutting down, how could I let something like this happen? How *did* something like this happen? Had I changed my mind in my intoxicated state? Did Nathan change his? I know I had been contemplating the idea before, but I never would have acted on it without talking to Audra. Something like that needed a great amount of consideration. I hadn't even completely decided myself. I had wanted to make a choice for myself and once I knew for certain I could do it, I would then talk to Audra before anything was set in stone. This wasn't like me. I could be sporadic but not about something like this. This would've been the perfect example of something I would not have been hasty to decide. When I drank, I could become either very fun or very somber, but even drunk I was very conscious of whether something was a good idea or not. If I wasn't comfortable with something, I wasn't one to jump into it in any state. I remember walking home drunk with Audra one time, and she wanted to kiss me in the street. I was so scared, and I didn't want to, but she did everything in her power to convince me. If it took that much convincing for me to kiss the love of my life in public, then I couldn't imagine what I was told or what I was thinking to agree to hop into bed with Nathan. I knew by sleeping with him I'd have to be in the right state of mind and recognize the consequences. I'd have to consider my relationship with Audra, how it would affect Will and Nathan, and even my own comfort level, especially since we'd have to try multiple times. It didn't seem like much, but I had always been really proud of the fact that I'd never slept with a man. There were so many women who hadn't come to recognize the truth about themselves until after they were married or intimate with someone of the opposite sex. In my experience, it was rare that someone realized it, or even accepted it, on their own. I had, so for me that was something I was thankful for, especially growing up in a world that was rigid in its actions and beliefs. I knew it sounded foolish, but I suddenly felt like I lost a little part of myself.

My mind flashed to Nathan, wondering if he had noticed anything was different. Was he as upset as I was or was he completely fine? I suddenly found myself feeling angry that he hadn't reacted as much as I had. I tried to tell myself that he had a headache and was confused, that he was probably just as shaken as I was, but the other part of me couldn't help but wonder. He didn't seem upset, and he had tricked me into drinking last night. Of course, I decided to dive into the gin, but maybe if I hadn't had those first few glasses of wine… I stopped myself. No. He wouldn't do that. I could recall exactly how upset he was when I confronted him, and his intentions were innocent. It was Nathan, for God's sake.

When the water turned cold, I finally pulled myself out of the tub. I wrapped the towel around my body and dried myself off. I threw my hair up with a clip and got myself dressed into something comfortable. Once I was finished, I walked down the hallway, conscious not to look into Nathan's room as I passed it in fear that I would just get upset again. I got halfway down the staircase before I stopped, hearing Nathan in the kitchen. I took a deep breath before I moved just as he came out, carrying a tray. I immediately noticed the living room was clean. Either we were very tidy drunks, or he had taken the liberty of clearing away the bottles before I came down. I sighed in relief, grateful that I didn't have to see them; the thought of alcohol made my stomach twist again.

"Feeling any better?" he asked, offering me a cup of English breakfast. I took it from him and sat on the edge of the sofa. He seemed to have picked up on my body language and chose to sit on the chair next to the couch, to provide a bit of distance.

"I don't smell of liquor anymore, so that's an improvement," I replied. I tried to steady my shaking hand as I took a sip and placed the cup back on its saucer. Nathan passed me a napkin when he noticed the trembling had caused my tea to spill a bit. I placed my drink on the table before I thanked him, dabbing the part of my dress that I'd gotten tea on.

"About last night-"

"We had sex."

"What?" he responded, confused. He leaned forward, shaking his head. "Are you sure?"

"I'm pretty positive," I replied, sounding monotone. I cried so hard in the bath, that I found myself emotionally drained.

"I-uh-I mean," he fumbled for words, pausing as he

looked at me. "Are you feeling okay?"

I wish he'd stop asking me if I was all right, I'd already stated I wasn't. However, I noticed his tone changed this time. He didn't just mean emotionally. He stared at my arms which I had unconsciously wrapped around my waist. I found myself struggling to look at him, and I hated it. Nathan was my best friend and there I was resenting him for something that wasn't his fault. I knew it wasn't fair, but I couldn't help but find myself feeling that way. I needed some time alone to comprehend what had happened before I was ready to deal with it.

"I think I'm going to lay down," I replied as I started to get up, "I'm really nauseous."

"Did you want me to bring you anything? Toast? Water?"

"No, thank you," I responded. I was angry with myself for being frustrated with his kindness. It was hard to be mad at someone who was so sweet.

"I know you don't want to, but I still think we should talk about what happened," he said as he stood up. "Maybe after you're feeling better?"

"Perhaps," I wasn't sure I was ever going to feel better.

"Vivian, please," he said firmly as I began walking towards the staircase. "You're not the only one who's upset."

I wasn't sure if it was the exhaustion or the stress, but something took over me and suddenly I was furious at his statement. I couldn't control myself as I whipped my head around, "how do *you* feel, Nathan?"

"What do you mean?" Nathan replied cautiously,

seeming to sense that I was about to back him into a corner, "look, Vivi, can we just take a step back?"

"Oh, you want to take a step back? When would you like to step back to, *exactly*?" I snapped at him.

"Vivian-" he pleaded with his eyes. I was prepared to make a harsh retort back at him but, suddenly, as I looked into his eyes, I was possessed by my own wave of sadness and found myself unable to continue.

"I'm sorry," I shook my head, "I just need to be alone right now."

I didn't wait for him to reply before I turned on my heels and walked up the stairs. I didn't want to fight with him, but I knew I would pick one if I stayed there any longer. Besides, my legs were starting to give out again and my head was swimming. All I wanted to do was lay in my own bed and pass out. Any bad dream I could possibly have could be nothing compared to the nightmare of the reality I was living.

CHAPTER FOURTEEN

WILLIAM

Atlanta was much bigger than I had anticipated, but I knew the town outside Albany where Audra grew up would not be. Just as she had said, everybody knew everybody. The first day we were there, Francine was quick to invite us out with her to get some groceries for dinner. Just about everyone she passed by she had to stop to say hello to, and if we didn't stop, she was quick to point out who they were and a tidbit of information about them. She introduced us to everyone she could think of. It didn't take a genius to realize she'd only invited us to run errands so that she could show us off. I could tell Audra was a bit annoyed as she kept her conversations short and her head low when she could. It was obvious Francine liked to gloat from the way she spoke, and how she seemed to exaggerate when sharing a story. According to Audra, her sister tended to be the subject of conversation, but it was the first time her mother actually had a reason to brag about Audra herself. She was trying her best to keep a calm demeanor, but I could see in her eyes that she was getting overwhelmed by the attention, especially from those she wasn't fond of. I was just as taken off guard as she was. My uncle liked to talk about my accomplishments, but he didn't do it to show off to anyone. He was just proud, and he wanted me to know it. I think Francine wanted to drag us around more for her own ego than for our benefit.

We had managed to stray away from one of the many conversations her mother had gotten into with one of her neighbors on the street. Seizing our opportunity, we decided to go to the store across the road. Her mother barely noticed when we slipped away. Audra rolled her eyes as I laughed. I couldn't believe how oblivious she was. As we walked towards the convenience store, I turned to look at Audra when I noticed her stop dead in her tracks. She took a moment to collect herself before she returned to my side. I looked back to see what had taken her off guard and saw two women who appeared to have just come out of the store, staring at her. I could sense a bit of tension but pretended not to notice anything as we continued walking.

"Well, look who rolled back into town," the taller woman with auburn hair said coyly as she watched Audra. "Never thought we'd see you again."

"Ain't you gonna introduce us to your friend?" I glanced at the other woman with done-up golden blonde hair, and bright red lipstick.

"Will, this is Connie and Mirabelle. We went to school together," Audra said quietly.

I wasn't sure of their exact relationship, but I could tell it wasn't a friendly one. Based on the way Audra hung her head low, and the way the women stood with their arms crossed, I had a feeling they may've bullied her in the past. It was odd for me to see Audra, who was usually bold in personality, suddenly seem so insecure. She could barely maintain eye contact and was clearly trying not to engage in conversation. I'd never really been bullied before, but I had friends who were, and I'd seen what it did to them. Some of my closest friends seemed like completely different people when they crossed paths with those who had picked on them. It was exactly what was happening to Audra. I had figured she'd be a bit snippier and stand her ground, as her usual personality would display. She'd told us about how she'd lash back at her bullies, but that wasn't what I was witnessing. She was timid, and unsure of what to say. I couldn't tell if she was trying to hold back because she didn't care, didn't want to make a scene, or if she legitimately felt knocked down a peg. The girls hadn't really said anything mean, but their tone was condescending. However, I couldn't help but notice the change in their personality when they turned their attention to me.

"It's a pleasure to meet you," the blonde one, who I think was Mirabelle, purred as she extended her hand to me and batted her eyelashes. I glanced from her to Connie who stood twirling her hair, staring at me. I tried to hide my smirk as I watched them flirt with me. I decided to indulge them and use it to my advantage.

"The pleasure is all mine," I took her hand and kissed

it, making her blush.

"So, how do you know Audi?" Connie asked.

"*Audra*," I emphasized pointedly to correct her, making her eyes grow wide in embarrassment, "is my fiancée."

"Your *fiancée*?" she repeated, glancing from me to Audra in disbelief. I could've sworn both their jaws dropped in unison. I noticed Audra's hunched over back straightened up a bit as she heard me speak.

"I know, it's hard to believe," I started as I reached around Audra's waist and pulled her close to me, "I still can't believe I managed to catch this one."

"You mean, *you*… went after… *her*?" Mirabelle said slowly as if she was trying to comprehend what I had said.

"I don't know how I got so lucky," I glanced down at Audra who seemed to have the light flickering back into her eyes. "It's hard to believe we're getting married in a couple of months."

"Wow, Audi – I mean, Audra, I must say we're a bit surprised," Connie replied, glancing at Mirabelle in shock. Neither of them knew what to say, which brought me some joy and, I could tell, made Audra feel better.

"If you'll excuse us, ladies."

We left them on the porch before going into the store. We moved towards the back of one of the aisles so that we couldn't be heard by the man at the cash register.

"Sorry, I didn't mean to catch you off guard," I apologized, unsure if I overstepped. "I just thought it'd get a rile out of them."

"It's all right, I kind of enjoyed that… the reaction I mean," she replied, grinning. I think it was the first time since we had arrived in town that I saw her smile.

"If I go too far or say too much just let me know. We haven't really needed to play these roles before, so I'm just going by gut feeling," I said as we began to walk down the aisles.

"I'll let you know," she replied as she slipped her arm through mine and rested her head on my shoulder, much to my surprise. "Thanks for bein' here with me, Will."

"What're friends for?" I retorted, "so, how're you feeling about being back and all?"

"So far it ain't as bad as I thought it'd be. I think havin' you here has really helped," she answered, grabbing a few things off the shelf. She stayed quiet for a few minutes as she continued strolling through the aisle somberly. I didn't know what to say. I wasn't used to this Audra. She normally had a fire in her eyes and was quick to react. She kept her head high and stood her ground. Even when she was upset, she had some passion in her, but she just seemed a bit subdued. I thought maybe we'd get into town, and she'd feel a bit more empowered and confident. Although our relationship wasn't real in the traditional sense, no one knew that. It occurred to me that might've been her issue. She had already been beaten down for years, and to come back and face the people who had harassed her for so long with a lie as her only defense probably didn't feel great. Not for someone as truthful as Audra. I doubt she ever denied the rumors, but rather neglected to confirm them. She spent so many years just keeping her head low until she got out of there that this probably felt contradictory. For someone like Vivian, her relationship with Nathan was perfect because she had no problem walking around with a mask, but for Audra she wanted to be free, to live as she wished without needing any kind of cover.

"I'm glad," I replied as we paid the cashier and headed out of the store. As we walked out the door, we both stopped and sighed almost in unison. Her mother was still talking to the same people across the street. "Can we walk back?"

"It's a bit of a hike," she answered before she looked at me, "but I could use the fresh air... and silence."

"Should we let her know?" It was as though Francine had heard me. She turned her head to see where we had gone, and Audra waved to catch her attention. She motioned that we were going to go, and although I'm not sure Francine understood exactly what Audra was saying, she didn't seem to care when we began to walk away.

We had only been walking along the road for about twenty minutes when she stopped over the bridge we were crossing. She leaned over the wooden railing and stared at the river that lazily flowed under it.

"How'd you feel 'bout a detour?" she replied, waiting for my reaction. I shrugged, not sure what she meant by a detour, but I was up for doing anything that kept me out of her house. Her family had been unexpectedly kind to me, however, I still found them to be overwhelming.

I'm not sure why I felt so on edge, maybe I just wasn't used to so much attention. The only other time I got attention like that was back when I was younger and going to bars every night, but it was a completely different kind of attention, and it was actually wanted. I could tell Audra was getting overwhelmed herself, but for different reasons. She was quickly growing tired of dodging everyone's prodding questions. Luckily, we had used our private drive down to Georgia as some much-needed time to come up with our answers and stories for whatever questions they might ask. Where did we meet? How did I propose? How many kids did we want? I think Audra and I both had more sympathy for Vivian and Nathan after we were subjected to our own interrogation.

I followed her as we walked back over the bridge in the direction we had come, but instead of walking down the trail we stepped onto the grass and began to make our own path as we headed south, following the stream. We walked mostly on grass, but on occasion stepped through some patches of dirt that left my shoes dusty. I think Audra was concerned that I was upset about it, but it didn't bother me. Unlike our significant others, we both didn't mind getting our hands – or shoes – dirty. We walked for another fifteen minutes or so, with Audra continuously ignored my questions of where we were headed. She was being secretive, and the anticipation was making me antsy.

Finally, we stopped in front of a large area blocked off by bushes and tree branches. Audra pulled the branches aside and motioned for me to go through the opening.

"You're kidding, right?" I asked as I pushed past the excess branches she had missed and squeezed through, while trying not to get caught on any stray pieces. As I made it through to the other side I stopped and looked around. I laughed as Audra came through the bushes and bumped into me. I thought I'd left her more space than I had. "Sorry."

"Well, what do you think?"

I glanced around; if I was being honest, it was picturesque. It was like a peaceful sanctuary. The creek had widened this far down and flowed slow enough for a serene and relaxing sound, but fast enough that you could see the ripples through the water. I noticed several large stones in the water that allowed you to easily cross from one side of the creek to the other without getting your shoes wet. The grass was lush and soft, the large trees cast enough of a shadow to keep the sweltering heat from drying it out. It also provided some much-needed shade for the both of us. I narrowed my eyes as I saw what looked like a handmade swing hanging from a large tree branch.

"What is this place?"

"My home away from home," she replied as she walked past me and down towards the water. She hopped on each stone carefully to stay dry and made her way to where the swing hung. She sat on it with her full weight without flinching. It must've been years since she last sat on it and who knew how sturdy it was. I followed her to the other side and when I reached her, I placed the small bag of snacks we had purchased down and sat on the grass at her feet. "This was the place where I came to get away from ev'rythin' goin' on in my life. It was my safe space."

"It's really beautiful," I replied as I passed her a piece of beef jerky, something I hadn't had in years. "Peaceful, too."

"This is where I realized I liked women," she admitted to me. I looked at her a little surprised. I wasn't sure what I had expected, but I didn't exactly think she'd stumble upon that discovery in the woods. "After the friends I told you about disappeared, I spent a lot of time alone here until one day this girl named Irene appeared out of nowhere, and one thing led to another."

"Did you-?" she knew exactly what my partial question was implying. I couldn't help it, I was curious.

"Yeah," she answered, honestly. She blushed as she thought back. I knew exactly what she was recalling. You always remembered your first, whether it was good or bad. There was something about the nervousness, the curious and adventurous part of yourself you got to explore, and there was a rush of it all that made it very memorable.

I had always thought that the first time I stumbled into bed with someone would be this amazing and fantastic experience, but in reality, I was a bit awkward. At the time, it seemed like everyone I knew had slept with someone, except me. I began to feel as though I was missing out on this whole world of excitement by waiting for a perfect person that I wasn't sure existed. Finally, one night, I decided I was through waiting. I got my hands on a couple of drinks and there was this woman who was quite a bit older than me that caught my eye. She introduced herself, and she made her intentions very clear. She brought me back to her place and I remember wanting to seem confident, as if I had all sorts of experience, but she knew I was full of it, yet she didn't seem to mind. In fact, she was aroused by the idea of being with someone so young and inexperienced. I was incredibly awkward and unsure, but she seemed to find me charming. She enjoyed being in charge, and truthfully, I enjoyed being led. I think in a way I was lucky that I had experienced my first time with her because had it been with anybody else, it could've gone very differently. It didn't take long before I gained my confidence and found myself in the arms of a woman more often than I thought I would. I didn't go out with the intention of ending up in bed with someone frequently, it just sort of happened. My awkwardness had completely dissipated, that is, until the first time a man flirted with me, and I found myself back at square one, feeling like a lost puppy. However, the first time I slept with a man went a lot smoother than I'd anticipated. Everything just seemed to flow a lot more naturally, and I experienced a whole new level of sensation. There were things I didn't know I liked, and feelings I never knew I could feel. Over the years, I continued to sleep with women that I was attracted to, but I couldn't deny that my desires more often led me into the arms of stunning men – and now, I had the most dashing one of all. It made me laugh to think of all the fun I'd had over the years and how my sexual experiences so vastly differed from Nathan and the girls.

I looked at Audra as she glowed, recounting her past love.

"She made the first move," she said to me as she let out a soft laugh, "it sort of dawned on me, you know? How did I not realize? The rumors were made up over somethin' so silly, but it turned out they were true. I'll always wonder what would've happened if she hadn't kissed me."

I couldn't help but think about what she said. Had Irene not made her move on Audra first, it was possible Audra could've gone down the same path that I had – despite her denial of the fact. I figured it was even more possible especially since she lived in such a conservative Christian environment. She had rumors circulating around her for so long that she was a lesbian, that had she not discovered so quickly that they were true, I could imagine she might've tried being with a man before she realized. Sometimes it takes a bit to realize the truth. It almost seemed so complicated but was yet so simple. It was like looking at a red car and you know that it's red, but one day it really dawns on you that it's *red*.

I laughed as she continued to talk about Irene and some of the other relationships she had after her. I couldn't help but smile and realize how many similarities we had. I was glad I came down to Georgia with her, I'd always loved and trusted her, but I also always felt there was a part of me that didn't know her as well as I'd hoped. Perhaps it was because she was always a bit guarded. It was a shame since there was something in her spirited nature that I could see in myself. I was glad to finally start to see the real her.

I raised my eyebrow as I looked past Audra, realizing someone was heading towards us. I wasn't sure if the man could see me, or if Audra's back blocked his sightline. At first, I assumed he was just passing through, but quickly disregarded the thought as he stopped and stared at Audra intently. Before I was able to say anything he spoke.

"I knew I'd find you here," he said.

I watched as Audra's eyes widened and her back stiffened at the sound of his voice. I didn't know who he was but by the look on Audra's face – she did.

CHAPTER FIFTEEN

AUDRA

I knew I'd find you here."

I couldn't move; it was like I was frozen in place. I kept running what I had heard in my head over and over again. My eyes glossed over, and I felt my chest tighten. I stared past Will and into the distance. I didn't want to turn around because I wasn't sure I wanted the truth. I wasn't sure if I had heard what I thought I heard. I couldn't tell if my mind was jumping to conclusions or if my suspicions were correct. I felt everything spin as I held onto the rope of the swing. Out of the corner of my eye I saw Will stand up, ready to support me if I tipped over. I wasn't one to faint but if I ever had a reason to, this would be it.

Finally, I turned my head to get a good look at the man who spoke. It was over a decade later and I still recognized the smooth and gentle voice that I once knew so well. I felt my heart pounding in my chest as my eyes watered up. I tried my best to keep my composure and not let him see how worked up I really was.

"Don't recognize me, Audra?" he asked as he took a step forward. His voice was much deeper than I remembered.

"No, I do," I replied so quietly it was almost under my breath. I didn't know what else to say. I looked him up and down; he was no longer the scrawny little boy I knew, but a full-grown man. He was taller and broader than I had imagined he'd be. It seemed everything about him had changed, except for his soft eyes - those had stayed the same.

"I'm sure you're a little shocked to see me."

"Shocked? Well, I'd say that's an understatement," I didn't know why but I felt a bit of anger rising in me. It seemed crazy. I wasn't sure why, or even how, this was happening. There I was standing face to face with one of my childhood best friends, the same best friend who had just up and left one day and never came back. I guess somewhere deep down I felt a sense of resentment and abandonment. We spent nearly every day together and I didn't even get a goodbye, from either Taye or his sister. Maybe it was easier for me to be upset about it than to have mourned the loss of our friendship.

I watched as Taye took a few steps forward, "you look good, Audra."

"Thanks," I replied sharply. I sighed as I glanced at Will before realizing that he seemed a bit lost. "Sorry. Um, Will, this is Taye."

"Taye, your-" he didn't need to finish asking the question before I nodded to answer him. I watched as he walked over to Taye and shook his hand, introducing himself. For the first time since we'd been in Georgia, Will didn't introduce himself as my fiancée. I didn't know if that was intentional or not, but the gesture was enough to make me notice.

"What're you doin' here, Taye?" I asked, confused what he was doing back in town after all these years.

"I wanted to see you," he replied, I could hear the honesty in his voice.

"How'd you know I'd be here?"

"Your sister," he responded without the slightest hesitation.

I felt the hair on the back of my neck stand up. When would Faith and Taye have crossed paths? Better yet, what was she doing talking to him? It didn't make sense to me. I had never seen her, or her friends, willingly talk to anyone of color when we were growing up so what changed? Did Taye approach her? He had to have; she wouldn't have even known who he was. Did he corner her so that she had no choice but to talk to him, or was Vivian right and she'd changed? Faith had been quick and desperate to convince me to come home, and although I had enjoyed my quality time with Mamaw, she had been surprised we came down with everything going on. I couldn't help but feel there was some other reason she had pulled that trick to get me to come down. Could Taye have been the reason?

"What do you mean?" I asked, confused. "When'd you meet Faith? How'd you meet Faith?"

"Years ago," he replied with a heavy sigh, "when I came back here lookin' for you."

"What're you talkin' 'bout?" I suddenly recalled overhearing Faith tell Vivian she had something to tell me about Taye and Nan. I shook my head in disbelief; I just figured she was going to bring something about the past up. I would have never imagined she'd tell me that she met Taye, let alone that he was back in town.

"Our paths crossed 'bout five years ago when I came back lookin' for you, but I found her instead," he answered, staring at me. "I came here, hopin' by some weird chance of luck you'd still be on the swing, but I ended up seein' Faith. I caught her off guard, and she said she'd been comin' here alone for years. I asked if she happened to know you, and that's when she told me she was your sister."

I stood there for a minute unsure what question to ask first. There were hundreds running through my mind. Finally, I settled on one, "why?"

"Why?" he asked, not sure what I was referring to in my vague response.

"Why come back after all these years?"

"Audra-"

"Don't *Audra* me. I deserve an answer," I responded, trying to fight back the tears that were glossing my eyes over. "Do you realize how that felt? What I went through? I showed up here *ev'ry* day lookin' for you, and you just vanished without a word. I kept wonderin' what happened to you, and then I would wonder if I did somethin' that made you not come back."

"Audra, how could you think that?" he tried to take a step forward but stopped as I took a step back to keep the distance. "You were our best friend."

"What was I s'pose't think? The only people in my life I gave a damn 'bout and who I thought gave a damn 'bout me just picked up and left without a word."

I suddenly felt myself sway. Will reached out to grab my arm, taking a tight grip in case I fell. I wasn't sure what was happening, I wasn't one of those women who felt faint anytime they got overwhelmed. I took things head on, as best I could, and dealt with each thing as it came. Sure, maybe I was prone to getting upset and storming off but it's because I needed to clear my head. Think about what I wanted to do. The one thing I never did was get so flustered that I'd topple over like a damsel in distress from one of those God-awful books Vivian read before bed. Yet, there I was, trying my best to stay grounded.

I always dreamt about what would happen if Taye and I ever crossed paths again, but it wasn't going the way I had imagined. I thought I'd be overwhelmed with happiness and pure joy to see him again, and yet there I was being crushed by waves of frustration and confusion. I wanted to push my feelings away and embrace the ones I'd always dreamt I'd have, but that was easier said than done.

"I'm all right," I said to Will, who stared at me with concerned eyes. He nodded and loosened his grip on me but still stayed by my side as a precaution. I looked back at Taye as I spoke, "my heart broke that day, Taye."

"Mine did too, Audra," he responded. I watched as he looked down at his feet, holding back his own tears of emotions. I stared at him, and if I thought I was confused before - I was wrong. He tried to speak but struggled to get the words out. I stepped away from Will and closed the gap between Taye and myself as I walked closer to get a better look at his face. As I stood no more than a foot away from him, I sighed and tilted my head.

"Why didn't you come back?"

"We moved."

"You *moved*?" I asked, almost angrily as I repeated his response. "That's your answer? You moved away? What? Did y'all pack up and leave in one night? So quickly that you couldn't even pop over for a goodbye? Even just to give me a head's up?"

"It was more complicated than that."

"Really? Please, enlighten me," I was surprised by the sharpness in my voice, but I felt my anger was justified. I didn't think it was possible for Taye to lower his head anymore, but he did. After a moment, he finally looked at me and I felt my heart shatter a bit as I stared into his soulful eyes and realized just how much sadness they possessed. I suddenly felt horrible for my behavior, and the way I spoke. I hadn't even truly given him a chance to explain. I didn't think it was possible for him to feel as bad as I did, but as I stared into those dark eyes, I realized that I could be wrong. I finally asked my question, softly but bluntly, just wanting to know, "what happened, Taye?"

"She got sick."

"Your Ma?"

"Nan."

"What? When?"

"Just after the last time we saw each other. The dog ran out and she went lookin' for it in the rain. It was so cold that night and she got pneumonia," he replied. "She got real sick, Audra."

"So, you left to find a doctor, right?" I asked, praying for him to say yes, because I feared where his story was headed. The sound of his voice did not instill confidence in me. "Right?"

"In a matter of two days she went from bad to worse. I would have sold my soul to make her better," he shook his head, "but God doesn't work that way."

"Where is Nan now, Taye?" my voice trembled, holding onto the last speck of hope I had. He had not directly said what I feared but what he implied made my knees go weak again. "Taye?"

"She died," he finally answered, matter of fact. It was like there was no other way for him to say it without breaking down. I took a few steps back, trying to process what he had just said. It was no longer possible for me to hold back my tears. I tried to wipe them away as they fell but they kept coming and it was no use. "We left the next day. Our parents couldn't bear to be in the house anymore with the memory of her. It was too hard for 'em. I wanted to stay but I didn't have a choice... Audra, I came lookin' for you, to try and tell you but I couldn't find you and I had so little time to do anythin' before we left."

"Where did you bury her?" I asked between my hiccupped sobs that I was still trying to hold back.

"Here."

"What?" I felt my heart skip a beat as my body trembled. I wasn't sure if I heard right. I looked around, confused. "What're you talkin' 'bout?"

He walked towards me. His parents struggled to

live with the memory of her, but he couldn't live without it. Everyone handled death differently, and they were on opposite ends. They didn't have a lot of money, and he had overheard them talking in the kitchen, unsure what to do. Finally, he stepped forward and shared his idea. The only thing Nan loved more than her family, and reading, was the creek and the time we'd spent there. So that day they went down to the creek and buried her body. He pointed towards the large tree to the left of the one our swing hung from. After they buried her body, he planted the tree there so that she would always be a part of the place that made her so happy. The tree had been so small at the time that I'd never noticed it. I didn't even notice the disturbed dirt; I had been too focused on myself to notice anything was different.

I slowly walked towards the tree and placed a hand on the bark. I wept as I leaned against the tree. I trembled, completely grief stricken, struggling to catch my breath between sobs. Suddenly, my tears seemed to come to a stop as everything went fuzzy. I found myself no longer gripping the tree for comfort, but rather for support.

"Will-" I tried to say his name but couldn't tell if I had said it loud enough to be heard. I gasped for air as I tried to call it again.

The next thing I knew my legs were giving out and I found myself collapsing to the ground. I wasn't sure if it was Will or Taye who had managed to catch me, but I landed in someone's arms before being placed gently on the ground. It was the last thing I remembered before I passed out.

CHAPTER SIXTEEN

VIVIAN

I wasn't sure how Nathan seemed to lose his grip on the English language but despite telling him multiple times over the last two days to *go away,* each time he would come back and knock on my bedroom door as if he'd get a different answer. I didn't want to see him, and I wanted to be left alone. I thought I had made that quite clear. He kept walking by to see if I needed anything and while I understood it was well-intended, I was still getting agitated. I sighed as he knocked again, and when I neglected to say anything, he knocked a second time.

"Go away, Nathan," I felt as though I were a broken record.

I heard silence for a moment, but I knew he was still there as I didn't hear his footsteps fade into the distance. I sat up in my bed as my attention was grabbed by the sound of the door handle turning. I watched as the door opened and just as I was ready to say something, I held my tongue, realizing it wasn't him. I leaned back into the pillows behind me.

"What're you doing here?" I asked as I watched Elaine balance a tray with two cups on it as she closed the door with her free hand. She placed the tray on the side table before she took a seat on the edge of the bed and looked me up and down. I unconsciously pulled the blanket up higher as if it'd stop me from feeling emotionally exposed.

"Nathan is worried about you," she replied as she handed me the cup of tea that she'd brought me before taking her own. "And frankly I am too."

"You don't need to be."

"You look like crap," she said bluntly, which caught me off guard. She'd never spoken to me that way before. "Besides, you've called in sick to work for two days now and you've never missed a day. I've seen you almost pass out at your desk rather than take a day off, so I knew it had to be serious. Now, while you look like a mess, you don't look sick. Talk to me, what's going on?"

"Nothing," I replied as I took a sip of tea and avoided eye contact.

She glared at me, clearly not believing my answer. She put her drink down before she leaned towards me, eyeing me seriously.

"What happened between you and Nathan?"

"What do you mean?" I questioned. I wasn't sure what, or if, Nathan had said anything to her or if she was just taking a guess. For all she knew we simply had a fight.

"Don't do that, Vivi. If you're not talking to Nathan that means something more than a little squabble happened," she put her hand on my thigh and gave it a comforting squeeze. "I'm here for you, but I need you to be honest with me."

She was right, there was no use in lying to her, it would get me nowhere, just as laying in my bed for two days hadn't. Truthfully, it made me feel worse. I had closed myself off and done nothing but given myself the opportunity to stew in my emotions. I couldn't stop playing out different situations, but every conceivable thing that ran through my mind made my stomach twist in knots. The mere implication that we had been intimate made my chest feel as though I had bricks stacked upon it, making me struggle to catch my breath. I almost didn't want Audra to come home because I was too afraid of what would happen when I told her. If Elaine could so noticeably see something was off, Audra would be able to as well.

I didn't even have to say anything, I simply looked at her and she knew. She sighed and tilted her head.

"Oh, honey," she said softly as she took my hand. She gave it a squeeze as I held back tears. "What happened?"

"I don't know," I responded as she raised an eyebrow, confused by my answer. "I mean it. I don't know how it happened. We were drinking and decided against it. It would make things too complicated, and it was better for us to adopt. Next thing I knew, I woke up in his bed sick and with a splitting headache."

"What did Nathan have to say?"

"Nothing, he can't remember."

"So, neither of you can recall that night?"

"No," I shook my head, looking down at my lap. "I wanted to remember what happened, to piece everything together, but now that a few of my memories are coming back I wish they'd stop. They aren't helping figure out what made us change our mind or what led to it, they're just making me sick."

"What sort of memories are coming back?"

"I recall partially undressing, and um, I just have this really vivid image of him on top of me," I said as I put a hand to my chest, struggling to breathe. Elaine was quick to pick up on the cue as she took the teacup from my hand and helped me sit up a bit before handing me my water.

"Shh, it's okay," she stood over me, rubbing my back, telling me to breathe. I kept experiencing minor panic attacks every time my mind flashed back to that night. My chest would grow tight, and my breathing labored. I found myself unable to do anything until they passed. "Do you know if Nathan made you do something you didn't want to?"

"What?" I looked up at her with wide eyes, surprised by her question. "No, I mean, I don't think so. I don't remember, but this is my fault. If I'd just kept my mouth shut, we never would have ended up in this situation."

"Vivian, listen to me," I felt Elaine put a hand on each of my shoulders and held me tightly as she looked into my eyes with a serious expression, "it is not your fault. If someone forces themselves on you against your wishes, even if you had flirted the night away, it is not your fault. This whole thing may've stemmed from an idea, but no decision was made. If you said no, and Nathan still wanted to, that makes him in the wrong. Not you. Do you understand?"

"I do, I just don't think it's like that," I replied as she sat back down beside me. I understood where she was coming from, and I was so thankful to have a friend like her. For all she knew, Nathan had taken advantage of a situation and it was her duty to me to ensure I was all right and knew that, if that was the case, that I didn't place any blame on myself. The thing was, I may've been too drunk to say no, but he may've been too drunk to object had it been my idea. For all I knew we had mutually decided. Nathan had been just as unsure as I had been, if not more, so I couldn't see him initiating anything entirely on his own. I knew my drunken self must've had some part but based on my memory I was quick to regret the decision. I didn't want to see or talk to Nathan, not because I blamed him for anything but because I could not wipe the image of him from my mind and it killed me. At first, I just recalled the weight of his body on me and the feeling of his chest against mine. I remember I kept my shirt on, which would've made sense; I had no reason to take it off. It would've just made things weirder. The thing was, the more the image replayed in my mind the more of that night I was starting to recall. I recalled how much it hurt when he got on top of me, and I had heard stories about what it might be like, but it wasn't the same. Having heard stories and experiencing something yourself were two completely separate things. When I closed my eyes I could smell the scotch, and I didn't even know if it came from him or me.

"I just want to make sure," she said as she took my hand again. I thanked her as she handed me back my tea now that I had calmed down a bit. "I didn't get the sense that he had pressured you, but I wasn't there so I needed to check."

"I'm fairly positive," I replied as I took a sip.

"I think you need to talk to him about what happened."

"I can't do that."

"Why not?"

"I just *can't*," I said, stressing the word. I couldn't tell her why, but I could barely pull myself from my bed, let alone confront Nathan. I wondered if his memory was coming back like mine was or if he was still in the dark. I wanted to put it behind me more than anything but the idea of talking to him made me tremble.

"He's really worried about you."

"I don't care," I was surprised at how snappy I sounded. I hadn't anticipated my voice to come across so harsh, but I was unable to change it.

"Okay," she said softly as she nodded. I could tell she was just as shocked as I was to hear what came out of my mouth. "Vivi, do you need to come and stay at my place for a few days?"

"What?"

"If you don't feel safe here-"

"It's not about feeling safe."

"All right, if you're not feeling comfortable here, maybe a change of scenery will help," she replied. "My husband is away for the weekend, so it will just be us."

"That's very generous Elaine, but-"

"You need to get up. You can't stay barricaded in your room," she cut me off, not wanting to listen to my objection. "Nathan called me because he was worried about you. You haven't left this room in two days, you've barely eaten, and I bet you've not opened those curtains once. He asked me to help you, and I think the best way for me to do that is to help prevent you from shutting down. Don't block him out. Nathan is one of your best friends and if this whole situation was an accident, as you say it was, then he doesn't deserve this."

"He's not even upset," I said with tears in my eyes.

"What are you talking about?"

"When we woke up, I was mortified, and he was acting as though nothing had happened."

"I thought you said neither of you remembered."

"I've never fallen asleep next to him, so I knew something was up. Then, when I went to the bathroom I-" I couldn't finish my sentence.

"Honey, all I can say is that for the most part men and women treat sex very differently. You can't blame him for not feeling the same way as you. Had you not said anything he might've never known. But you can't tell me that Nathan isn't upset about it. I don't think I've ever heard someone so flustered on the phone," she put her hand under my chin and tilted my head up to look at her when I tried to look away. "You're fixated on your emotions and that is understandable. It's a lot to process. I will say though, Nathan's clearly worried about how you're feeling too. He probably isn't thinking about himself and what's going on in his head right now. I really think you should come to my place to just relax and clear your mind. It'll give him space to clear his too. Maybe when you've both had some time apart, you'll be able to sit down and talk about things."

"I don't know."

"What's the worst that can happen?" Elaine replied with a gentle smile. "At the very least you and I get to spend some quality time together."

As much as I didn't want to go, I thought Elaine had a point. Maybe some time apart would help. Maybe a change of scenery would take away some of the stress I felt, and I could have a clear head when I was finally ready to talk to

Nathan. Being in Elaine's company already made me feel better, so perhaps a few days at her place was exactly what I needed. Nathan would also get a break, as he wouldn't feel inclined to check on me every hour as he'd been doing. It would also give him some time to reflect. For all I knew, maybe he'd get his memory back and we could piece things together. As much as I didn't want to remember, I was starting to think knowing the truth could give us some closure on the situation.

Finally, I nodded, agreeing that she was right. I just prayed it would help me feel better. I worried if I couldn't collect myself in the next couple of days, then Audra would notice something as soon as she walked through the door. I needed time to prepare what I should say, and in my current state I could barely function.

I sighed; I could do nothing but hope for the best.

CHAPTER SEVENTEEN

AUDRA

I stirred as I felt something cold press against my forehead. I tried to open my eyes but struggled to do so. My body felt like it was filled with rocks as every limb felt so heavy. I could feel people hovering above me and could hear the sounds of their voices, but I was unable to respond. My mind was fuzzy but at least it seemed more willing to work with me than my body.

"Should we take her to the doctor?" a deep voice asked.

"Nah, she'll be fine. She's probably just in shock," a female voice followed, "see... she's stirrin' now."

I recognized the female voice, but I couldn't put my finger on who it was. Was it Faith? Was I still at the creek? Finally, my eyes fluttered open as I felt the damp cloth press against my cheek. I laid there for a moment, trying to steady the spinning feeling that was taking over me. As I stared up at the sky and saw the large branches overhead, I realized I was still at the creek as I'd thought.

"Welcome back," I looked at Will, who stared down at me with a relieved expression. I glanced from him to Taye and Faith, who seemed just as comforted that I had woken up. How long was I out for?

I struggled to sit up, welcoming Will's assistance as he held onto one of my hands and used his free arm to wrap around my back to help me slowly rise. He kept his hand on my back even after I was sitting up for support in case I got light-headed again.

"What happened?" I asked. I knew what happened, I passed out. What I really wanted to know was for how long, but the question had seemed to be the only thing I could get out mouth.

"You fainted," Taye answered, "lucky Will was quick enough to break your fall."

"Thanks," I said to him, he just nodded and rubbed his hand on my back for comfort.

"How you feelin'?" I glanced at my sister. Before I could answer, Taye was quick to say they were lucky she showed up right as I was blacking out because she was quick to respond. My attention turned to the damp material she held in her hands, the one I was certain she'd used to cool me down. The material perfectly matched the pretty pink dress she had on, and that was when my eyes shifted to the hem. She had torn her dress to use the material as a cooling cloth for me. I offered a soft smile of appreciation for her gesture.

"Better."

"Boys, would you mind if I had a few minutes with my sister alone?" she asked them, leaving me a bit confused. Taye was quick to agree, but Will waited for my response before he answered. I nodded to him that it was all right and watched as he got up from the grass to follow Taye down the stream towards the clearing, disappearing out of sight. I waited for my sister to say something for I didn't know why she wanted a moment alone since we'd barely spoken most of the trip. "How you really doin'?"

I looked in her eyes as she stared back at me with genuine concern and empathy. She didn't mean physically, she meant emotionally. I sighed and shook my head, "I don't know, I guess I was kind of taken off guard."

"I'm real sorry 'bout your friend," she said to me as she reached out and tucked the damp pieces of hair that had fallen in front of my face behind my ear. I watched as she took my hand and gave it a squeeze. "I know how much you cared 'bout her."

"No, you don't," I couldn't seem to bite my tongue. There Faith was, trying to be caring and supportive, and my first reaction was to snip back at her. It wasn't fair. As I went to take what I said back, she opened her mouth.

"Actually, I do. I know you used to sneak out here ev'ry day to play with 'em," she said, implying both Nan and Taye. "And I know what you're thinkin', that Taye told me all 'bout your adventures down here. Well, it's true he told me 'bout the games you played, but I already knew when we were young that you were comin' out here after school ev'ry day. I was born at night but not *last* night."

"How'd you know I came here?"

"I knew ev'ry inch of this town where us kids liked

to spend time and I ain't never seen you *anywhere*, not a single person did when we asked 'em. After school you'd just vanish, so one day I followed you," she laughed. "I watched y'all play from the bushes for an hour."

"And you never said nothin'?"

"Audra, I *rarely* saw you happy. In that single hour, it was like I saw the light in my big sister's eyes shine for the first time in my life," she said, surprised when a tear had fallen. She let out a small laugh before she smiled and shook her head, trying to stop another one from falling. "I wanted nothin' more than to be your friend and not just your annoyin' little sister, but I didn't think that was ever goin' happen. So, if keepin' my mouth shut was my way of keepin' you happy so be it."

"I can't believe you never said nothin'," I replied, a bit unsure. I found it difficult to believe that she had known about my friendship with Taye and Nan for so long and never once breathed a word of it. She could barely keep it a secret if she saw me sneak a cookie before dinner, so how was it she was able to bite her tongue about a relationship she knew our Pa would lose his mind over? Was she telling me the truth? Did she truly care about me that much? If that was the case, why did she go the next several years in school ignoring me or why was she never by my side when I was an outcast?

"I know you think I was against you, but that wasn't the case," her voice was strained as she tried to get me to believe the words she said. "I didn't feel like I was ever good enough for you. It was like you never saw me for me and you had me painted in a different light than what and who I was. Maybe, I didn't do ev'rythin' I could've done to be there for you and maybe I was friends with the wrong people at the wrong time, but I tried to be there for you, and I tried to defend you but you didn't want to see it. You didn't want to see me."

"That's not true."

"Really? Back in New York I tried to get you to talk to me, but you kept findin' any excuse not to be alone with me. You were quick to assume somethin' I hadn't even said or done. Maybe I did hastily convince you to come down here 'cause I hoped we could talk, but you've done ev'rythin' in your damn power to avoid me," she sternly said. "Now, can you really sit there and tell me that's not true?"

I wanted to tell her it wasn't, but we both knew I'd be lying. She said exactly what Vivian had been trying to tell me, but I refused to listen. I was struggling to listen now, and I knew I couldn't deny it. I tried to look back and recall my memories, had I really been so blind to her actions? Maybe if I had just given her a chance to redeem herself, the hostility that I had towards her wouldn't exist. Maybe the relationship with my sister that I so desperately wished for could have been a reality. There was a large enough age gap between us that we didn't always see eye to eye and maybe years ago I expected too much of her. I wanted her to think for herself and not like everyone else in town with their God damn negativity and nastiness. The thing was, I never stopped to realize how young she was. When she was little, she was focused on making friends in school, she hadn't yet realized how the world really was. She was surrounded by people who had the same opinions as our folks, and by the time she was old enough to realize what I had been saying all along, I had already cast her aside. In my mind, I grouped her with the folks who made those jokes about me. I grouped her with the folks who treated people like Nan and Taye as second-class citizens. I grouped her with the folks who thought so damn highly of themselves that they believed they could step on *anyone* different and not bat an eyelash. Maybe in my mind I had pushed her so hard into the people that shared those mentalities that she struggled to claw her way out. Looking back, maybe if I had been more patient or had tried to spend more time alone with her, I'd have seen that she wasn't who I'd decided she was.

"Taye told me what happened years ago, how they'd disappeared," she said to me, sadly. "I knew exactly when he meant. I didn't know what had happened, but I remember you comin' home out of nowhere and you were so different. I had thought maybe the timin' of that whole Bobby Michaels thing was to blame, but I always knew it was somethin' more. Rumors don't just break a spirit like yours but losin' a friend would do the trick."

"Why didn't you ever say anythin' if you were so certain that somethin' was wrong?"

"What was I goin' say, Audra?" she shook her head. "You barely gave me the time of day as it was. In your mind I was the last person who was s'posed to notice anythin' 'bout you. If I had said anythin' you would've just lashed out at me, and I didn't need to be yelled at again."

"I'm sorry," they were the only words I could

manage to say. I wasn't sure what else I could voice that could rectify the situation. I spent most of my childhood isolated and angry, and I never stopped to notice that maybe my sister had felt lonely too. I walked around with such anger because I felt the effects of people's words, and I felt that the only way I could protect myself was to shut everyone out, and apparently that included my sister. So, in return, she walked around with a burden of sadness that I only contributed to. Maybe if her voice had been louder, and mine a bit softer, we would've met in the middle and realized what we were missing in our lives was each other.

"The past is the past," she said as she took my hand back and gave it a squeeze. "We can only accept what we can't change and grow from it."

"You're right," I said as I glanced at the large tree behind us that Taye had said he planted over Nan's body. I sighed, I had always wanted to know what happened to Taye and Nan, and although I hated the answer, at least I could lay my wonder to rest along with Nan.

"You know," Faith started with a soft voice. "In a way, it's like she never left you at all."

I turned and looked at my sister, overcome with warmth in my heart. I suddenly found myself unable to control my actions and leaped forward and wrapped my arms around her. I smiled as she I felt her arms wrap around my back, squeezing tightly, returning my affection. I couldn't remember the last time I had hugged her, *actually* hugged her, but it felt so nice and comforting. After a minute of embrace I felt her pull away from me, though she kept her eyes locked with mine. I studied her face, unsure why she had a sudden look of hesitance and worry. She gulped. It was obvious she was trying to say something but was holding back. I wasn't sure why, but I put my hand on her lap. I didn't know what she was about to say but her worry made me nervous.

"I was real selfish makin' you come down here, but I really needed you to know 'cause you're the only one who'd understand."

"Understand what?"

"The moment I met Taye and realized who he was I wanted to call you and tell you, but I didn't know how. I couldn't just tell you that your childhood friend came back lookin' for you and that Nan had died. I just couldn't," she said, shakily. "It wasn't enough to just tell you that I'd met Taye, I needed you to see for yourself that he'd come back. I just didn't know how to convince you to come down sooner without tellin' you exactly why."

I paused for a moment, I understood why she had convinced me to come down and she knew I did, so what was she trying to confess to me? Suddenly, a thought crossed my mind, "how long have you known 'bout Taye?"

"A little over a year."

"You knew for a year, and you never thought to-" I stopped as I saw her flinch. Like she had said, the past was the past. Even if she had tried to convince me, we both knew I never would've come down. "It's all right. At least I know now."

"That's not all," she said as I raised an eyebrow,

unsure where this was headed. I watched as her hand trailed her neck along the chain she wore. The chain was long enough that the pendant hung past the top of her dress and sat hidden in her chest. She slowly took the chain off and placed it in my palm. I glanced at it confused, wondering why she was handing me her necklace, until I took a second look and realized it wasn't a pendant at all but a ring.

"Faith, what is this?" I asked, shocked. It wasn't hers, was it? If she were engaged, why was she hiding it? Our folks would've been thrilled. My eyes grew even wider as I pieced everything together. There was only one reason I could think of as to why she would keep her engagement a secret. I looked at her for confirmation because the only thing that made sense also somehow confused me even more. My heart began to pound so loudly I swear she could hear it. "Are you-? I mean, how did you-? What?"

"I'd been comin' here for years just for some silence and peace of mind. Plus, a part of me felt closer to you when I was here. Taye only came back lookin' for you, but as we started talkin', somethin' just clicked, you know?" I watched as she blushed and watched my face for a reaction. I just sat there, stunned. I didn't know what to say. I could tell my silence was making her anxious but in the span an hour I'd gotten way more information than I felt I was able to keep up with. "Say somethin', Audra, you're makin' me nervous."

"Do you love him?" I asked.

"I do," she replied, timidly but filled with glee. "More than anyone I've met in my whole life."

"It's not-"

"Legal? Not here… but heard we can in California," she replied with hope in her voice.

"You're goin' move to California?"

"We've talked 'bout it," she answered. "We still have things to figure out. It may not be easy for us, but if goin' to California means we can be somewhere that's safer, and in a place where we can hold hands down the street, then I wanna make it happen."

"Faith, please be careful," I warned. "Just because it's legal to get married there doesn't mean it's accepted, or safe, for that matter."

My heart felt for her. I knew better than anyone what it was like to love someone and have society ridicule and object against you. Every day I wanted nothing more than to walk down the street and hold Vivian's hand, and yet, out of safety we never did. We walked as though we were merely friends. I heaved a heavy sigh as I stared at my sister, and despite her optimism, I worried she wouldn't even be able to do that. Vivian and I could walk down the street, and no one would know by looking at us that we were lesbians. Taye and Faith, on the other hand, couldn't exactly hide the fact that they were different races. I wanted to be positive, but I feared for them. The world was not a kind place. I was certain Taye knew what he was getting himself into, but I wasn't sure my sister did. I don't think she'd ever experienced any kind of mistreatment in her life. She had always been the picture of a perfect Southern belle, not only in looks but in demeanor too. Everyone we knew held her high up on a pedestal. If she chose to stay with Taye, her whole world would change. I wasn't sure she would be able to handle that. Then again, I'd just come to realize I didn't know her quite like I thought I did.

"Audra, I know it won't be an easy road, and I know we're puttin' each other in a risky situation but I can't be without him, and he's said the same for me," she went on as her eyes glossed over. "All my life I did and said what other people wanted me to, and I looked happy, but I wasn't. I was tired of puttin' on a show. I tried so hard to be the person that people expected me to be, and in turn I said some awfully ignorant things. For that, I'm so sorry. I wanna be better. I wanna do what I wanna do, and what I wanna do is follow my heart no matter what happens. Our folks don't know a thing because we both know what'll happen if I tell 'em."

"And his?"

"They've known for a few weeks. Understandably they're unhappy and have expressed their concerns."

"Have you talked 'bout kids?"

"We have," she replied, keeping her answer brief. I could tell that was a discussion for another time. I nodded and took her hand, giving it a squeeze. Amidst my concern, I also felt overwhelmed with happiness for her. I couldn't imagine in a million years that something like this could happen. Not only was my sister in love, but she was also in love with someone I held so dear in my heart. Although I worried for the two of them, I could tell they had deliberated on the trials to come. I hoped she was truly prepared for the consequences but either way, in that moment, I made a silent vow that I would be by her side. "I just hope we're half as happy as you and Will."

Her kind words made my stomach ache. There she was, being completely honest with me and I was sitting here like a damn fraud.

I had to admit I had liked having Will as my fiancé since we'd arrived in Georgia. I didn't understand before. I couldn't grasp how someone would be so willing to pretend to be someone they're not. I think it was because it was the first opportunity that I had to personally experience the benefits. I didn't have the most understanding or cooperative family, but since moving to New York I didn't have to deal with them. I talked to them on the phone, but all I really had to do was avoid the conversations I didn't want to talk about, and I was fine. I knew I could've had it worse, like Vivian, who not only had to deal with constant phone calls and letters but also lived in a close driving distance to her folks.

We had only been in town for two days and I had done everything I could to keep my head low and avoid as many people as possible. My Ma had tried to convince us to go to church while we were around, and I'd flat out refused. That would be throwing myself to the wolves. The other day when we ran into those women at the convenience store, I couldn't describe the appreciation for Will in that moment. When they heard Will was my fiancé, I swore their jaws hit the ground. At first, I didn't know if they were shocked to see I'd actually stepped foot back into town, but I was quick to realize their attention had snapped straight to Will. I couldn't say it surprised me. Will was very good-looking, and incredibly kind. He's always had a softness to him that made people feel drawn to him. Unlike Nathan who was a bit more suave and masculine, Will had a bit more of a rugged persona. Nathan had always been put together, held his head high, and came across as a protective patriarch at times, which earned him a lot of female attention. It seemed a bit opposite to Will. Granted, Will was generally well-dressed but was more likely just to throw on any clean shirt. He wasn't afraid to get his hands dirty. He had a confident demeanor, and prided himself on his actions, but had a bit more of a teddy bear personality. He seemed like the kind of guy who'd take you out for a hike before treating you to a homemade dinner. I had seen them both be flirted with before, but Nathan by far got more attention in New York. I was curious to see if it'd be the same in the South. In New York, women were looking for handsome high-power men who could take care of them and that was exactly the tone Nathan could give off. But down in Georgia, I think Will might've been a bit more of a catch. He definitely could give off the husband vibe, but it was easier to see his fun laid-back side. Granted, Will had a very different upbringing than Nathan.

It brought me a sense of satisfaction when he had introduced himself as my fiancé and they had to take a minute to realize what he'd said. I tried my best not to laugh but I'd been able to feel the edges of my lips rolling up. I couldn't help but notice he was quicker on his feet than I had previously seen. Nathan was a smooth talker, but his natural grace was what had women falling all over him. I'd never heard or seen him do anything that resembled flirting, in fact, he'd always made an effort to escape a conversation or situation where he felt someone getting too close. I knew Will hadn't picked up his flirty demeanor from Nathan, so I couldn't help but wonder if he was drawing from his past dating days. I appreciated that he was tasteful in the way he toyed with them. He never once said anything that was a direct compliment, it was in the way he talked and the way he narrowed his eyes. He drew them in with the tone of his voice before turning back and motioning to me. He began telling them how lucky he was to have found me and continued to talk me up. I could see their confusion was mixed with a bit of envy. I didn't anticipate him turning to kiss me, but I didn't pull away. I knew it was for show, and their reaction was worth it.

I had experienced so many mixed emotions about getting engaged to Will. I hated the idea at first and then it grew on me a bit when Vivian explained the benefits, showing me how it worked for her. It wasn't until I arrived in Georgia that I really understood Vivian's point of view. For days, I had felt comfort by having Will keep up our charade. I wasn't walking around in fear of people's commentary, or of them asking me awkward questions, or of them treating me differently. Suddenly, I was just like everyone else and blended in. As far as anyone could tell, I was no longer *Audi the Odd Girl.*

However, suddenly with Faith's confession, I felt sick about the whole thing. Sure, Faith was hiding her relationship for now, but it was only a matter of time before the truth came out. It wasn't like Faith could continue in a masked relationship like Will and I could. She either had to bite the bullet or marry someone else. I knew from the look in her eyes when she spoke about him, that she wasn't giving Taye up for anything. If that meant straining or losing her relationship with our family, so be it. Yet, there I was. The one who preached equality and standing up for what you believe in, was hiding like a coward and acting like a hypocrite - it killed me.

"Will's not really my fiancé," I finally said, catching myself off guard as the words escaped my lips. I couldn't do it anymore; I couldn't lie, especially if she was being so truthful.

"What?"

"I mean, *technically* he is, but I'm not in a relationship with him in the traditional sense," I said as she watched me, waiting for me to elaborate. "Will's my beard."

"Your what?"

"My beard. Will's gay, and so am I," I admitted, unable to look at her. "We made the decision to get married to hide the truth in order to... in order to blend in, I guess."

"Nathan and Vivian... they did that too, didn't they?" she asked me, watching as I stared at her confused. How could she possibly have known that? She continued to speak, "and you're in a relationship with Vivian, yeah?"

"How did you know?"

"At the bridal store she wasn't as excited as I'd thought a best friend would be, and when I came back before Ma to drop off a dress, I saw you two kiss," she replied, sadly. "I just don't understand."

"I just feel 'bout Vivian the way you do 'bout Taye. I can't help that I fell in love with her."

"Nah, silly, I understand that. What I can't understand is why *you* of all people would put yourself through this circus?" she said. I was taken aback. Her response was not as I had anticipated. I suddenly realized that she wasn't upset or even shocked that I was a lesbian, but she was struggling to wrap her head around how, after years of being myself and standing tall, I'd be so quick to hide. I wished I had an explanation for her. "I think times are changin' for Taye and me, slowly but surely. I guess times are just a bit further away for you and Vivian. I can understand if you're afraid."

"I'm not afraid," I said, and I wasn't. At least, I didn't think I was. Sure, we couldn't just walk freely down the street, and we had to move in more secretive circles, but I felt more liberated in New York than I ever had in Georgia, but maybe that was everyone's overall mentality. Maybe fear was why Vivian was so quick to marry Nathan. She claimed she only did it for the security and for people to leave her be, but she wanted to feel safe even if it was a façade. Maybe for Vivian, she felt safer with everyone believing she was in love with Nathan. She came from a society of prudes, where women looked down on each other, and men were quick to puff their chests. From her stories, they did not take rejection well; I could only image what would happen if they knew why. She must've lived in a state of panic for years when she was younger. We had heard so many stories of men being beaten up, or women being attacked for turning a man down, that in theory I ought've had a bit of fear in me too.

Maybe she was so insistent that I should marry Will, not because it'd be easier to explain our situation or that it could further our careers and social lives as it had theirs, but because she worried what would happen in a few years to me if I was still unwed. How I could be viewed and treated? I could only speculate, but it was in Vivian's nature to worry about those things unlike myself.

"As long as you know what you're doin'," Faith said to me. "You'll always be my sister and I'll always love you. I understand if you want to keep the truth from Ma and Pa, but I just want to make sure you're doin' what you're doin' for the right reasons."

I couldn't help but laugh, and it wasn't long before she joined me. What were the chances? If only our folks could see us now, between the two of us we would give them each a stroke. Their eldest daughter a lesbian, and their youngest in a relationship with a black man. Damn, we were quite the pair.

I reached out and gave her another hug as she took me in her arms. I had never felt such love and support in my entire life from anyone other than Vivian, Nathan, or Will. To have someone who I had so longed to have a relationship with accept me for me, and to have her trust me enough to confide her own secret made me so overwhelmed with tears of happiness.

Having had Faith wholeheartedly accept me, and even worry for me, made me really begin to wonder if I was making the right decision marrying Will. A part of me felt it was too late to do anything and it didn't seem like there was any harm being done with our secret, but a part of me still felt off about the whole thing. I would have to make a hasty decision whether I wanted to call the whole thing off or teach myself that I didn't need to feel guilty for the decision we made. Whatever I decided, I'd have to do it quick.

In the meantime, I planned on using the rest of our time in Georgia to get to know my little sister, and to finally reconnect with the best friend I thought I'd lost forever.

CHAPTER EIGHTEEN

NATHAN

I wasn't used to the house being so quiet. On occasion, one of us might've been alone for a bit, but generally no more than a few hours. Two days had passed and, though I didn't want to admit it, I was lonely. I tried to keep myself busy with work and errands during the day, but I couldn't do anything about the evenings. With Will in Georgia, I went home to an empty bed. It didn't seem so bad when I had Vivian around to socialize with when I got home, but ever since our drunken encounter I'd been apart from her too. She'd refused to talk to me for two days and that was a turning point for me. She'd not come out of her room once and with Audra gone I called the only person I could think of to help.

Elaine was her best friend outside of our circle and I knew Vivian would confide in her with most, if not all, the things going on in her life. I had always admired their friendship and was thankful Vivian had someone to talk to that could be on her side and yet remain unbiased since she wasn't directly involved. I didn't know if Vivian had talked to her about what she'd been thinking or how she'd been feeling but I had to take the chance. I was careful not to tell her exactly what had been going on but simply said that Vivian was upset, and I was concerned. I could tell she was wary and trying to think of reasons that Vivian and I wouldn't be on speaking terms since we never argued and rarely had any big disagreements. I held my tongue and refused to breathe a word of the truth. I'd leave that to Vivian to share, *if* she wanted to.

Elaine came to the house almost immediately after I called. I opened the door and before I could say a word, she had walked past me asking, "where is she?"

I silently pointed towards the stairs and watched as she walked straight towards them without even a glance in my direction.

"Elaine?" I asked, catching her attention. "I made tea if you want to bring some up."

She nodded as she came back down the steps and followed me into the kitchen. She asked how I was doing but I told her I wasn't the one she should be worried about. I wasn't locked up in my room, refusing to come out. I felt odd as she watched me, waiting for me to say something but I remained silent.

I quietly sighed to myself, the truth was that I wasn't doing well at all, but I didn't know what else to do other than push my thoughts aside and focus on Vivian. I tried to recall our evening over and over but for the most part I still had no memory. What I did recollect was so faint and I couldn't confirm anything. All I remembered was being in bed and Vivian standing in the doorway in her nightgown, drunkenly leaning against the frame for support. The only other thing I thought I might've recalled was a feeling, if that was even possible, of awkwardness. I vaguely remembered being uneasy in my body and that something was off, but I wasn't sure what. I sighed, for all I knew I was just recalling how I felt during our conversation, or even a completely different event. The morning we woke up, I was sick and nauseous from the alcohol but that was it - I didn't feel any different and, had Vivian not said anything, I would never have jumped to that conclusion. I honestly thought us waking up next to each other was innocent, but she strongly believed otherwise. She seemed too certain and was not only ill from drinking so much, but she seemed different. I tried to get her to talk to me so we could calmly assess the situation, but she was too overcome with emotion that she refused. I couldn't blame her. She was so convinced we had slept together, that I had no choice but to believe her. It would've explained some of the memories I had, but I wished I had something more concrete on my side. Maybe, at some point, the memories would come back. I couldn't help but wonder what exactly made Vivian so confident it had happened when she, herself, said she couldn't remember the events of that night. I was too scared to ask, and she was already so hesitant to be near me that I didn't want to push it. Maybe she'd tell me later, but I'd leave that up to her.

I kept feeling responsible. I knew I might not have done anything wrong, but that didn't help me from feeling guilty. She was my best friend and I felt like I betrayed her trust. I wanted to know. Did I do or say something to her that made her apprehensive towards me? Would she even tell me if I had? I could rack my brain and question all I wanted but it didn't change the fact that Vivian was upset, and I had no recollection of anything.

I didn't know what Elaine had said to her, but it wasn't long before she informed me that Vivian was going to spend a few days with her until she could calm down. I didn't like that their solution was to walk away from the situation rather than talk about it, but I understood. I recognized that Vivian wasn't me, and while I might've been ready to sit down and talk about things, she wasn't. She needed to back away and work things out in her own mind before she'd be ready to work them out with me.

She barely said goodbye as she left and could only manage to give me a forced but soft half smile. She wasn't in a good state so I appreciated her gesture, and I could only pray next time I saw her she'd be able to look at me again.

I sat on the couch watching television until my attention was turned towards the front door when I heard the latch click and keys jingle. I turned the television off as I stood to see who was walking through the door. Vivian wasn't due back until tomorrow but there she was, bag in hand.

"Vivian," I said, surprised to see her. I quickly walked towards her and took her bag as she struggled to take her jacket off. "You're back early... is everything all right?"

"Yes, I just wanted to come home," she replied as I put her bag down and motioned for her to sit, she looked exhausted. She sighed as she relaxed on the couch. "There's nothing like home."

"You sure?" I asked, considering the state she was in when she left and how anxious she had been to leave. I sighed, I knew it wasn't home she was running from, it was me. I rubbed my face, wishing I had held my tongue and not said anything. She seemed calm and the last thing I wanted to do was upset her, "Vivi-."

"Nathan, I'm so sorry," she said to me, catching me off guard. "I shouldn't have reacted the way I did, and I feel terrible about the way I treated you."

I took a minute before I brought the chair closer to the couch so I could sit across from her but still be close. I cautiously reached out and took her hand in mine, giving it a comforting squeeze.

"Vivi, you have nothing to be sorry for," I told her. "If I-"

"It wasn't you."

"What?"

"It wasn't you," she heaved a heavy sigh, holding back the tears that began to form. I looked at her confused, I didn't understand what she meant. From the look on my face, she seemed to realize that I was at a loss. "I started to remember."

"You did?"

"I think it was my fault that all of this happened," she took the tissue I handed her as a few tears trickled down her cheek. "I remember struggling to put my nightgown on and it really dawned on me that we had made a decision. I was so happy about our choice but was suddenly mourning not carrying a child. I went to your room to talk about it because I unexpectedly felt so sad."

"I remember you in the doorway," I said slowly as my mind flashed back, suddenly it was as though more pieces of the puzzle were drifting into place. She was holding onto the doorframe the best she could; her eyes were glossed over and sad. I recalled telling her to come and she stumbled over. She laid next to me, her head on my chest for comfort. I remember saying something and her responding back but I didn't know what we said. It was as though I was watching a motion picture in my mind, but without any sound. I attempted to focus, trying my hardest to recall what had been said.

"Nathan?" I heard her say as I snapped out my thoughts. I had gone quiet for longer than I had realized. "What is it?"

"What did you say?" I asked her.

"What? Just now?"

"No, after you came into the room."

"I don't know *exactly*, but something about courage or wishing it'd be easier or..." she shook her head as she trailed off. "Honestly, I can't remember."

I gulped as I slowly felt my stomach tighten as the voices in my head became clearer, as if the volume was slowly being turned up. Suddenly, I wished my memories had stayed blocked. The more of the conversation I recalled, the more the blurry images in my mind began to take shape.

"*It's not like we'd remember in the morning,*" I said.

"What?"

"That's what I said to you. *It's not like we'd remember in the morning,*" I responded, repeating the exact phrase I had said the first time. I watched her expression, which I could only assume looked similar to mine as she began to connect the pieces. I watched as her eyebrows scrunched together as she ran through the events that followed.

It was as though that one phrase was the key to our memories. I watched as she tried to process what was going through her mind, while I simultaneously watched the same visions roll through my own.

After she had come and laid down next to me, she did

her best to try and express how she felt, but her drunken state made her trip over both her words and her thoughts. She was upset that it was so easy for some people. Not only for a traditional couple who could naturally try and get pregnant, but for the women who either had a liking for both sexes, or who could just get over the idea of sleeping with a man. Maybe it wasn't their preference, but they had an ability to treat sex more nonchalantly than women like herself. However, Vivian struggled to say 'nonchalantly' so had substituted the word for 'wishy-washy'. Women like her couldn't just do that.

She began to recount a conversation she had with a friend she'd met years ago during a private event on 67th Street. Jayne had been completely beside herself after a conversation with her sister, and immediately reached out to Vivian who would listen and understand her pain. Her sister had urged her to get married for stability and to have a family, determined that her interest in women was just a phase and once she was wed, she'd see that. Despite explaining she had no interest in men and couldn't fathom sleeping with one, her sister continued to press on. She'd told her to just lay back and close her eyes, that it wasn't a big deal and she'd get over it. Although Jayne tried to explain she couldn't do that and how wrong it was, but she kept being told she was being dramatic. Unfortunately for her, it wasn't the first time she'd encountered a similar topic of conversation. People couldn't grasp even the idea of sleeping with someone of the same sex yet told her *she* was being ridiculous. Apparently, it was completely sane for them to be turned off by the concept, but for her to be turned off by sleeping with the opposite sex wasn't the same thing. There were some people who understood and supported you, and then there were some people who tried to support you but lacked an understanding. Vivian had come home feeling awful for her friend. She couldn't imagine being told to just *get over it* as Jayne had. She was exactly like her. They both had realized their sexuality early, they both had been as true to themselves as they could be in this day and age, and they both had very strong views of how they regarded sex. Neither could just sleep with anyone that caught their eye, and they both felt the same way about even the concept of being with the opposite sex. Yet, there Jayne was, feeling utterly burdened by the commentary surrounding her and when she spoke, Vivian could see the pain and frustration in her eyes. She felt for her, and somehow felt personally affected because she knew the exact remarks would be said to her if she had shared her secret to her family and friends the way Jayne did. Vivian wanted to more than anything, but she knew whatever Jayne was experiencing, she would have it worse.

As Vivian continued on a rampage of run-on sentences and jumping thoughts, it made my mind wander. I understood where Vivian was coming from. I was always surrounded by men who wanted to show off how masculine they were. They somehow felt a great deal of pride by voicing the number of women, or type of woman, they had been with. I had never felt any desire to try my hand as I knew at a young age where my interests lie, but I also knew how I would be viewed or what would be said if I ever admitted I was gay. It would ruin my career, my reputation, everything. I'd heard those men make harsh jokes about people who are gay, and even voice threats they thought were funny when in fact they were incredibly ignorant and cruel. Whenever they'd make comments, I'd have to excuse myself from the conversation.

I wanted more than anything to talk back but I couldn't. As much as I hated it, I was stuck. I didn't know if their threats were malicious jokes or if there was some truth in them, in which I'd be putting myself at risk. So, all I could do was keep my head low and blend in.

I had spoken before I even processed the meaning of my words, and interrupted Vivian in the middle of her rant, "it's not like we'd remember in the morning."

"Huh?" she was confused by what I said. She attempted to get up and look me in the eyes but fell back on her elbows, unable to hold her own weight.

The conversation following that was a bit hazy, and I wasn't sure if it was the alcohol talking or not, but we both knew we'd never really be able to bring ourselves to do anything. We could talk about it all we wanted, but at the end of the day it would never happen. Vivian was too undecided and uncomfortable, and I felt even more so. Having that much scotch in my system made me a bit more confident, and even that inebriated I knew if I didn't do something in that very moment, in that state, we'd lose our window forever.

"It's not like we'd remember in the morning," she repeated what I had said quietly as if she was still trying to wrap her head around my words. Her mind was distant, and it was as though she was trying to guide herself through a fog of uncertainty. She couldn't seem to convince herself that she could do it, even consumed by that much liquor. She shook her head, "I don't know, Nate."

I couldn't seem to stop talking. For all we knew we could do it and it would be nothing. If that was the case, if we were okay with it, we could try a few more times until she did get pregnant - or it would end in a disaster and at least we tried.

We exchanged a few more words, and I wished I could recall exactly what was spoken but nothing came. I do remember hesitance in Vivian's voice and sternness in mine. Perhaps I was giving her a now or never ultimatum, or maybe the scotch brought out a firm tone in me. Truthfully, I didn't know. All I did know was that it was after those last few exchanges that I remember Vivian going silent and getting a glossy look over her eyes as she stared into the distance for a minute. She finally locked her eyes with mine, searching for what I could only assume was trust because no more than a moment later, she laid down on her back. I moved towards her cautiously, waiting for a reaction but she gave none. I took a deep breath to settle the nerves that were rapidly rising and realized I needed to do exactly what Vivian was trying to do – distance herself from the situation. She lifted her hips as I warily reached under her nightgown and removed her undergarment. She broke eye contact with me and just stared at the ceiling while I fumbled and tried to adjust myself, feeling incredibly awkward as I moved closer to her.

"It wasn't your fault," I said to her as I searched her face, trying to gage her reaction as she sank back against the couch. Her face was expressionless, and she seemed lost in thought. I sat there and waited a few seconds, watching for a reaction, but she just stared blankly. "Did you hear what I said, Vivi? It wasn't your fault, it was mine."

I almost jumped as she burst into laughter. I felt frozen in place and looked around as if someone else was in the room that could give me a clue of what to do. I couldn't move as I watched her laugh, was she hysterical? She had already gone through a depressive state, was this her mind's new way to respond? Nothing about that night or this situation was funny. Yet there Vivian was, howling. Finally, she wiped away a few stray tears. I couldn't tell what kind they were.

"I'm so sorry," she gasped for breath.

"I don't understand. Why are you laughing?"

"It was so awful."

"And that's funny?" I asked slowly, proceeding with caution. I was at a loss.

"I just – what were we thinking?" she finally caught her breath, and I handed her my glass of water from the table, waiting while she took a sip. "I think we were both at fault."

"I don't know. If I hadn't encouraged us to drink that much or if I hadn't pressured you-"

"Nate, stop," she reached for my hand. "I'm sorry for how I reacted. I was in shock. We just – our intoxicated selves just didn't listen to what our sober logic had to say, and now we have to deal with those consequences. There's nothing else we can do."

I looked into her green eyes and nodded. She was right. I couldn't believe how much her mentality had changed in a matter of days. She could barely look at me before and now I was beginning to feel like we were returning to our old selves. Whatever she and Elaine talked about, or whatever Vivian had done to process what had happened, had really helped her. I felt a wave of relief as I started to see a glimpse of my best friend again, only an hour ago I was sitting on the couch scared I'd lost her.

"I think we shouldn't tell them," I said.

"What?"

"Audra and Will."

"I don't think I can-"

"Look, what happened between us was a mistake. We

both know that, and we know it will never happen again. They're going through a lot right now and maybe it's better for everyone, including us, to just sweep it under the rug."

"You would keep that from William?" she asked me with an arched brow.

"I can't very well tell Will and make Audra the only one in the cold. No, if we keep it a secret, we keep it a secret from everyone," I said honestly. Although Will was not against the idea, he wasn't for it either. He merely understood why we had initially contemplated the idea of having sex, but if it were his choice, it would never happen. Vivian seemed reluctant at first, we were never ones to keep secrets from our spouses, but we agreed that it might cause more harm than good if we said anything – especially between Vivian and Audra who had not even discussed the idea of it. The whole mistake had almost cost Vivian and me our relationship, the last thing we needed was to damage our *real* relationships.

CHAPTER NINETEEN

I smiled as I sat on my usual bench in the courtyard and as I watched my new colleague Gregory walk towards me with his lunch. I moved over to make some space for him, welcoming the company.

It was about two weeks ago that I stood at the chalkboard in the empty classroom and began writing some of the key notes we would be speaking about that afternoon. I was copying what I had first drafted on a piece of paper as I let my mind wander. I yawned, feeling exhausted. I had felt that way for days and the fact that I had been going to bed at a decent hour ever day did not seem to help in the slightest. I wasn't sure what had me so spent because in addition to the full night's rest I'd been getting, the house was back to a comfortable state since our better halves returned.

I was shocked at how unsurprised I was when Audra and William got home from their trip to Georgia and informed us that they had agreed to call off the wedding. Audra had always been uneasy about the idea, and after reconciling with her sister and finding out about her sister's soon-to-be public relationship, she found herself finally admitting that she couldn't go through with it. Will seemed to be on the same page with her and agreed after much talk and deliberation, deciding that although it worked for Nathan and me, they just did not have the same struggles. I supported their decision and couldn't help but feel responsible for putting them through everything only to have them call it off. I knew Audra was never fond of the idea but marrying Nathan had helped me so much and taken such a burden of stress off my shoulders, I only wanted the same for her.

I had to admit over the last week, since they'd returned, they both seemed noticeably less anxious, which benefitted everyone. We all seemed in a better mood. Will was back to his more carefree demeanor and Audra lost her short temper. She'd never lose her edge, but she came home every day much more relaxed and was no longer consumed by the stress that made her snip more than usual.

Over the last couple of months, between my absurd workload and her uncontrolled anxiety over the wedding that she didn't even want, we had not found many opportunities to be alone with one another. The times we did find ourselves alone, we had ended up bickering over absolutely nothing just because we were both on edge. However, despite my usual workload, once the heavy weight was lifted from her shoulders and she got her free time back, were able to make the time to spend together and reconnect.

The other day when Audra was due to work late and Nathan and Will had gone out for dinner, I was doing the dishes as it was my turn, and I knew I tended to be the one who got out of doing the chores the most. I hadn't even heard Audra come in and jumped when I felt her behind me. My momentary shock swiftly disappeared as I felt her arms wrap around me and her body pressed against mine. I grabbed the towel and dried my hands right before she turned me around. She placed her hands on my waist as she pressed her hips against mine, leaning us into the counter. She began to kiss my neck as her hand trailed up thigh, slowly slipping under my dress. It had been a long time since we'd been so spontaneous, and I couldn't do anything but let my body take over. We had barely made it up to the bedroom as our clothing began to drop along the way leaving a trail. We had simply laughed; it wasn't as if Nathan and Will hadn't done that before. I'd missed the sensation of her soft skin against mine, the taste of her lips, the feeling of her hands as she caressed my body.

I bit my lip as I recalled the other night. I shook my head, snapping myself back to reality, and tried to focus as I made another point on the board. I couldn't help but smile to myself, Audra and I had shared many intimate nights in a row, perhaps they had winded me more than I anticipated. However, I couldn't exactly complain about it. I yawned once again and shook my head, trying to shake off the fatigue I was feeling.

"Well, you know there's something wrong with a lesson plan if the teacher is falling asleep thinking about it," someone had said in a joking manner.

I jumped and turned to see who spoke. I observed a man standing in the doorway, not too much older than myself, no more than maybe five or ten years, which seemed barely like anything compared to the dinosaurs that I had been surrounded by. He had dark hair similar to Nathan's, was clean-shaven, and gave me an almost a suave smile. He had a very distinguished jawline and deep, soulful eyes.

"Sorry to frighten you," his voice rang low as he took a few steps in, "are you Mrs. Porter?"

"It depends on who's asking."

"I'll take that as a yes," he laughed as he walked towards me, reaching his hand out to shake mine. "I'm Gregory Miller."

"It's a pleasure, Mr. Miller," I responded, "how can I help you?"

"I- uh," he scratched his head confused and waited a moment before he spoke, "didn't anyone tell you I was coming?"

"No, I'm sorry."

"I'm here to replace Professor McKay."

"You are?" I asked in shock; it was the first time I had heard of that. "Has he had to take time off?"

"No… he… uh… so nobody's come to talk to you?"

"No, they haven't," I was beginning to get annoyed. What did I not know?

"I'm sorry, Mrs. Porter, but he passed away over the weekend. I just assumed being his assistant, someone would've contacted you by now to discuss what was going to happen for the rest of the semester."

I had to excuse myself whilst I took a seat. The news had caught me off guard. I wasn't sure if I was more shocked about his passing or by the fact that not one person I had seen all morning had breathed a word about it. How did no one stop to say anything to me? I placed my hand to my head and rubbed my temples as I collected my thoughts.

"Do you need me to get you anything?" he asked as he took a seat across from me at the desk, watching me with concern. "Did you need to take the rest of the day off?"

I shook my head. I was fine. I couldn't help but feel somewhat relieved by the news, and it created a guilty pain in my gut. I did not like to think ill of the dead, but he had been horrible to me. Not only did he purposefully overwhelm me with work, but he was a sexist pig. He was consistently making inappropriate remarks, excluding me from things, talking down to me, and always taking credit for *my* work. I sighed as I looked at the man across from me. I'd been preparing the lesson plans, and helping Professor McKay teach for years, yet of course the university would bring in some man from somewhere else to do the job I was more than capable of, and would in fact, excel at doing. Although Gregory Miller hadn't actually said he was taking over the class, he didn't need to - it was obvious.

"I heard you tend to be in class early and I was hoping to catch you to go over the lesson plans, if you're up to it," he said. "All the administers I've talked to say you're very good at what you do, and I really don't want to be the guy who comes in here and starts taking over. I don't know how you and Professor McKay did things, but you know this class well and I was hoping maybe we could collaborate and be a bit more of team for the rest of the semester if that's all right with you."

I raised an eyebrow as I stared at him. I tried to search his eyes to see if I could read what kind of man he was. Did he truly want to collaborate or was he just saying that? Either way, I had no choice but to share the lesson plans with him, but he spoke kindly and seemed to have an honest air about him that I couldn't help but sense trust.

Gregory was the first professor I called by first name, as he had insisted. Over the course of the day, he treated me with the kindness and respect that no other educator at the institution had, and I felt grateful for it. I was careful to observe and see if it felt forced, as if he was just trying to get on my good side, but he seemed like a genuinely nice individual. I couldn't help but be thankful that if anyone was going to take over his class instead of me, it was him and not one of Professor McKay's equally aggravating colleagues.

That evening, for the first time in a long time, I didn't come home with a stack of paperwork. In fact, for the following two weeks I barely brought anything home, or at least, that was what it felt like. Gregory made true on his partnership agreement, and we rotated the workload or split it equally. There were a few evenings he'd asked if I'd rather just stick around for an extra hour or two in order to work together and finish the assignments quicker, so we didn't have to take anything home. Unlike Professor McKay, Gregory didn't think it was fair if only one of us was doing all the work. At home he had two beautiful little girls he talked about all the time, and a wife he equally adored. Although I didn't have children, he was quick to note that quality time alone with my husband was just as important. Even though it wasn't Nathan I'd been spending my evenings with, it was nice to go home and actually spend time with Audra. I think everyone was glad to see the mountains of paperwork swiftly disappearing off the dining table so we could have regular meals there for the first time in what felt like years.

In addition to the luxury of finally getting home at a

decent hour and being able to enjoy the company of those I loved, I also suddenly felt more secure in my position. I knew Gregory had only been there for a short period of time but for the first time in years I was experiencing the respect that I had only dreamt about. He also spoke highly about me in front of others which was a nice change compared to the previous years where I was simply ignored.

"Thank you," he said as he took a seat beside me on the bench. I watched as he pulled an apple out of the brown paper bag he had and took a bite, staring at me as I sat there with my food untouched, "not hungry?"

"Not really," I replied, I didn't want to admit I was a little nauseous. I wasn't sure why, just the idea of the pasta I had in my bag made my stomach twist. I had a feeling that maybe I ate something bad for breakfast and I was still reeling from the aftermath. I didn't quite feel like I had to throw up, but I definitely felt a sickly feeling in my stomach. I took a sip of the tea I had purchased from the cafeteria and welcomed its warmth as the wind blew a cool breeze.

"Perfect day for a warm beverage at least," he smiled as he finished his apple and wrapped the core in a tissue. He placed it on the ground by his foot before he opened the sandwich he had brought. "So, I had an idea for next week. I know it may not seem traditional, but I figured what if we forwent the test."

"What?" I asked, as I put my hand over my mouth, and tried to distract myself from the bologna smell coming from his sandwich. The mere whiff of it was beginning to make me queasy.

"In substitution for the test, I say we lead a debate."

"A debate?"

"Yes, have the students study the themes and morals of the text and split them into teams, have them on opposing sides and run an educational debate. I'd be interested to see what concepts they draw from in a completely different sort of setting," he replied, watching me for an answer. Although I really loved the idea and thought it would be incredibly interesting to see, my facial expression seemed to not reflect my feelings. "You don't like the idea."

"No, I do," I apologized, as I shook my head. "My stomach is just feeling a little off and the smell of your sandwich is not helping."

"I'm so sorry," he apologized, I felt awful as he wrapped it back up and put it back in his bag. I watched as he reached into his blazer and pulled out a little container, offering me a mint, "it always helps if I'm feeling sick."

"Thanks," I accepted it, grateful for the peppermint taste in my mouth. Like Gregory, I always found mints comforting whether I felt well or not. "Do you need to take a half day?"

"Oh gosh, no," I shook my head. "It'll pass. I think I just ate something weird for breakfast and the feeling just hasn't subsided. I'll be fine."

"Are you sure?" he searched my eyes. "I don't mean to pry, and I haven't known you for long, but you've just seemed really exhausted lately. For someone who's said they've had a lighter workload than they've ever had at the university, you'd think you'd have more energy."

"I don't know what you're getting at," I replied, feeling uncomfortable with his words. I wasn't sure where he was going with his thoughts, but I felt uneasy. Although I was growing to appreciate Gregory and respect him as both a colleague and newly found friend, I didn't feel we had known each other long enough for him to comment on my state of being.

"I didn't mean to offend you, I just, well," he said flustered, cautiously proceeding, "the last two times my wife was pregnant she had similar symptoms. She was perpetually exhausted and was nauseated at the smell of almost everything."

"I'm not pregnant. Trust me," I laughed. My smile faded as he stared at me seriously. I shook my head, "I'm not; I just ate something bad this morning."

"So, you haven't been feeling sensitive to smells all week?" he asked, raising an eyebrow. "You know, around the time my wife started to get nauseous she would also complain her body was starting to ache."

"That's incredibly inappropriate to say to a colleague," I snapped back angrily as I tried to stand up, wanting to leave the conversation. I looked at him as he grabbed my arm and gently pulled me back down, keeping his hand on my arm.

"I didn't mean to upset you. I was just being frank. I'm sorry, Vivian. Please, stay," he said as he released my arm, sensing I wasn't about to walk off again. "All I was trying to say, is it could be a possibility."

"Well, it's not," I responded.

"Just, maybe go to the doctor and see," he said, unconvinced by my response. "If you're not, great, but if you are I'll make sure your position is secure for the rest of the school year."

"Gregory, that's very kind but-"

"I understand how hard you've worked to get where

you are, and how this might not be coming at a great time but if there's the slightest chance you could be pregnant, you're better off to find out now so you can take a care of yourself," he said with a great deal of compassion. "I'm on your side. I'm not trying to be your enemy."

I took a deep breath before I took a sip of my tea. I wasn't pregnant; there was no way I could be. My mind flashed back to my night with Nathan. I had tried so hard to suppress my memories that, for a brief moment, I had forgotten about it. It had been easier than I had anticipated keeping the truth from Audra, because I was so desperate to forget the night that my mind seemed to block out the event. I didn't have to try to keep a secret, because I hadn't thought of it for weeks until now. Was it possible that I could be pregnant after that one single time? I glanced at Gregory as I thought. I had been exhausted, and I was feeling nauseous, and in all honesty my chest had been hurting more than usual, but I just assumed I was due to have my time of the month. Although I found it very hard to believe, Gregory did have a point, it was worth at least looking into. If, by the smallest chance I was, I would do everything I could to keep myself in perfect health to finish off the school year. If it was possible to feel more nauseated, I did at the thought of actually being pregnant. On the one hand, it would make what Nathan and I had gone through worth the stress and pain, but on the other hand my stomach turned at the thought of how we would even begin to explain what we vowed to keep a secret from Audra and William.

I had to do my best to keep my head on straight. There was no use in panicking until I knew for sure.

CHAPTER TWENTY

WILLIAM

I wrapped my arms around Nathan and gently placed a kiss on his lips before he headed towards the door with Audra. I always enjoyed Monday mornings when I could wake up, have my coffee, and see everyone off at the door before enjoying some time to myself. Since I worked at the market on Saturdays, I generally took Mondays as a day off in substitution. I waved them both off as they headed out quickly, running a bit later than usual. Normally, Vivian also joined them as her work was on the way and she'd catch a ride, but Audra said she had taken the day off to go to a doctor's appointment for a routine checkup. I was proud of her for finally making an appointment; I think we all were as she usually avoided the doctor like the plague. For someone so well-educated, she couldn't seem to grasp the importance of having a checkup as the rest of us did. When I asked what her aversion to doctors was, she had no answer. I don't think she knew herself; she'd just always avoided them if she could. I remember a dinner we had where we mentioned that as we got older it was more and more important, and she was quick to dismiss the conversation. I couldn't tell if she'd had a bad experience or not. Nathan and Audra seemed to be on the same thought: that her family didn't really discuss those sorts of things because it wasn't proper. They were uncomfortable discussing anything medically related, which in turn, left Vivian uncomfortable herself. Vivian had once, however, mentioned that she did tend to get flustered and self-conscious at even the thought of going so I had to believe that Nathan and Audra had hit the nail on the head.

I waved them off as the car left the driveway and closed the door behind me. I walked towards the kitchen to grab myself a cup of coffee when I stopped, hearing a bang come from upstairs.

"Vivian?" I called from the bottom of the stairs, trying to listen for a response. When I heard nothing, I decided to go up and make sure she was all right. I gently knocked on the bathroom door, "Vivian?"

When I didn't hear a response, I began to worry. Noticing the door wasn't locked, I let myself in to check on her. I sighed as I saw her on the tile leaning over the toilet trying to catch her breath from vomiting. I quickly grabbed two cloths and ran them under the sink so they could soak up some cold water before I rung them both out. I placed one on the edge of the counter and the other one I took in my hand as I knelt beside her, placing it on the back of her neck. Luckily, her hair had already been pulled back out of her face and was out of the way. I placed a hand on her back as she shivered, holding onto the rim for dear life. It wasn't a moment later that her body convulsed, and she began throwing up again. I just rubbed her back, trying to comfort her as tears streamed down her face while she was sick. Finally, she began to cough as if her body still needed to throw up, but she had nothing left in her stomach. She stayed leaning over the rim, seemingly scared she would experience a third round but after a moment, she seemed to feel safe and finally sat back. I helped her lean against the tub on her right then stood up to fill the empty glass on the sink with water. I handed it to her and crouched as she took a sip. I reached over and grabbed the other cloth and gently dabbed it over her sweating forehead. I watched as she tried her best to drink the water but struggled to as she attempted to catch her breath. I worried as I stared at her droopy eyes and paler than usual complexion. She looked exhausted and as if all the color had been drained from her face.

I reached up to the robe behind me and swung it off the hook as she began to shiver again. I helped her slip the robe on and rubbed her shoulders. Shakily, she passed me the half-drunk glass of water that I put back on the counter before she pulled the robe more tightly around her as if it would secure and protect her. She silently shifted onto her side and lay down in my lap. I stroked her hair with one hand while the other wrapped around her as if I was a blanket of support. I just sat there with her on my lap in silence as her breathing gradually became more regulated, and I could feel her once rapid heartbeat slow down as she calmed.

"Are you okay?" I asked very quietly as to not startle her.

"No."

My heart broke a bit at her sad and weak response. I finally helped her into a seated position, she seemed dazed and out of it. I sighed as I helped her up and kept my arm around her as I guided down the hall and into her bedroom. She slowly laid down on her bed; I could tell she was still in pain from her body tensing as she was ill. I sat on the edge of her bed and pulled the blanket over her to try and steady the trembling. I put the cloth I'd previously used over her forehead to cease whatever headache I knew would be on the horizon. I had spent too many mornings hung over and vomiting to not know the side effects that followed. Although I doubted that she was hung over, it still didn't change the fact that you'd feel just as awful no matter the reason your stomach decided to turn on you.

"Can I get you anything?" I watched as she shook her head, staring off into the distance. She looked so small and frail. I couldn't help but begin to worry that most of her color still hadn't returned, except for spots of bright red that were overwhelming her cheeks. "Are you starting to feel a little better?"

"I'm scared, Will," she finally said to me, her voice trembling.

"Scared of what?" I asked and watched as she turned her head from me, tears streaming down her cheeks. My heart began to pound in my chest as she remained silent, panic starting to take over. "Vivi, talk to me, you're worrying me."

"I can't – oh god," she began to break into a crying fit, unable to control herself. She tried her best to speak but I could barely hear her between the hiccupped gasps for air. "Will, I'm sorry."

"Vivi, you need to calm down or you're going to make yourself sick again," I grabbed onto her shoulders tightly and forced her to lock eyes with me. I was finally able to get her to steady her breathing. Although the tears continued to fall, her breath was consistent, and she seemed more lucid. "Please talk to me, what's going on?"

"I can't," she replied, broken.

I took a moment and studied her face; she could barely look at me. Finally, I sat back, and nodded. I rubbed my forehead and took a deep breath. It didn't take a genius to put two and two together. If I had to take an educated guess, I assumed it happened while I was in Georgia with Audra. It was really the only time they could've been alone. I felt frustrated, not because of what happened but because Nathan hadn't been honest and told me when I got back. I didn't understand. He had come to me, and I had been willing to support him if that was the decision they made. Although I wasn't thrilled about the idea of my partner sleeping with someone else, I was willing to accept it because of the circumstances and because I knew if they had made the decision, it wouldn't have been made lightly from either party involved. I just wished I knew why he hadn't been upfront about what happened. It didn't make any sense to me. As the wheels began to turn, many questions popped into my mind. When did they make the decision? Were either of them all right? How many times did they sleep together? Finally, I caught myself and stopped myself from letting my thoughts spiral out of control. I reached for her hand and gave it a squeeze. She turned and looked at me, mortified, realizing I knew.

"It's okay, I'm not mad," I said to her watching as she heaved a heavy sigh of relief. "I'm frustrated that Nathan didn't tell me, but I'm not upset."

"We weren't going to say anything to you or Audra," she replied, holding back tears. "It was a mistake. We didn't know."

"What are you talking about?"

"We decided not to, but we got really drunk and we didn't even remember what happened at first. We just wanted to put it behind us. I hadn't even told Audra that we'd talked about it, and since we decided not to go through with it, I was never going to, and then-" she paused between trembling breaths. "We vowed not to say anything because it almost wrecked us, I was a mess, and I didn't want to risk losing you or Audra either."

"Nathan should've said something to me, especially considering my views."

"We didn't think it was fair to tell you and not Audra."

I nodded. Although I didn't agree, I understood their choice. It was an equality thing; I just wished I had been told. It wasn't as though I could change anything, but it didn't help my frustrated feelings, especially since I'd been so verbally accepting to the prospect. I sighed as I pushed my feelings aside and stared at Vivian's horrified expression. I needed to focus on her. The fear in her eyes made me believe she hadn't even considered it a possibility that she could fall pregnant after one mistake, and her guilt was consuming her.

"I don't know for sure," she finally said, breaking me from my thought as she tried to sit up.

"Vivian-"

"It's not for sure. That's why I made the appointment today," she said. I rubbed my forehead; I knew it was out of character for her to willingly go to the doctor without a real cause. She wasn't one to volunteer for a routine checkup, and she wasn't going to one. She was going to find out if her nightmare was a reality.

"Okay," I responded. From the timing and her symptoms, I'd be surprised if she wasn't, but I could tell she was holding onto a shred of hope. "Let me come with you."

"What?"

"I have the day off, and I think it'd be good to have someone there for support, no matter the outcome," I responded. From my understanding, she had kept Nathan in the dark. She had been holding everything in and trying to deal with the stress of it herself. It wasn't healthy. The cat was already out of the bag, having me there even just to lean on might do her good. I was relieved when she agreed to let me come with her. She refused to breathe a word to

Nathan about anything until she knew for certain. By the sounds of it, they were still trying to fully repair their relationship and she didn't want to place any additional stress on their friendship if she didn't have to. She also planned on waiting as long as possible before she had to talk to Audra about it - *if* she had to talk to her about it.

I held Vivian's hand all the way to the doctor's office and offered as much support as I could to calm her nerves, especially in the waiting room. Her leg shook as she began to get anxious. I had originally thought she was going to have some tests run, but she told me she had gone in a couple days ago, and today they'd be giving her the results. I couldn't believe she had kept everything a secret for so long and had acted so normally amidst her fears and sickness.

When the doctor called her name, I squeezed her hand before she went in alone. A part of me wanted to go into the room with her, to be able to stand by her and comfort her if she needed, but the other part of me knew that waiting for her was the right decision.

For the first time since I'd found her in the bathroom earlier that morning, I had a minute to myself to try to comprehend the situation. I felt horrible for Vivian and couldn't imagine what she was going through. I'm sure she had the same thoughts that were running through my mind, there were pros and cons to the potential outcomes. If she wasn't pregnant, then she wouldn't have to worry about uprooting her life. Although her new professor said her job would be secure until the end of the semester, he couldn't exactly promise that. The fighting chance she had was that she was the only person who was familiar with the current curriculum since Professor McKay's passing. With his replacement just starting at the university, the new professor needed time to get acquainted with the lesson plans, and it would be unfair to the students to lose another teacher within the same year, let alone semester. She also wouldn't have to worry about telling Audra.

I heaved a heavy sigh. I was so irritated that Nathan didn't talk to me about what had happened between him and Vivian, even if it was a mistake. I could only imagine Audra's response. Even if she could wrap her mind around what happened, I knew for a fact she would not be nearly as understanding as I was, and it would certainly cause a rift in her relationship. Although I didn't agree, I understood why Vivian felt the need to hide the truth. It would certainly be easier if she wasn't pregnant, and she could go back to pretending what happened between her and Nathan had never occurred and bury it like she intended. However, I couldn't help but think about the fact that the whole reason the conversation came up in the first place was because Vivian wanted to have a baby. Even though she and Nathan had initially decided against it, clearly deep down the feelings were still there – otherwise they wouldn't be in this situation. If, by some miracle, she did fall pregnant on the first and only try, it would make what they'd gone through worth it and they'd have a beautiful little baby in the end.

After what felt like hours, Vivian finally emerged. She thanked the receptionist and walked right past me towards the door, without even acknowledging my presence. I felt like I had to sprint to catch up with her.

"Vivian, Vivian!" I grabbed her arm and spun her towards me. I put my hand under her chin and tilted her head up to look at me. I searched her piercing green eyes for an explanation. "Whatever he said, we'll make it through it together. You don't have to run."

"I can't tell her."

She didn't need to say another word. I took her into a large bear hug and held her. I felt her arms wrap around my back and squeeze. I could tell she was scared, but we would work through this together like a family. This was a good thing, she was going to have a baby, she was going to bring life into the world. Perhaps it wasn't in the best circumstances, but do things ever go quite as we hope? I'd help her talk to Audra; maybe I could help her see things in a different light as I did. I was in the exact same position with Nathan as she was with Vivian. If anyone could try to make her understand, I think it could be me. Either way, Vivian had to let her stress go. It wouldn't be a comfortable conversation but there was no way around it. There was nothing she could do now; she couldn't turn back the hands of time and undo what was done.

The fact of the matter was that she was pregnant, and no matter what happened, she needed to focus on that. She didn't need any additional stress. She would have Nathan and my support, and hopefully with some convincing and time to adjust, Audra's as well. We would just need to take everything one step at a time.

CHAPTER TWENTY-ONE

NATHAN

I waved to Vivian as she walked out of the school looking for me. She returned the gesture before she put on her sunglasses and used the railing to support herself as she headed down the stairs towards me. I offered her my arm as support while we walked along the cobblestone path until we reached the paved road. I asked why she insisted on wearing those heels when going to work considering the walkway made it challenging for her, but she'd argued the heels were both comfortable and pretty. She only had to deal with a slight unbalance in the courtyard, so it was worth the struggle.

She stopped me as I was about to turn left towards our usual lunch spot and suggested maybe we could grab a tea from the café next door and take a walk instead, insisting that she wanted to enjoy the weather. I had to admit it was a beautiful day. The breeze was cool, but the sun was out, making it the perfect temperature for a light jacket or shawl. Autumn was both of our favorite season because of the colors and smells. With winter on the horizon, she wanted to enjoy every last day she could before the snow came.

Vivian was rather quiet while I purchased our teas, adding two pastries for something to snack on. I tried to get her to tell me more about the new professor, for so far, I'd only heard good things. I began to worry when she barely said anything. She never missed the opportunity to share what was going on in her professional life, whether it was good or bad, yet now with such big changes she hardly utters a word? I watched her as I took a sip of my tea, she could tell I was eyeing her, but she didn't give me much of a choice. I was concerned.

"Is everything all right, Vivi?" I asked as she looked down. I was hoping I'd just been imaging things, but it turned out that I hadn't. I sighed and motioned to an empty wooden bench for us to sit on as I waited for her to talk to me. She hadn't asked me to lunch just to sit in silence, but I didn't want to push her.

"Will knows," she finally said, quietly.

"What?" I didn't understand. I thought we'd agreed not to say anything to them. I knew for a fact that I hadn't breathed a word of what happened and based on Vivian's guilty expression it was obvious how he came to find out. I rubbed my forehead and tried not to get worked up. I just wasn't excited about the conversation that was to come. Will was generally very easy to talk to and we had an open-minded relationship, which worked for us. We had always gone into every conversation with a passive nature so even if we didn't agree on something we'd both take a step back and it always prevented an argument - unlike Vivian and Audra who'd both jump to defensive mode which caused most of their spats. Now, I'd have to go home to my partner and explain why I'd kept a secret like that from him, especially when his initial reaction was so understanding.

I looked at Vivian who waited for me to get upset but I found it hard to as I looked at her puppy dog eyes. I just wanted to know how or why she told him, so at the very least I could go into my conversation with him prepared.

"I didn't exactly tell him," she answered. "He put two and two together."

"What're you talking about, Vivi? You had to have let something slip, he wouldn't have just come up with it on his own," I watched for her response. If she hadn't said anything there would be nothing to put together. Perhaps if we had still been painfully uncomfortable with each other he would've noticed, but at that rate Audra would've been the first to sense the tension.

"I didn't," she admitted before she continued, "he walked in on me."

I took a second to register what she'd said, I needed her to elaborate, she couldn't have meant what I was thinking. She caught herself before I needed to say anything.

"Throwing up. I mean, he walked in on me throwing up."

"Vivi, what are you talk-" I stopped myself, it was as if something suddenly clicked. I shifted my body and turned to her, staring into her petrified eyes. As her breath quickened, I placed my hand on top of hers which was rested on her lap curled in a tight fist. I felt her relax at my touch, "are you positive?"

"Yes, my doctor confirmed it himself," she answered. I found myself taking a moment to soak in the information. I couldn't deny it came at a bit of a shock and I must've had it written all over my face for she leaned forward, staring at me, waiting for me to speak but I had no words. I needed a minute. Had I truly heard right? Vivian was pregnant? With my child? I mean, I knew it was possible for a woman to get pregnant after one time, but the likelihood was incredibly slim. I'd known couples who had been trying for months or even years before any success. How was it possible we could be that drunk, that uncoordinated, that quick, and yet *still* have her fall pregnant? I finally turned to look at her. I could tell she was more worried about my response than her own reaction, as if she had settled into the fact. "Nate, are you okay?"

"Okay? I'm ecstatic," I answered her with a smile, "I guess I'm just shocked."

"You and me both."

"So wait, you said Will knows we slept together... does he know you're pregnant?"

"Yes, he came with me to the doctor's on Monday."

"He came with you? On *Monday*?" I asked. I didn't intend to react to the way I did, but I suddenly felt an overwhelming sense of envy and confusion. Why hadn't Vivian said anything sooner? And if not Vivian, why wouldn't Will? It was Thursday, which meant for three nights I had laid in bed next to Will and he didn't breathe a word to me about it. Nothing even seemed out of the ordinary. Neither my best friend - the mother of my child, or the love of my life - my other half, said a single thing.

"Nathan, don't get upset with him, I begged him not to say anything," she said. It was as if she could hear the thoughts running through my mind.

"You should've told me sooner," I replied.

"I know, but when did we have a minute alone? Today was the first lunch we both had free to meet," she answered me. She put her hand on my cheek, "I'm sorry."

I took her hand in mine and gave it a squeeze; she had nothing to be sorry about. I was overreacting. There I was, upset that Will hadn't said anything to me, when I'd kept such a big secret from him. When he found out he probably jumped to a compassionate understanding than a jealous pout like I did. He had walked in on Vivian sick and offered to go with her for support. For all they knew at the time, she wasn't pregnant. She was probably panicking and upset and instead of getting anyone else worked up, myself included, they kept it between themselves until they knew for sure. She was right, it was her secret to share with me and if I really thought about it, I would have probably been upset if I had heard it from Will first. Besides, how would he have even started the conversation? First, I kept a secret from him about what happened and he in turn kept the secret about the aftermath. As far as I was concerned, and I was sure he was too, we were on par.

"You have nothing to be sorry for, I was just getting upset over nothing. We're a family and I'm glad Will was able to be there for you. I'm just sorry I wasn't," I answered her. She offered a soft smile as she took a sip of her tea and sighed. I took a minute, waiting for her to say something, knowing that something was on her mind. When she said nothing, I put my hand on her back and leaned forward to look at her when her eyes faded down to the ground. "What is it, Vivi?"

"I'm really happy you know," she replied.

"But?" I sensed a bit of hesitation in her voice.

"It just makes everything real now and since you and

Will both know, that means-"

"You have to tell Audra," I nodded, seeing the panic in her eyes. I gently pulled her closer as I rubbed her arm, trying to comfort her. I couldn't even imagine what she must be feeling. I could almost feel her heart pounding as she leaned against me, resting her head on my shoulder. I felt horrible she'd been sitting with this secret for days. She undoubtedly ran through her conversations with Audra and me in her head, thinking of every possible outcome and fear. Talking to me must have seemed like a piece of cake in comparison to what her conversation with Audra would be. Although Will was incredibly understanding and logical about the whole thing, if the situation were reversed I wasn't sure I'd be able to wrap my head around it. I would hope I could but wasn't certain. The difference was, even though I knew Will had been with women in the past, I never had the slightest fear that something would happen between him and Vivian. It just was never a fear that crossed my mind. Yet, the idea of something potentially happening between Vivian and me had crossed Audra's on more than one occasion. I wasn't sure if it was because we were technically married or not, but it was an unease she never quite shook. We used to think she was being ridiculous, but now, given the circumstances, I understood her worry. Granted, from our experience it was something that would never happen again, but it didn't dismiss the fact that we did sleep together.

"I don't even know where to begin," she said, looking up at me. "I keep thinking of ways to say something, to bring it up, but nothing seems right."

"There'll never be a perfect time and there will never be a perfect way. All we can do is pray that she sees that it was a mistake," I paused as I caught myself glancing at her stomach, "a wonderful mistake, but a mistake none the less."

She placed a hand on her abdomen and nodded. I could tell she felt the same way. At least we were being blessed with something so good in the midst of a bad situation. I could only hope, for Vivian's sake, that Audra could see the error we made, and feel the remorse Vivian expelled. At the end of the day, Vivian was having a baby and if Audra wanted to be with her, she'd have to accept that fact and learn to forgive Vivian as she was learning to forgive herself for what we had done.

I brought my arm back down to my lap as Vivian looked at her watch and sat up, wiping away the tear that fell down her cheek. She stood, having to get back to class. I couldn't believe how fast the time had gone. We didn't say much on the walk back, but after I helped her over the cobblestone to the front steps of the university, I gave her a kiss on the cheek.

"It'll all work out," I said to her. She nodded but didn't reply as she turned and headed into the school. I wasn't sure my statement convinced her, and I understood why. Truthfully, I didn't mean it would work out in her relationship with Audra. I couldn't predict that. I meant that, no matter what happened between the two of them, she'd still have Will and me. She wouldn't be alone through all of this, that was for certain. I hoped Audra could wrap her mind around what had happened and accept the situation. I knew she loved Vivian more than anything, and it was that love that made me hope she could live with the knowledge and salvage the relationship. However, her love and protectiveness of Vivian was also what made me scared she'd react the opposite way. I feared it'd be too much for her to deal with and that it'd be the end for them. Audra was strong-willed, and she'd been through a lot, but having the love of her life fall pregnant to someone else was something I wasn't sure her heart could take. I could only pray I was very wrong, for Vivian's sake, and for all of our sake's because at the end of the day, Audra was part of our family, and I didn't want to lose her either.

CHAPTER TWENTY-TWO

AUDRA

I pinned Vivian's wrists above her head and smiled as she moaned while I kissed her neck. I loved the way she sounded as she lied there and allowed me to seduce her. I missed her, I missed this, I missed *us*.

Since calling off the wedding, I felt the weight of the world lift off my shoulders. I was no longer feeling the unbearable pressure that the stress was putting on me. Although my parents were mad as all hell, I was thrilled. I did feel bad for terrible timing though. Unfortunately, Faith had decided to announce her decision to move to California on the same day we called off the wedding. She apologized to us profusely, but there was nothing to be sorry for – she didn't know. Ma had gotten so dramatic when we shared the news, she kept on wailing, "where on God's green earth did I go wrong?" Will and I ended up fibbing a little to make her feel better. We told her we weren't separating, just that we weren't quite ready to be wed. I figured in a few months I'd tell her we decided to go our separate ways. I felt bad, she was mortified that Faith was leaving. I listened to her for nearly an hour, ranting and raving about how Faith was going to ruin her life. It didn't take me long to realize that my sister had omitted some information herself. It took everything in me to bite my tongue as Ma complained. Faith had told her she was traveling to California to meet a friend and that there were exciting opportunities for her there. She didn't breathe a word about Taye to either of them, and for good reason. They were already madder than a wet hen, I could only imagine their response if they knew the truth about who she was going with. Regardless, I was happy for my sister and my childhood friend. I was glad they made the decision to go sooner rather than later. A fresh start would do them good, and I was starting to think that maybe a new beginning was what I needed too.

I slowly moved my hands from Vivian's wrists and slid them down her arms until they reached her neck. I watched as she smiled while I untied the knot that held her robe together and opened it. I gently and seductively ran my hands over her silky, almost see-through, baby pink nightgown and could feel her squirm at my touch. She grabbed the collar of my gown and pulled me in to kiss me. I lingered as I took in her soft lips. While I used one hand to support myself, I ran my other one down her side until I reached her hip and began sliding the gown up higher. I gently pulled away to get a good look at her, to take her in. She looked so peaceful, so serene. The moments alone we shared were some of the few where I saw her relax and just let go. She was always so worked up and so stressed that it physically hurt me some evenings to see her. If she wasn't physically exhausted from all the extra work she had to do, she was completely rung out emotionally between work, her family drama, or whatever else was going on. When it was only us, she could just be. Whether we were being intimate, on a little road trip, or even simply spending an afternoon having a picnic – it didn't matter, she could just unwind. I'd always had this dream that we would run off together, just the two of us, and start fresh. She could get a job that didn't leave her exhausted at the end of each day, and we wouldn't have family drama or fake marital problems. We could live without all the mess that currently surrounded us. Since Will and I called off the wedding, the dream felt more obtainable. Our lives would be so much simpler and happier if we could just go and be ourselves. That was all I wanted when I left Georgia, to be free. Yet, somehow, I got caught up in this whole mess and felt trapped again. With the new freedom of losing my title as fiancée I suddenly felt I could do whatever I wanted again, if I could just get Vivian to see how liberating it was. She could choose freedom by leaving Nathan, if she could only see how much better off she'd be.

I wasn't sure what came over me, but I was tired of dreaming and of keeping the fantasy to myself, "let's run away together."

"What?" she asked faintly as she slowly opened her eyes when I stopped kissing her neck.

"Let's run away. You and me," I said as I stayed sitting on her hips with my hands stroking her body, dreamily.

"Where do you suppose we go?" she asked as she rubbed my thighs and looked at me romantically.

"What do you think 'bout San Francisco?"

"San Francisco?" she smirked.

"I hear there's big things happenin' there. We could have a life, Vivi, a *real* life. Just you and me," I replied. She stopped stroking my thighs, as she looked me in the eyes, realizing that I wasn't joking. I watched her for a moment, waiting for a response before I continued. "Think 'bout it, Vivi. We'd be far enough from our families to not have to worry 'bout what they're thinkin' or have 'em intrude in our lives. Besides, just think 'bout how much more stress free we'd be."

"I can't just leave."

"Why not? You can get a teachin' job in San Francisco. Sure, Professor Miller seems nice and all, but who knows if the university is goin' to keep him next year. What if he's replaced by someone worse than McKay?" I replied, trying to convince her. With Professor McKay, she came home with piles and piles of paperwork and was perpetually exhausted. Things were supposed to change with Professor Miller, and although it seemed like she had way less paperwork, she still looked weary. "I have a lot of money saved, we could afford to find a real nice place and settle in until we find work we actually like. For all you know, you could get a teachin' job right off the bat."

"Audra-"

"Come on, Vivi," I begged excitedly, "can't you just imagine it? You and me takin' on the world. There'd be no politics involved, no fake fancy dinners, no coordinatin' our lives 'round the boys, no more-"

"It's very tempting, Audra," she laughed. I couldn't help but frown at her lightheartedness. I was being serious. I'd never loved anyone so much in my entire life, was it so wrong for me to want us to be completely free and happy? "Don't look at me like that. I'm being realistic."

"So am I. Vivi, I've thought 'bout it for years."

"You have?"

"Yes," I answered her truthfully. Although San Francisco had only recently caught my attention after my conversations with Faith, my dream to run away with Vivian had always weighed heavily on my mind. I wasn't sure where we would go or what we would do, all I knew is that I wanted her and only her. I always felt the only way to get that was to get away. "I just never said anythin' because you were workin' so hard at the university and, at the time, we hadn't been together for long. Back then, I didn't think you'd give that up for me. Over the years, I was always tryin' to find the right time to say somethin' and then with the weddin'... just now it's *real*, you know. We could make it happen if you're willin' and wantin'."

"It's not about wanting to, I'd want nothing more than to run away with you," she said as she placed a hand on my cheek. "It's just that I can't. It's complicated."

"How? How's it complicated?" I asked, as far as I could see it was pretty black and white.

"I can't just up and leave Nathan like that."

"Nathan?" I knew I shouldn't have been shocked or upset at her response. Nathan always seemed to be her biggest concern. They had been friends for over a decade, I had to accept that it wouldn't be easy for her to leave him. "Vivi, what if this was Nathan and Will?"

"What do you mean?"

"If Nathan really wanted to pursue his own life with Will, would you stop him? Or would you be happy for him?" I asked, watching her expression. I ran my hand over her bare chest before I slid it up the side of her neck and stroked her cheek. I could see the wheels in her mind turning. She'd be happy for him; she knew it and I knew it. "How is this any different? I know if you tell him that this is what you want, he'd support you... that's what friends do."

"It's different, Audra."

"No, it ain't."

"I want to go with you. I truly do, but I just- I can't."

"Why? What's holdin' you here, Vivi? If it's your friendship with Nathan he'll understand, he has to," I said.

She kept saying no but her eyes were screaming yes. I could tell she wanted to escape just as badly as I did, but I couldn't tell why she was so hesitant. I suddenly felt bad, it wasn't fair for me to spring this on her and expect a quick and easy response. She wasn't impulsive like I was. She needed time to think and deliberate. She couldn't just jump and go at a moment's notice. I sighed.

"Audra, I'm sorry. I just can't."

"Look, Vivi, you ain't got to make a decision now. Just think 'bout it, all right?" I replied as she took a deep breath, I could tell she was tense. I sighed as I placed my hand on her cheek. "For now, just relax."

I bit my lip as I undid the ribbon on her nightgown and opened the top, exposing her bare chest. She couldn't help but close her eyes and let out a soft moan as I ran my hands up and down her torso. I gently caressed her breasts, watching as she unconsciously smiled, before I leaned forward and began kissing her neck. My right hand gradually moved down her leg until I reached the hem of the fabric. I sensually slid my hand back up her inner thigh when she suddenly stopped me. I felt my heart skip a beat before it sank into my chest as she uttered words I'd never thought I'd hear her say.

"I'm pregnant."

I pulled my hand out from beneath her nightgown and propped myself up, staring at her. It was as if my mind couldn't grasp what I heard, as if I had imagined what had come out of her mouth. It took a minute for me to be able to move or speak, as I tried comprehending what was said.

"Audra?"

"Sorry, I thought I heard you say you were pregnant," I shook my head. "But that's crazy 'cause to get pregnant you have to have sex with a man and the last I checked I don't have a pe-"

"Audra, please."

I quickly got out of the bed and began looking around. Vivian pulled her nightgown closed as she sat up, fumbling as she attempted to tie the ribbon back into a bow. I began to panic as I searched for the trash can. I grabbed it just in time as I felt my stomach turn. I sat on the edge of the bed and threw up in it. I felt Vivian come closer, placing her hand on my back, but I shifted not wanting to be touched. I put the bin on the ground when I was finished and grabbed a tissue to wipe my mouth before taking a sip of the water that I'd brought up earlier. Vivian remained silent as I began to pace back and forth in the room, I didn't know what I wanted to say. I was overwhelmed with too many emotions for my mind to function properly. I felt overcome with extreme jealousy, anger, and above all, sadness. It was like every fear I had ever had since Vivian and I began dating had come true and I wasn't sure how to respond. I kept telling myself for years that I was just being envious for no reason, that nothing would ever happen, and that I was insane for thinking such things. Yet, there I was in the midst of it all.

"Audra?"

"How long?"

"What?"

"How long have you been sleepin' together behind my back?"

"We haven't been."

"I may not be a doctor, but I know you don't just wake up pregnant one day without cause, Vivian," I snapped at her.

"Once," she replied, shakily. "It was just the one time, I promise. It was a stupid, drunken mistake, and we regretted it immediately after."

"Oh, please."

"It's true, Audra, please believe me. We didn't even remember what happened when we woke up, it was a blur. I couldn't even look at him after; I had to go stay with Elaine for days afterwards. What little memories did come back we just wanted to forget. It was horrible, and I am so sorry."

"You know, for a long time I thought I was crazy - that I was being irrational. I loved you so much and I was so consumed with a fear of somethin' like this happenin' that I thought my apprehension was goin' wreck us. I felt that way, and you made me feel that way. It took ev'ry strength in my body to get over my worries and trust that all of this madness was goin' work," I wiped away the tears that began to fall. "I came to believe that this crazy wonderful household would work because I was the only one worried, and I know I can have a jealous edge. But now – you *knew* that I was terrified of this happenin', you knew and yet you and him-"

"We didn't mean to. Audra, we were so drunk-"

"It doesn't matter. Even that drunk somewhere deep down you knew what this would do to me, what this would do to *us*, and still you hopped in bed with him."

I had to sit back down for a minute, I wasn't sure if I was about to throw up again or not. I didn't say a word, and neither did Vivian. I could hear her choking back tears behind me. I felt so sick, and I was getting light-headed. I grabbed my chest as I struggled to breathe, feeling a panic attack coming on that I tried to subside. I put my head between my legs and took a few deep breaths. My world was spinning. I was almost certain I was going to pass out, but the only thing keeping me grounded was my rage that I was unable to control.

I felt as though I had been punched and then kicked to the ground. Not only was I trying to soak in the information that she had slept with Nathan, but on top of that I also had to absorb the fact that she was carrying his child. I adored children but wasn't sure I'd be able to look at that child without the constant reminder that the love of my life had slept with someone else. I also wasn't sure if I'd be able to look at Nathan the same way again. The idea of him with Vivian made me shake with anger. I couldn't contain my resentment and frustration; it was too overwhelming.

"Audra, honey?" I heard Vivian's shaky voice behind me. I could feel her close, wanting to reach for me but scared to touch me since I'd shaken her off only minutes before.

I turned and looked at her, feeling my heart shatter. I could barely look at her and she knew it. A part of me wanted to cry and be there for her. She was so scared and upset and I wanted nothing more than to wrap my arms around her and protect her. However, the other feelings that were consuming me were stronger. It was if my unconscious reaction to the news was anger and spite, and as much as I wanted to be there for Vivian, I had to focus on myself. I could take a lot of things, but this was one thing I wasn't sure I'd be able to get over. Not only had she slept with Nathan and fallen pregnant, but had that not been the case, was she just going to lie and keep the truth a secret from me for the rest of our lives? Did Will know they slept together?

"I can't do this," I finally said, trying to wipe the tears away as I stood. I began to strip in front of her and quickly grabbed the clothing I had hanging on the hook to my left.

"What?"

"I need some space," I replied as I finished buttoning my red dress and grabbed the small suitcase that sat beside our closet.

"Audra… Audra, what are you doing?" I could hear the panic in her voice as she watched me pack a few of my clothes.

"I just, I just can't do this right now with you."

"Please don't go. Audra, please, I'm begging you. I love you and I need you. This whole thing was just a big mistake."

"The thing 'bout mistakes is that they still come with consequences," I shot back in a nasty tone which was much meaner than I had anticipated, but I found myself unable to withdraw it.

"Audra, please… Audra!" I heard her yell my name between sobs as I stormed out of the bedroom. I couldn't continue our conversation; I couldn't even spend another minute in that room with her because I feared what would come out of my mouth. I needed some space to think. I needed to be alone to really see if this was something I could get over or forgive. I knew if I stayed, we'd have no chance in the future because something would certainly be said that couldn't be taken back. I wasn't sure if we could salvage our relationship or the situation, but the only chance in hell we had was if I left.

"Audra, what's going on?" I saw Nathan walk towards me rapidly as I came barreling down the stairs. I glanced to the top of the staircase, the sound of Vivian weeping was echoing from the bedroom.

"You know *exactly* what's goin' on," I replied between gritted teeth, as I pushed past him towards the front door.

"So… what? That's it? You're just leaving?"

"You're kiddin', right?"

"No, I'm not. The moment trouble arises, you bolt?"

"Trouble? You call this trouble?" I dropped my suitcase and took several steps closer to him, I could feel the steam flowing out of my ears. "This is far more than just *trouble*, Nathan. I'm gone for a matter of *days,* and you take it upon yourself to get her pregnant?"

"You make it sound like I planned for this!"

"Didn't you?"

"No. Despite what you think it was not my master plan to wait until we had a moment alone to get drunk enough to do something we couldn't even remember. If I *really* wanted to get Vivian into bed, I would've done it long before she met you. You can huff and puff and sulk all you want but at the end of the day it was an accident," he snipped back at me. "Do you realize she couldn't even *look* at me for days? That she had to physically leave the house because she couldn't stand being around me? Does that sound like something that either of us would've planned or wanted? Listen to her crying, Audra. Do you think that sounds like a woman who intentionally wanted to hurt you?"

"It doesn't matter if she meant to hurt me or not, the fact is she did and I'm entitled to react the way I damn well see fit," I shot back at him. "I knew walkin' into this that it was a bad idea, and I didn't trust my better judgment. This whole damn charade was goin' catch up with us eventually. Well, Nathan, guess what? You're just playin' your role, right? Married the perfect woman, have the perfect house and job, and now you'll have the *perfect* kid. You're just the all-around American family, ain't you?"

"That's not fair, Audra."

"I know, but it's also not fair you slept with the woman I love," I replied, my anger subsiding and my sadness taking its place. "I'd say it's a lose-lose situation, but here I am broken and alone and soon you'll have a little baby that loves you unconditionally. So, as far as I'm concerned, I got the shorter straw."

"You don't have to be alone."

"Actually, right now I do," I replied as I walked back and picked up my suitcase. Nathan didn't say another word and let me go. I listened as he turned and headed up the stairs. I stopped at the door and as I opened it, I took a minute when I heard Vivian crying. If my heart wasn't already shattered, her tears would've broken it. I needed to go; I couldn't turn back. I was no use to Vivian, if I went back up, I wouldn't be able to conquer my feelings and be there to soothe her. I knew my spitefulness would just hurt her even more. She'd have Will and Nathan. I hoped I was able to accept what happened and go back to her but, truthfully, I wasn't sure I would be able to. Either way, I'd be back – whether it be to rekindle the relationship, or to grab my belongings. I just didn't know which.

I barely made it off the front steps when I heard the door open behind me. I caught myself as I was about to snap at Nathan, realizing it was Will who had followed me out instead.

"Hi," he said as he slowly walked towards me. "Where are you going?"

"I don't know, I just can't be here right now," I replied as I wiped the tears from my eyes. "Did you know?"

"Which part?" he asked, shaking his head as he sat on the step.

"Why didn't you say anythin'?"

"It wasn't my secret to share," he replied. "Are you and Vivi over?"

"I ain't sure. I just know I can't even look at her right now," I answered him honestly. Since our trip to Georgia, I had found a connection to Will that I didn't have before. I trusted him, I confided in him. "I need some time to myself to think 'bout things."

"Where are you going to go?"

"A motel maybe? I didn't really think it through, I just, I had to get out of there."

"Here," I raised an eyebrow as he held his hand out. I walked towards him and picked up a pair of keys he had pulled from his pocket. "When Nathan and I started dating I refused to sell my apartment. I guess I was always waiting for the other shoe to drop. It was weird, you know, the whole Vivian and Nathan married thing, but it grew on me. Vivian and I became friends and I think our friendship helped strengthen the relationship Nathan and I had. Eventually, when I was ready to sell the apartment, you started seeing Vivian, and I decided to keep it in case Nathan and I wanted a weekend away. Anyways, it's yours until you decide what you want to do."

"You sure?"

"Of course," he replied. I placed my suitcase on the ground so that I was free to wrap my arms around him and gave him a tight squeeze. No one had ever been so kind and selfless like that for me before. The gesture in itself spoke wonders of Will and for a moment I regretted not marrying him. "Just promise to let me know if you need anything."

"I will. Thank you," I said.

"I hope you decide to come back because you and Vivian are a beautiful couple. You know just by looking at each other what the other is thinking. I've watched you both have so many ups and downs throughout the years and no matter the challenge life throws at you, you've been there for one another. I know we all have each other to lean on, but it's different when you love someone the way you love her. I can see it anytime you look at her, and she at you – even in an argument. I've watched you love and support each other unconditionally. These circumstances, they're... well..." he sighed as he looked for the right words but seemed to be unable to find them. I couldn't blame him; I wasn't sure how to describe the situation myself. "This whole thing is hard to process... trust me, I know. But hopefully you can one day look past this because it'd be a shame to lose a relationship like yours."

I picked my suitcase back up and as I turned to leave, I stopped, glancing back at him, "how do you do it?"

"Do what?"

"Accept that somethin' like this has happened?"

"What else can I do? It was a mistake that they

both regretted. I could see it in Vivian's eyes when I realized what had happened. I love Nathan, and Vivian's like family. Although I hate the idea of them together, in the end, we're only human," I could tell he was holding something back, but whatever it was, maybe it was better he didn't tell me.

I glanced at the keys in my hand and thanked him again before I headed down the street to catch a cab. If only I could have the mindset of Will.

Unfortunately, I wasn't Will, and I had to cope with the situation in my own way: alone.

CHAPTER TWENTY-THREE

NATHAN

I wanted to be mad at Audra, furious even, for picking up and leaving Vivian in haste. I understood she was upset but her actions were so harsh. I wanted to be bitter and disappointed, but I couldn't. When she snapped at me all I could see was pain and it broke my heart because I knew I'd contributed to it. What happened was partially my fault, and I had to accept that.

It took hours to finally calm Vivian down as she entered a state of panic. We knew Audra would react poorly to the news, but we didn't think she'd grab her bag and leave just like that. Vivian could barely catch her breath between sobs. I felt useless as I sat next to her, trying to soothe her. I was worried she'd make herself so sick she'd throw up. She needed to calm down. Eventually, she exhausted herself and completely passed out. I had grabbed a cold cloth and put it over her swollen eyes before covering her with a blanket. Hopefully the cloth would help ease and minimize the headache I was certain was on the horizon. After I was positive that she was asleep, I turned the lights off and closed the door almost all the way. I wanted to leave it cracked opened so that it'd be easier to hear her if she woke up. Afterwards, I had gone downstairs to find Will sitting at the table sipping his coffee. I joined him, taking the tea he had left for me. I took a seat in the empty chair next to him. I sighed, feeling drained.

Will and I had always been good at talking things through and discussing what was on our minds, but neither of us had said a word about what happened. I looked at him and smiled as he placed his hand on mine, offering me support. It occurred to me that we didn't have much to say. What was done was done and all we could do was move forward and learn from our mistakes. I couldn't imagine being with a more understanding and loving partner. When I had originally gone to him, he met me with love and support, not once did he meet me with judgment. When he found out I'd kept what we'd done a secret, he could've reacted with frustration and resentment. Instead, it was a bit of disappointment but overall, he understood why we reacted the way we did. Audra, on the other hand, didn't want to hear it. She couldn't even stop for a moment to listen, even if she didn't agree or if she couldn't handle it, if she could've just stopped and realized how much remorse we carried maybe she'd feel differently.

Vivian lied in bed for days and barely spoke. I had called the school and told them she was getting over the flu and would be off for a few days. Will and I took it upon ourselves to take a few days off as well and just sit around the house in case she needed us. Neither he nor I felt comfortable leaving her alone after what happened. If I thought things were bad the morning after we slept together, I had no idea. At least she had expressed her grief towards me but this time, she just seemed vacant. If she wasn't asleep when we went to check on her, she was lying awake staring at the ceiling. We tried to talk to her, see if we could do anything or if she was hungry, but she gave us no response. She couldn't even look at us. It was as though she was empty inside, and we were just looking at a hollow shell. Will said she needed time, but I was beginning to worry. I wanted her to be angry, I wanted her to cry, I wanted her to give us some sign that she was still in there. I couldn't stand seeing her lost. Each time I walked by her room, I was scared she was disappearing further and further into her mind. Will had brought some soup up to her the other day and tried to get her to eat, but she barely touched it. It was at that point that he began to share the same concerns I had. He said the effort it took for her to even sit up was painful to see. She'd barely had anything to eat or drink in three days and did nothing but lie in bed in silence. She was beginning to get pale, and her eyes were swollen. It was clear to see she'd been crying when we weren't present. I wanted to hold her and take away her pain but unfortunately it didn't work that way, so all I could do was be there for her.

We sat at the dining table the next morning as we ate our breakfast. I yawned as Will poured himself another cup of coffee, welcoming the caffeine since neither of us had slept much over the last few days. As I flipped through the paper, I almost choked on the piece of apple I was eating when I saw Vivian walk down the stairs out of the corner of my eye.

"Vivi!" I said surprised, as I looked her up and down. I couldn't believe she was out of bed and dressed no less. She had her blonde locks pulled back into a tight bun and out of her face. "You're up."

She just nodded without a word as she walked towards

the front door. She was dressed in her beige blazer with a black pencil skirt. I watched as she slipped on her matching heels before she walked back towards the table that her bag was leaning against.

"Uh, where are you going?" I asked as I got up and headed towards her, confused.

"To work."

"Work?"

"Yes, Gregory will be here any minute to pick me up."

"I, uh," I couldn't find my words. I glanced at my partner for support.

"Are you sure you're feeling up to going?" Will quickly got up and walked around the table, careful to stay his distance so it didn't look as though we were cornering her.

"I have the new lesson plans."

"Yes, but I'm sure they'd be okay if you gave them the paperwork and stayed here if you wanted."

"I'm fine," she replied firmly. She barely glanced back at us as she headed out the door without another word.

I stood dumbfounded after she left; it took me a minute before I turned to Will with a confused and questioning expression. I didn't know what just happened. It didn't even look like the same woman. No more than twelve hours ago she could barely sit up to eat, and now she was out the door dressed to the nines heading to work just like that? Something wasn't right.

"We should go after her."

"And say what, Nathan?" he sighed as he walked towards me and put his hands on my shoulders, giving them a tight squeeze. "If she wants to go to work-"

"This isn't her," I turned to him, feeling stressed. "In

all the years I've known that woman she has kept her composure, her sanity. There were nights she'd cry her eyes out because she'd gotten into a fight with her father or yelled because she was furious about something at school. Whatever her reaction, she'd always been Vivian. In the last two months since all this started, I feel like I've barely seen her."

"Nathan-"

"I'm not being dramatic, Will. Have you seen her lately? She's had every emotion under the rainbow, and it's like each day a piece of her is fading away. The fact that she's spent the last three days like a corpse and now she's acting like nothing happened?"

"Maybe that's what she needs right now," Will sighed as he sat himself down on the couch. "Maybe she couldn't lie in bed anymore and getting up and going to work was her solution."

"She didn't even say good morning, she just left."

"She needs some time to figure things out for herself. Don't take it personally," he said.

I knew he was right, but I found it hard not to. Vivian and I had always led our separate lives but were there to support and lean on each other as friends did. We never dictated what the other should do. At the very most we offered our opinion. I wasn't sure what it was, but suddenly I was feeling overly protective and a bit too controlling for even my own taste. I couldn't tell her if she could go out or not, it wasn't my place. There was a fine line between being opinionated and telling someone how to run their life. It wasn't right for me to tell Vivian if she should stay home, or how she could feel. I had to be careful not to cross that line. I'd seen it in other couples or friends, where one becomes so concerned about the other that they've hovered to the point that it feels like a controlling situation. I didn't want Vivian to feel like that was the case; I just worried about her. I wasn't sure if it was because of the recent stress between us, the fact that she was carrying my child, or some other reason, but my guard was up.

I sighed as Will wrapped his arms around me and pulled me into a hug, "she's a grown woman, she'll be okay."

"I know," I replied as I looked into his piercing blue eyes. I smiled softly as I placed my lips against his and ran my fingers through his shaggy locks. I slid my hands down his backside and pulled him closer to me. He was right, Vivian was an independent woman. If she needed space, she was entitled to have some. She'd come back when she needed us.

I smiled as he placed his hands on my chest and kissed me once more before I took his hand and lead him upstairs. What I really needed was to clear my mind, and I knew just how to do that.

CHAPTER TWENTY-FOUR

VIVIAN

I thought getting up and going to school would help, as if putting on a nice outfit and holding my head high would somehow instantly make me feel better, but it didn't. I felt exhausted from using every fragment of willpower I had to stay focused on our class and not let my mind wander because I knew if it did, I would crack. I lied awake early this morning and found myself unable to cry any longer. The last three days had been a blur. When I wasn't sleeping, all I was able to do was just lie there feeling empty. I could barely think, I could barely speak, and I was barely a person. I suddenly felt an overwhelming sense of pity and frustration towards myself. I knew Audra would be upset at the news and I knew we would fight about it, but never in a million years did I anticipate a reaction like that. I think I'd gone into shock when she grabbed her bag and bolted. She said she needed time to think but I didn't know what that meant. I didn't even know if we were still a couple. I hadn't heard from her in days, and I didn't even know where she was staying. I just wanted to know if she was all right and that she was safe. I had thought about calling all the hotels in the area to see if she was staying in one of those, but for all I knew she could've hopped on a train to Georgia. The situation there was terrible, but it probably seemed better than here.

I sighed and glanced around to make sure no one could see me as I placed a hand on my abdomen. Gregory had been a sweetheart and had so far kept my secret. I didn't want anyone to know I was pregnant until absolutely necessary as a precaution. Although he said he'd fight for me to keep my position until I had to leave, we couldn't control his bosses from making a rash and uncalled for decision. If anything, they'd try to move me to administration to cover their behinds, but that removed me from the position I'd worked so hard to get. When the thought of having a child originally crossed my mind, I hadn't quite worked out all the quirks and issues I'd run into, and now I wasn't left with a lot of time to be strategic. I was thankful to have Gregory's support, for if Professor McKay was still around, I'd be out of the classroom in a matter of months. Even when I called Gregory earlier to see if he'd be able to pick me up on the way in, he was quick to ask if I was feeling better before graciously saying he'd be more than happy to come and get me. On the car ride, he said he missed me and made a joke that the classroom was dull without our witty conversation. I couldn't help but smile at his words.

I could tell Nathan and Will were shocked at my sudden turnaround this morning. I didn't give them the opportunity to say anything because I was scared if I let them speak, I'd either change my mind and stay home or break into tears. They'd been so incredibly kind the last few days, taking multiple opportunities to check on me and make sure I was all right. I felt embarrassed to have leaned on them for support, but I was unable to do anything else. I wasn't used to relying on others like that. Sure, in the past when it was just Nathan and me, and one of us was sick, the other would bring soup or whatever was needed. We obviously helped look after one another, but it wasn't to the degree that Nathan and Will had cared for me over the last while. Maybe throughout the years of having partners that we leaned on and looked out for had changed us in ways we didn't know, maybe it made us realize a sense of protectiveness and compassion we possessed that years ago we didn't grasp.

I was so thankful to have Will and Nathan by my side, but I didn't want to go through this without Audra. It wasn't the same.

As I kept a hand on my stomach, I took a deep breath. When I got dressed that morning, before our fight, I'd stopped in front of the mirror. Without my clothing on I was beginning to show, not much, but I could tell. I was surprised Audra hadn't noticed while I was getting dressed, she was always quick to notice things, but perhaps she'd just assumed I was a bit bloated. As I thought of her, I'd quickly moved from the mirror and had gotten dressed. With my clothing on I didn't look any different than normal, which was good. Until I was ready to tell people, I wanted to keep it that way. I had already made the mistake of telling my mother which I immediately regretted the moment it came out of my mouth.

I sighed, all I seemed to be doing lately was regretting my growing list of awful choices. I had managed to pull myself out of bed that morning to go to the bathroom. As I made my way towards my bedroom door, I stopped by the dresser that I had my letters stacked on. At the top of the pile was the most recent letter from my mother. I stared at it for a moment before I picked it up and brought it to the bed. I began to read through it. It wasn't the most recent letter I had gotten from her, but it was the one that I had received around the time I first let slip to Nathan that I wanted to carry a child. I wasn't sure what was different about the letter compared to her other ones. They all outlined the same subjects: the current drama going on at the country club, a strong commentary about me getting older in age, and of course, her desire for grandchildren. I wish I knew what possessed me to pick up the phone in that moment, but without really thinking about it, I dialed her number. Normally, she was excited to get me on the phone and couldn't wait to carry out what felt like a three-hour conversation, but she was in a bit of a rush to get to an event at the country club. That's when I idiotically told her, "I just called – uh- I wanted you to be the first to know, that Nathan and I are expecting."

I wasn't sure what I was anticipating her reaction to be, but I suppose I had thought she'd be a bit more thrilled about the news. She definitely seemed happy, but she expressed more relief than excitement. I wasn't sure why I was surprised, but I guess I just expected more of her. That's what I always did with my family, I always hoped for more than they'd ever deliver. They were who they were and set in their high-class mentality. I knew I had my flaws, but nothing compared to them. I was so grateful that my child would not be raised in the same environment that I was -

where every action you took was judged, and you were expected to say and do certain things. God, if I hadn't married Nathan years ago, there was no doubt in my mind that I would've eventually been disowned by them or crumbled under their pressure. They had a way of making me do what they said, and as hard as I tried to stand up to them, I was conditioned to do as I was told. Even after all these years, I often still struggled to say no. It was without question that they would've pushed me to marry some moron who had his head shoved so far up his own rear that he'd never be able to listen to reason. I would've been stripped of my career, my life, and my autonomy. I felt disgusted by the thought of marrying any one of the suitors my parents had introduced to me over the years, I could only imagine if I had been forced to wed one of them. I would have been so miserable beyond compare; I wasn't sure how I would've been able to cope – if at all.

"How're you doing?" I jumped as Elaine took a seat next to me; I was too caught up in my own thoughts to have noticed her walk towards me. "Didn't mean to scare you."

"It's all right, I just wasn't paying attention," I replied as I looked at her. I sighed as I stared at her concerned expression as she looked me up and down. I shook my head, "Nathan called and asked you to check up on me, didn't he?"

"Can you blame him?"

"I suppose not," I sighed.

"He told me about Audra."

"Of course he did."

"He's just worried, Vivian," she said to me as she took my hand. "It's going to be okay."

"It's just a lot to handle," I took a deep breath as I

shook my head trying to hold back tears. "Between almost destroying my relationship with Nathan over this, finding out I'm pregnant, having possibly lost Audra for good, telling my mother-"

"You told your mother?" she asked, apprehensive if that was the wisest choice. "What did she say?"

"She seemed more concerned about bragging to her friends than how I'm doing."

"Classic Mrs. Montgomery," she shook her head. "Does Nathan know you told her?"

"No, and I don't want to tell him yet. He'll just get upset I did something so senseless, especially given everything going on. He thinks I'm rung out as it is, and it'd be *unnecessary stress*."

"He's right."

"I don't know what I was expecting. Before I even had the chance to talk to Audra, he asked if I was all right with him telling his mother. Martha was concerned given the situation but, after we assured her that we were fine, she was so happy and asked to speak to me. I could almost hear her cries of excitement," I said. Nathan had always shared everything with his mother; they were joined at the hip. When we first told her we were getting married she was on edge because she knew Nathan was gay and worried about the repercussions of him marrying someone he wasn't romantically involved with, but when we told her the truth about me, she understood why we were making the decision and has always supported us. Sometimes I felt she was more of a mother to me than my own was. Martha was a mother to all of us really – including Will and Audra. The only reason I agreed to let Nathan tell her before I had the chance to tell Audra was because the secret was killing him, and I knew she wouldn't tell anyone. Martha's initial reaction was to worry about the two of us. She knew neither of us had ever crossed a line, and that doing so could cause problems. The potential emotional repercussions for us if we did overstep our boundaries were even bigger than normal friends given our other relationships. Once Nathan assured her that we were all right, she couldn't help but be excited for us, saying if we needed anything to let her know and she'd be over in a jiffy. I suppose a part of me had hoped my mother would be even a fraction as supportive as Martha. Granted, my mother had no inkling of the truth about Nathan and my relationship, but even if she just asked how I was doing or if I needed anything - something other than the fact that she was *relieved* that I'd gotten pregnant. I shook my head; I wanted to move on from the conversation. The more I thought about my mother, the livider I became.

"I just wished everything could go back to normal," I admitted. "Don't get me wrong, I'm thankful to be having a baby, but none of this is what I wanted or expected. I didn't think so many people would get hurt. That was our biggest issue, we didn't *think*, we just did."

"Nothing in life ever goes according to plan, Vivian," Elaine said, taking a brief pause as she caught my eye. "No matter what it is, we can plan and plan but at the end of the day things happen as they will. You and Nathan ending up in bed together was a big mistake, but from that mistake you're going to have a world of a miracle. Sometimes something bad has to happen for something good to happen."

"What about Audra?" I asked. "What good was supposed to come from her being hurt like that?"

"I don't know, honey," she answered as she rubbed my arm. "I don't have all the answers, but I have to believe God has a plan."

I scoffed and shook my head as she smirked knowing that'd be my reaction. I sighed. I'd always had a conflicting relationship with religion, and she knew that. Unlike Elaine, who always had it be a part of her life and who went to church with her husband every week, and I felt confused by it. It struck me as odd when I'd originally found out how involved in the church Elaine was considering how open and liberal her views were. I rarely went to church, only on special occasions such as Easter or Christmas Eve. I felt a mixture of emotions whenever I went. On the one hand, I was often overcome with a sense of comfort and serenity. I felt at peace whenever I heard the organ play and breathless when I saw the beauty of the stained-glass windows. I couldn't deny that I often felt moved and inspired by many of the passages that were shared, and yet, on the other hand, I would feel an overwhelming sense of fear and retribution that I couldn't shake.

When I was younger, I would occasionally attend church with my family, they went mostly for the social aspect of it, but I always felt out of place. I wanted to believe in everything the priest had to say but how do you believe in something that so publicly condemns who you are? As I got older, I grew to realize that I did believe there was a God out there watching all of us, and that there was a heaven. However, I didn't agree that he cast judgment or that he had some master plan for each person; he was there to listen if we needed and to help guide us in his own way. Audra felt the same way I did these days, only she struggled more to pull away from it. She grew up on the Bible Belt, where she was born and raised to live and breathe the words of the Lord. Growing up, she condemned it so much because the churchgoers would share words of acceptance and love yet turned around and do the opposite. Despite how much Audra struggled with the contradiction, and no matter how hard she tried, she admitted she couldn't completely cut herself off from the church. She said there were aspects of it that she couldn't help but appreciate and believe in. I understood exactly what she meant. I think I wanted to love going to church, but I couldn't bring myself to believe in the bible. That was the problem. I always found people would preach such beautiful words of God, and then they would turn around and use the bible to justify their hate towards others. Anytime I was in church, I felt as though I was being fed conflicting information. I struggled to understand how people could pick and choose what parts they wished to believe or act upon. For example, it's a sin to be gay and it's also a sin to kill another. Yet, if a religious man kills a gay man, suddenly one sin becomes admissible because the victim was queer. I'd read stories where murderers were let free because they said they were doing the work of the Lord. Not to mention those who'd been in jail for years on convicted crimes but were released early because they claimed they had found religion. If there was a God, I doubt he'd want his name used to justify malicious acts.

I shook my head, and almost laughed.

"What?" Elaine asked confused.

"Is it weird that I don't know if I really believe in the church but still want my baby to be baptized?" I asked. I didn't understand it. I had such a weird relationship with religion and struggled to understand the draw to it, and yet, I still wanted to have my baby baptized and I still wanted to take him or her to Sunday school and, in a way, be involved.

"Not at all," Elaine responded. "I think a lot of people feel the way you do, and I understand why, but there's nothing wrong with you wanting to be a part of the church for your baby. For all you know they could grow up to be a priest themselves, or they may be the opposite and never step foot in a church. Either way, if you expose them to the environment at least they'll know enough to make their own decision."

I nodded as I looked up at the sky. If I was ever going to pray, I suppose it'd be now. I wondered where Audra was and what she was doing. I could imagine her going to a church and asking for guidance. She'd never admit it, but I think she went more often than she ever let on in the years we'd been together.

I stared at the field as my mind flashed to the first time that I saw her. The butterflies in my stomach went crazy and I got goose bumps when she looked at me. I missed how every day, no matter what sort of mood we were in, she always looked at me with love in her eyes. Even when we were fighting, I could see the compassion she had for me. It had been less than a week since she'd stormed out and as each moment passed my heart ached more and more for her. I missed her touch. I missed the way she'd try to cuddle with me at night and how I'd make fun of her because her heat would make me sweat. I smirked as I thought of all the nights that we lied awake in bed holding hands and just talking about life, about plans for the future, about our dreams and aspirations. I didn't know I could love anyone so much until

I met her, and I ruined it.

I took the tissue Elaine offered to me as a tear rolled down my cheek. I wiped my cheek and under my eyes, trying to keep my makeup intact. I stood suddenly and straightened out my blazer before turning to face her, as collected as I could possibly be.

"Thank you for checking on me but I should head back to class," I replied as she stood and took my arms. She looked at me with the same concern that Will and Nathan had when I came down the stairs, dressed and put together. I sighed, "I'm fine. I just can't think about her right now or I'm going to start crying and not be able to stop."

"You're allowed to be upset, Vivi. Sometimes bottling things up can be worse than letting them out."

"I know, but I've already spent three days crying and I don't feel any better. I need to try something else."

"Okay, you know I'm just around the corner if you need me," she said as she rubbed my arms before pulling me into a hug.

As I reached the doors I stopped and glanced back towards the bench. Elaine hadn't moved and was standing there watching me. I nodded to her to let her know I was all right before I took a deep breath and headed into the school. There were only two more lectures before the end of the day, and I was determined to make it through them. I'd always said composure was my middle name, and I wasn't about to change that now.

CHAPTER TWENTY-FIVE

AUDRA

I threw my head back as I finished off my glass of whisky before nodding to the bartender to give me another one. I watched as someone approached me out of the corner of my eye and ignored them, hoping they'd walk right past me, but I wasn't so lucky. She leaned against the bar as she spoke to the bartender, "I'll have what she's having."

I glanced at her and raised an eyebrow as she stared at me, looking me up and down. I wasn't in the mood to be hit on. I was there to get as drunk as possible and stumble back to the empty bed at Will's apartment just like I'd been doing the last couple of nights at the lesbian bar I used to go to before I began dating Vivian. I still went there on occasion with her over the last couple of years but not as frequently as I used to. So far, I'd been successful at not drawing attention, so I wasn't sure what was special about tonight. This was the second woman to approach me, and I had a feeling this one wasn't going to get bored so quickly. I could feel her eyes on me.

"Look, I don't mean to be rude but I ain't all that interested," I replied as the bartender brought us our drinks. I took a sip before I turned to her, she hadn't moved nor responded, just stared. "What?"

"You just look familiar that's all."

"Well, I used to get 'round once upon a time so maybe our paths crossed."

"Used to?" she asked as she took a seat. "What changed?"

"I met someone," I replied as I took another sip. I watched as she ran her fingers through her short brown hair before she picked up her own glass to join me. I looked her up and down. She was dressed in a white button-down collar shirt and black trousers. She rolled up her sleeves to her elbows and leaned on the edge of the bar, smirking as she noticed I was watching her. I rolled my eyes; she clearly just assumed I was hitting on her, which was not the case. It wasn't as though she was unattractive, in fact, quite the opposite. She was tall and lean with a sharp jawline. Although she had a more masculine aura to her in the way she acted and dressed, she had an almost flirty feminine look in her eyes, specifically the way she seemed to be batting her eyelashes.

"From the way you're pounding down the whiskey, I get the feeling you don't see her anymore," she said, indicating a separation.

I chose not to respond. Truthfully, I didn't know what we were. I didn't even know what I wanted us to be.

The last week and a half had been brutal; I'd never missed anyone so much in my whole damn life. I went to bed lonely, crying my eyes out, and wanting nothing more than to show up at the house and make amends. Unfortunately, my bitterness prevented me from doing so. Every time I thought about going back to the house my mind flashed back to the idea of her and Nathan together and I felt almost as sick as I had when she first told me the truth. I wanted to be there for her but what they did was not so easily forgiven. I wished I had the mindset of Will who was able to accept what had happened and find forgiveness so fast. I was still barely wrapping my mind around the situation.

"Did I hit a nerve?" the woman smirked as I shook my head and remained silent. I heard her sigh before she changed her tone. "I'm sorry, I was just trying to lighten the mood. I'm Jean."

"Audra," I responded as I shook her hand when she offered it.

"So, tell me Audra, what happened between you and the lady?" she asked. "I've seen you in here the last couple of nights alone, so it couldn't have been good."

"It's complicated."

"It's always complicated."

"She cheated on me."

"Damn, the woman must be something to cheat on someone who looks like you," she replied as she threw back the rest of her drink before ordering us two more. I wasn't quite finished mine, but it'd only be a matter of minutes. "Do you at least know who she cheated on you with?"

That was it. I tossed back the rest of my drink before almost slamming the glass down on the table as I answered, "her *husband.*"

"Not to piss you off any more than you already are, but it's hard to blame a woman for cheating if you get yourself involved in their marriage."

"It ain't like that."

"Well then, enlighten me," she said.

I looked at the woman and bit my lip. I wasn't sure if it was the alcohol or her, but I found myself unable to hold my tongue. Although I was originally annoyed with her presence, once I felt she was no longer hitting on me and just engaging in friendly conversation I felt more inclined to talk. I was used to a household of people to chat with and now I was in an apartment all alone, so it felt nice to be able to complain to someone.

"They weren't really married in the traditional sense. He's gay and she's a lesbian," I said I heaved a heavy sigh and stared down into my glass. "They'd only gotten married to cover that up."

"They were each other's beards," Jean nodded as she took a sip.

"Exactly."

"Interesting. I haven't heard of it being a two-way street. Usually only one person realizes they're gay and just hides in a marriage while the other one is convinced it is true love," she laughed. She wasn't wrong. It was far too common that someone realized they were gay and yet married someone of the opposite sex anyways to try and hide the fact. Or, often they thought they were in love with their partner and later, down the road, realized the truth and began engaging in affairs while still staying in the marriage, too scared to leave and face the truth. Someone always got hurt no matter the situation. Whether it be the person who was hiding or the person who was blind to the fact, usually there were repercussions. "How long have they been married?"

"Ten years, give or take."

"And you're sure he's gay and not just pretending?"

"Yeah, he's been with his partner for 'bout seven years or so."

"And how long were you with the wife for?"

"Five," I replied as I took a sip of my drink. I was beginning to feel fuzzy inside as the alcohol numbed me. I think that was why my Pa's drink of choice was whiskey; it was quick to do the trick.

"Damn," she shook her head. "You sure they haven't been sleeping together the whole time behind your back?"

"I'm sure," I replied. That much I knew was true. Vivian was far too upset telling me the truth for this to have been a regular thing.

"So, they've been together for ten years, and in real relationships for over half the time, and *now* they decide to sleep together? What changed?"

"I don't know," I responded, honestly. Vivian had said they got drunk and made a mistake, but they'd gotten drunk many times before and never once came close to having anything happen - as far as I was aware. I held the glass to my lips and took as sip as my mind wandered, had there been moments between them that I didn't know about? Did Vivian get curious? Was Nathan restless with Will away? I had to stop myself from imagining things or I was going to drive myself crazy. I couldn't get into their inebriated mindset. I'd tried. The last several nights I'd gotten so drunk I could barely walk back to Will's apartment, and it was only a block away. Yet still, even drinking that much, I couldn't comprehend what they were thinking. I waved to the bartender for another whiskey.

"How'd you find out?" she asked. "Did you walk in on them?"

I sighed before I finished my glass, "he got her pregnant."

"You're kidding."

"I wish," I said. The bartender, Ralph, who moonlighted down the road at a drag bar on Friday nights as a beautiful lady named "Pheel Good Phyllis", was taking good care of us. Despite how busy the bar was becoming it seemed he was quick to watch for our signal that refills were needed. I wasn't sure if he knew I was having a rough couple of nights, or just knew he would be making a fortune off of me, but I was thankful for the quick service and attention. Regardless, he was a sweetheart.

"What does the boyfriend think of this?" Jean asked, her question was regarding Will. "I mean, did they break up or-?"

"Nah, they're still together," I replied. "I just needed some space, you know? He has a more forgivin' nature than I do."

"I get it, that's a lot to take in," she sympathized.

We spent the next couple of hours talking and drinking. We spent a while longer discussing my drama back home, before we began chatting about all sorts of other things. The whiskey seemed to guide our conversation because we began flipping topics like we were browsing through a magazine. It was after midnight when Ralph finally cut us off. I was pissed about it but, at the same time, I could barely stand straight. I found myself unable to control my laughter, and Jean was in a similar situation. The whiskey was bringing out the loud and outgoing sides of us.

We left the bar shortly after we'd finished our last drink and settled the tab. Jean didn't live far from me, so we began to walk down the street together as we were headed in the same direction anyway. There were a few times I had to lean on her when my legs went wobbly like a baby deer's.

Once we reached my apartment door, I turned to say goodbye, but before I was able to say the word, I felt her lips press against mine. My back hit the wall as she pushed me up against it. She bit my lip before she pulled away enough to see my reaction as she'd caught me off guard. My heart began to pound. I knew it was a terrible idea and I tried to stop myself, but my mind and body were saying two different things. I pulled her back towards me and groaned as she wrapped her arms around me and slid her hand up my shirt. We composed ourselves for a minute to make sure nobody caught us in a compromising position. I struggled to get the key into the door as my eyesight was blurred. Finally, I got the lock undone and as soon as we were through the doorway, she pushed me onto the couch at the first opportunity she got. I moaned as she kissed my neck, and I felt myself being taken over as my body tingled with each move she made. I lied there, letting her caress me. I undid the buttons on her shirt and as she undid mine in unison. My breath quickened as she unhooked my bra. She leaned down to press herself against me while continuing to kiss my neck. She undid my belt before she began unbuttoning my pants. As she pulled the zipper down, I felt her slip her hand between my legs.

I don't know what happened, but I suddenly grabbed her wrist to stop her. She looked at me confused as I laid beneath her, breathing heavily. She pulled her hand out of my pants and rested it on my chest as it heaved up and down swiftly.

"What's wrong?"

"I'm sorry, I just can't," I said. She sighed as she got up off me and leaned into the couch. I pulled the edges of my shirt over my exposed chest and ran my hand through my hair, "Jean, I'm sorry."

"Can't blame a girl for trying," she replied, before she reached out and placed her hand on mine. "Audra, it's okay. I get it. I've been through the breakup thing before. Sometimes rebounding isn't for everyone, or maybe you're not ready. Either way it's okay."

I nodded, relieved by her kindness. I didn't expect her to react that way, especially after I'd been the one to let her come up and, to that point, been so willing. Although I was desperately craving comfort and an escape, I was thankful that my mind and moral willpower were stronger. I reminded myself that the distraction and relief would've only been temporary. Luckily, I was quick to realize that if I'd slept with Jean, I would've regretted it.

I stopped for a minute. I didn't know why Vivian and Nathan had slept together, but in my heart, I believed they had remorse. Maybe they were so drunk they didn't even know what they were doing and at that point it was too late. Vivian and I hadn't officially separated, and there I was about to sleep with someone else. I wondered if I had slept with Jean if Vivian would've found it in her heart to forgive me and not just because she was asking me to exonerate her for her own actions. Would she be able to wrap her head around what I had done if I had actually gone through with it? I was so close to making a terrible mistake, and I was already guilty as all hell. I began to realize, if I was feeling so incredibly regretful over something I hadn't even done, I couldn't imagine how much worse Vivian felt. I may not be able to understand why she did what she did, but the least I could do was to try and forgive her because I realized she would do the same for me.

"I have to go," I said as I finished buttoning up my shirt, feeling her grab my arm as I stood up too quickly and almost lost my balance. "Thanks."

She escorted me outside the building after we'd both finished putting our shirts back on and fixing our messy hair. Our goodbye was slightly awkward and only made better by the fact that we still under the influence, which helped to mask the feelings of embarrassment on both our parts.

"I hope things work out for you two," she replied

as she kissed my cheek before she left down the street.

I sighed as I leaned against the wall, trying to stop the world from spinning before I made my way down the street in the opposite direction as Jean. I wanted to try to make it back to the house but wasn't sure if my legs could support my body for the reminder of the distance. I prayed I could catch a late-night cab. Either way, it wasn't a far walk so worst-case scenario, I'd have to take a couple of stops to catch my breath, but I'd make it. Maybe it was the whiskey talking, or maybe I was just being hard-headed, but I didn't want to wait until tomorrow to talk to Vivian. I didn't want to spend another night apart from her. I wanted to tell her I was sorry; sorry for the way I got upset, sorry for the way I made her feel, and sorry for the way I reacted. I wasn't happy about the situation, and I was mad as all hell, but at the end of the day I loved her, and I would do everything I could to accept what happened and try to move forward because I wanted everything we dreamed about. The road trips, the kid, the Sunday picnics, the entire life together. When we talked about kids, we spoke about adopting but at the end of the day come hell or high water, she was having a baby and I didn't want to miss that no matter how much distain I had for its father right now. Hopefully, in time that would come to pass, but for now I just had to talk to Vivian.

CHAPTER TWENTY-SIX

WILLIAM

Nathan?"

I thought I was dreaming when I heard someone call his name faintly from in distance. I stirred as my eyes cracked opened when I realized I wasn't dreaming. I rolled over, reaching my hand out to tap him and wake him up. I sighed as my hand hit the mattress. I rubbed my eyes, trying to make my vision less blurred as I looked at the clock. It was midnight and he still wasn't home from his work function. The firm held an annual fundraiser for a local charity each year, and this year was no different. Vivian had previously gone to them, but she'd described them more as a large party than a fundraiser. Based on her description it was no wonder she wanted to opt out this year, and why Nathan was still out even past midnight.

"Nathan?"

I yawned, I struggling to fully wake up as I pulled the covers off when I heard Vivian's voice call his name again. I decided to check on her, I thought maybe she was having a bad dream since her voice was rather faint when calling his name.

"Nathan!"

It was the third cry of his name that sent me running down the hallway, hearing the panic in her voice.

"Vivi, it's Will. I'm coming in," I said before I entered her room so that I wouldn't startle her. As I opened the door, I saw her in bed with a terrified look on her face. She held the sheet to her chest to cover herself as she was dressed in one of her thinner nightgowns. I grabbed her silk robe off the stand that it was hanging on and went to hand it to her.

"Please don't," she said nervously as I went to sit on the edge of her bed. I stood a foot away, confused. "Where's Nathan?"

"He's still out," I replied. My heart skipped a beat as I saw her trembling, she was becoming paler at each passing moment. When I told her he wasn't home it was as if all the remaining color drained from her face. "What is it? What's wrong?"

"I need you to take me to the hospital," she shakily said. I nodded and told her to stay put while I threw on some clothes.

I don't think I'd ever gotten dressed so quickly before in my life. I threw on a pair of pants and the first shirt I could find before making my way back to her room. She hadn't moved from the bed; I wasn't certain she had the strength. I went into her closet to find a loose-fitting dress.

As I brought it over to her, I noticed she wasn't paying attention, her eyes had glossed over as she stared into the distance.

"Vivi, can you put this on yourself, or do you need help?" I asked gently as I touched her arm to get her attention. I watched as she slowly turned her attention to me and stared at me uneasily.

"Will, I'm scared," she said, her voice trembling. "I'm bleeding."

I took a second to grasp what she just said and more importantly, what she meant. I looked into her petrified eyes and just nodded, saying the first thing that came to mind, "it's okay. You're going to be all right."

She nodded; she had no choice but to trust me. On the inside I was panicking, but on the outside, I was doing my best to keep a calm demeanor. Vivian had to take it easy or else it was just going to make matters worse. I pulled the blankets off her and helped her stand. She shakily managed to stand on her own two feet just long enough to be able to drop her nightgown and on put the dress I'd grabbed from the closet for her. While she was changing, she gave me permission to go into her drawer to grab her a change of panties and I passed them to her while keeping my eyes shut to provide some privacy. She let me know when she was finished so I could resume helping her. I opened my eyes to see her pulling the blanket back up to the pillow, trying to hide the blood-stained sheets thinking I hadn't seen them. I had, I just tried not to react no matter how nervous it made me. She glanced at me with a mortified expression, and it broke my heart, she had nothing to be embarrassed about and the fact she felt the need to hide anything was gut-wrenching. I took her hand as she leaned from the edge of the bed into me and looked up into my eyes, "Vivi, you don't need to do that."

"I just-" she stopped herself and just nodded. There needn't be secrets between us, and there was nothing she needed to hide from me for any reason. It killed me that she was clearly in pain and scared beyond belief and yet she felt the need to stop and adjust the sheets as if me seeing them would make me feel different about her or the situation.

I kept my arm around her waist as we headed out of the bedroom together and down the stairs. She waited at the door briefly as I quickly scribbled a note for Nathan, leaving it in plain sight so he noticed it when he returned home. After, I went to help her slide on a pair of her flat shoes before slipping on my own and grabbing her jacket. Hopefully the warmth of her coat would ease her shaking. I was thankful the Buick was still parked in the driveway. Sometimes sharing a car between the four of us could be a bit hectic, but with Audra gone and Nathan getting a ride home, it sat there for us. I held my arm out for her to hold onto as she took a seat. Once she was in, I closed the door and quickly went to driver's side.

I did my best to keep an eye on Vivian while still paying attention to the road. Her head rested against the window, and she was leaning onto the right side of her body while keeping her arms wrapped tightly around her waist. I glanced at her as she tried to hold back the whimper that escaped her lips.

"We're almost there," I said gently. She nodded. Her eyes were flickering as if she was about to fall asleep. My heart began to race as I picked up the pace. I pulled into the closest parking spot I could find, helping her out of the car and into the hospital. We barely made it three steps into the building before we caught a nurse's attention that rushed to our aid and took Vivian's free arm. She was followed by a second nurse who came and replaced me. I wanted to go with Vivian and be there for her, but they said it was best to stay out in the waiting room. I didn't even have the chance to argue with them and could only watch as they took Vivian through the white swinging doors. Right before they were out of sight, she glanced back at me and I nodded, letting her know I'd be there.

"As soon as they know anything, they'll inform you."

I turned to the woman at the administration desk who handed me a form to fill out on Vivian's behalf. I thanked her as I took the clipboard and went to sit down. I stared at the paper and filled it out to the best of my knowledge before returning it to the desk. I began to pace, panic finally setting in. I didn't want to stray too far from the waiting area, but I had to find a payphone. I wasn't sure when Nathan would be home, but I needed to get ahold of him. He didn't have a reachable number at the function so the only plan I had was to continuously call the house until he finally got home and answered. I luckily found a payphone around the corner from the waiting room, it was a bit further than I'd like to be but was still close enough to hear if someone called for me.

I put a nickel in and dialed the house, waiting a few minutes before I hung up the receiver. Nathan was usually quick to answer the telephone, so it was clear he hadn't returned yet. I decided I'd call every fifteen minutes or so until I got ahold of him. I had a lot of change and I didn't care how much it would cost me; I had to speak with him. I sighed as I picked the receiver back up, this time dialing the number for my apartment. Although the girls weren't exactly on speaking terms, I felt Audra should know that Vivian was in the hospital. The phone rang several times before I hung up and shook my head. I would just have to keep calling until she answered.

While I waited, I went back to the sitting area and found an empty chair. I tapped my foot, unable to control my nervousness. I ran my hands through my messy hair before I leaned back and let my head hit the wall. This couldn't be happening, not to her. After everything she'd been through, she couldn't lose the baby. I tried to think positively, I didn't know for certain that that was the case, but at the same time it didn't look good. I saw the amount of blood; I saw her fear. I had heard of women suffering miscarriages, but I'd never actually known someone who'd had one, let alone been there while they were experiencing it. I thought of Vivian, I couldn't imagine what was going on in her mind. I thought I was panicking, and I wasn't the one going through it. Then there was Nathan, I could only assume what his reaction would be.

The image of Vivian was stuck in my head. Her pale

face, her broken expression, her shaking body. When I'd helped her walk, I felt like I was practically carrying her for her weak legs could barely support her own weight. I should've just picked her up and carried her, I don't know why I let her try and make her own way.

I glanced at the clock before going to place another call to both the house and the apartment, but there was still no answer at either one. I slammed the receiver down and let out a frustrated groan, what the hell was everyone doing out? It was the middle of the night! I took a step back from the phone. This was exactly what I shouldn't be doing. Out of everyone I was the stress-free one, the peacekeeper. I looked at everything with a level head and tried to keep everyone else grounded. As soon as Nathan and Audra got word of what was going on they'd be a mess and all over the place. I needed to keep calm or else it would be a circus. No matter the outcome, Vivian was going to struggle with what happened. If she did lose the baby it'd take her a while to recover from that sort of loss, and if everything was fine the shock of the situation would still surely take a toll on her. Nathan and Audra needed to be there for her, but sometimes they could be too blinded by their own feelings to stop and assess a situation. They were wonderful partners and friends, and they would do anything for Vivian and me, but often it took them a minute to realize that they needed to push their own emotions aside first to be of any help. I felt as though it was my job to make them see reason. How could I help them cope if I could barely keep myself together?

I took a seat back in my chair and began to twiddle my thumbs. A part of me just wanted to stay at the phone and call and call but it would just be a waste of money. It was better I spaced it out every ten or fifteen minutes, then again, at least calling repeatedly would give me something to do other than stare at the floor and feel useless.

I sighed as I opened my wallet and pulled out a picture that I held onto of the four of us. It was from the state fair two years ago. I smiled, remembering the day so vividly. I'd asked someone to take a photo for us with my camera, and it turned out to be one of my favorites. I always chuckled when I looked at it. The girls had been so excited about a massive pretzel we'd purchased, that they held it proudly. However, it was in that moment that Nathan thought it'd be funny to lean forward between them and take a bite which caused them to gasp mid-photo. I was the only one who looked sane, except for the overdrawn smile on my face as I started to laugh when the picture was taken. I missed how we used to be. I yearned for the days when four of us would just go out together and enjoy an afternoon. Everything was much simpler before Vivian and Nathan got their promotions at work, and before all the stress overwhelmed Audra and me over the last year with the wedding. I couldn't express my relief when she told me that she couldn't go through with it. Although it had initially been my idea to get married, I didn't anticipate all the insanity that went with it. I also didn't foresee feeling as trapped as Audra did. I guess if I couldn't marry Nathan, I didn't really want to marry anyone. I didn't care if the world thought I was a single drifter for the rest of my life, I'd know that wasn't the case and so would everyone I cared about.

I frowned as I got up and headed for the phone, praying that this time I reached somebody. I didn't care who I got ahold of first, as long as I spoke to one of them. I couldn't bear the thought of them not knowing and when the doctor finally let me in to see Vivian, I wanted one of them there too. She needed her family there. As close as I was to Vivian and as much as I loved her, the fact of the matter was that I wasn't the father of her baby, and I wasn't the love of her life. She needed one of those two figures there with her. But, if they didn't make it in time, she would at least have me to hold her hand and be there for her no matter what the verdict was. I just prayed that I was wrong and that the baby would be okay.

CHAPTER TWENTY-SEVEN

NATHAN

I threw a hand to my chest as I gasped, caught off guard. I was at the front door, fumbling with my keys when I looked up and saw a figure walking towards me. I had a few too many drinks so my reaction was delayed and luckily, before I was able to get defensive, I noticed it was Audra as she came out of the shadows. I sighed and shook my head as I watched her stumble towards me, drunker than I was.

"Audra, you scared me."

"I forgot my keys," she replied. "Why're you gettin' home so late?"

"I was at my work benefit ... what're you doing here?" I changed the subject, confused about her sudden appearance in the middle of the night.

"I came to talk to Vivian," she answered me, avoiding eye contact. I knew I was the last person she wanted to see, but regardless, there we were. I could tell she was hammered from the way she was swaying as she stood in front of me. I'd had a couple drinks, but I was nothing in comparison to her.

"Audra, it's the middle of the night," I stated the obvious. The lights were off, and it was clear no one had answered when she knocked so they were probably fast asleep. Unless she stood there banging on the door furiously, chances were neither Will nor Vivian would be able to hear her, and I doubted she took that approach. She'd never been a disruptive drunk, so I didn't think now would be any different.

"I know," she replied as she stumbled forward. I reached out to catch her as she tried to regain her balance. She thanked me as she let go of my arm and stood back up. We stood in silence for a minute before she spoke again, "so, you goin' let me in or-?"

"Look, Audra," I rubbed my face and bit my lip before I continued, I had hoped she'd take the hint, but it had clearly gone over her head, "I'm happy to see you but I don't know if you being here right now is such a good idea."

"What're you talkin' 'bout?"

"It's just- it's late and Vivian's had a long day and could use the rest," I said as I watched her eyebrow raise and her lips pursed together, I could tell she was about to get defensive but still I continued. "I'm not trying to upset you, Audra. I'm just trying to look out for Vivian's best interests."

"And you don't think I'm lookin' out for her best interests?" she responded aggressively.

"No, I don't," I didn't mean to snap at her, but it just came out. I let out a sigh as she took a step back, shocked that I had raised my voice. I didn't mean to, and I certainly didn't want to start a fight, but I was tired and not in the mood to try to reason with her, especially when I could smell the alcohol off of her from a few feet away. Vivian wasn't back to her usual self, and I was worried about the way she was suppressing and handling everything. The fact that she'd been able to pull herself out of bed the last few days to go to work and try her best to get back on her feet was a huge step considering where she was following her fight with Audra.

"It's just that she's finally at a point now where she can function. She's gone back to her classes, and she's not stuck in bed crying all the time," I tried to take a step towards her, but she retreated. "Until you know what you *actually* want, I think you need to leave her alone."

"That ain't fair, Nathan."

"I know it's not, but you storming out like that wasn't fair either," I replied. "Audra, you are part of this family just as much as any of us are, and I love you, but you need to be certain you're going to be okay with everything before you come back. I don't think Vivian can handle you leaving a second time."

I watched her as she swayed back and forth on her heels. I could tell she was biting her lip, trying not to say something she'd regret. I was surprised by her level of restraint given her current distain for me. I couldn't blame her, and I completely accepted the fury she had towards me. I betrayed her trust and all I could do was try and earn it back in time, but right now this wasn't about Audra and me - it was about Vivian. I crossed my arms and shrugged as I looked at her. I wanted Audra in Vivian's life more than anything, but I needed to make sure that if she intended to step back into our family that she was doing it with a level head, not consumed by alcohol. It might've been harsh, but Vivian had already been through so much emotional turmoil that I couldn't bear to see her go through anymore.

"Just think about it. Come back tomorrow, *sober*. If you believe you can accept everything that happened, that we made a mistake, and that ultimately, we're having a child, then I will be here for you with open arms and so will everyone else," I said. I saw her huff and roll her eyes angrily as I spoke. "We miss you. *I* miss you. I miss your commentary and your hotheadedness, but mostly I miss the way Vivian smiled when you were around. I'm just scared right now that you being here and you saying that you're okay is only fueled by whatever you've been drinking. When you sober up are you going to have the same opinion?"

"I will."

"Then come back tomorrow Audra, and say it then," I replied as I went to reach for her arm. She shifted away from me with pain and frustration in her eyes. She pushed past me as quickly as she could in her tipsy state and headed down the path. "Audra, please!"

It was no use. She was gone. I sighed, that could've gone better. I just hoped that maybe when she sobered up in the morning, she would realize I wasn't trying to be mean. Did she really think it was fair to wake Vivian up in the middle of the night to talk about their relationship, especially drunk like that? Although she'd held her temper very well, who knew what she'd say in the heat of the moment if they'd started talking things through. We were all guilty of running our mouths when we started drinking. The risk of their conversation going sour was too high for me to willingly let her into the house. It'd be better for both of them if Audra came back tomorrow. I just prayed Audra saw that.

I shook my head as I walked back down to the edge of the driveway to see if I could still spot Audra walking down the street but there was no one in sight. For someone who couldn't exactly walk in a straight line, she moved awfully fast. I contemplated on rushing down the street to see where she had gone but I wasn't sure which direction she went. We had no idea where she'd been staying, and I suddenly felt guilty for letting her wander home alone in that state. The streets at night were no place for a lady, let alone a drunk one. I sighed as I pulled my keys out of my pocket and went to the garage to get the car. I decided I would drive around the block and see if I could find her. I wasn't sure she'd appreciate seeing me again, but I needed to make sure she was safe.

I immediately got a sickly feeling in the pit of my stomach when I opened the garage door and discovered the car was missing. Without hesitation, I quickly headed back to the front door. Neither Will nor Vivian had plans to go out that evening, and all the stores were closed. It was unlikely one of them would've made plans to go out, and if they did, they didn't tend to stay out late. The fact that I couldn't find one logical reason that the car would be missing in the middle of the night made me fear the worst.

I opened the front door, and I rushed up the stairs as fast as I could. I swung my head into my bedroom and felt my heart pound as I saw the empty bed. I truly began to panic as I realized Vivian's room was also unoccupied. I called their names as I headed back down to the living room, certain that neither of them were home, but I couldn't help but try. I began to pace back and forth, trying to think of where they could've gone before my attention snapped to the piece of paper on the coffee table with my name written on it. I rushed towards it and quickly picked it up, praying it just said they'd gone for a late night drive. Truthfully anything would have been better than what I'd read.

We've gone to the hospital. Meet us there when you can.

I felt my chest tighten as I struggled to breathe. I quickly dialed the number for a taxi and stressed the urgency that it arrive as quickly as possible. I paced in the living room as I waited for the taxi to show. I was certain I was wearing a hole through the hardwood as I walked back and forth in front of the window so I could see when the driver pulled up. I jumped as I heard the sudden ring of the phone. I was quick to grab it before it had the chance to ring a second time.

"Hello?"

"Nathan!" I heard Will heave a heavy sigh of relief. "You're home. I've been trying to call."

"I saw your note," I responded.

"I'm sorry, we were in too much of a rush for me to leave a lot of details."

"What happened? Is it Vivian? The baby?"

"I'm afraid so."

"How is she? Have you heard anything?" I waited for his response on the other end, my heart aching as I did so. Either he didn't know, or he didn't want to say, and based on his silence I knew it wasn't good. "Is she going to be all right?"

"The doctor is with her now, but they haven't told me anything," he answered, followed by a long and silent pause, not knowing what else to really say. "Just get down here as soon as you can, okay?"

"The taxi just pulled up, I'll be there shortly," I replied to him as I saw the lights shine into the house when it pulled into the driveway. "I love you."

I hung up the phone and quickly darted out of the house. The moment I got into the taxi, I offered the driver double his rate provided he get me to the hospital in under ten minutes, which he seemed more than happy to accept. As I sat in the backseat, I stared out the window, trying to grasp what was going on, it didn't seem real. I was so worried about Vivian; I couldn't even find it in me to be upset about the situation because my attention was entirely focused on her, and rightfully so. I could process my own thoughts later; she was my priority. I was so thankful that Will was with her, but it should've been me. I tried to push away my feelings of guilt for being out drinking when I should've been home and there for her. What mattered was she had someone there and she wasn't alone. It would only be a matter of minutes until I'd be by her side too. We'd get through all of this, we had to.

CHAPTER TWENTY-EIGHT

WILLIAM

We barely got any sleep after spending the evening with Vivian at the hospital. I had anticipated her keeping us at arm's length as she'd previously done, but this time was different. She didn't seem to be closing herself off, and actually welcomed the company. I think maybe she realized it was better to be surrounded by those who loved her than to be alone. The doctor had kept her overnight and released her by late morning. She was quiet for the duration of her stay and during the ride home, but I think it was mostly due to exhaustion. She wasn't only dealing with the physical implications of what happened but the emotional stress of it too.

I offered to escort her up to her room, as Nathan went to make her some tea and something to eat. As we had neared her bedroom, I felt her slow down and could sense her hesitance. She stopped before we reached the door and stared into the distance blankly. I rubbed her arm gently as a gesture of support; I don't think she realized that I knew exactly what had sparked her unease. She took a deep breath to prepare herself before she walked through the doorway. As she entered the bedroom she stopped and released such a relieved sigh that I could feel the stress leave her body. She'd noticed the cream sheets that had previously dressed the bed were now replaced with a warm beige color. She walked towards the bed and pulled the duvet back as if she needed to make sure she wasn't hallucinating.

"Did you-?" she began to ask, not needing to finish her question when I nodded. I held my arms open as she almost threw herself into my embrace. I felt her head rest against my chest as her arms wrapped around me. "Thank you."

During the night, after Nathan had arrived at the hospital, I'd excused myself to go home and change. Vivian had fallen asleep in the hospital bed, and there was no use in both of us sitting helplessly by her bedside. I took the car home and in an exhausted state tried to freshen up, splashing water on my face to wake myself up. I then, almost immediately after, went to her bedroom. The last thing she needed was to come home to a reminder of what had happened. I also knew she'd never just let me change her sheets for her; she'd ask me to leave and do them herself. She had already been uncomfortable with me seeing them, I couldn't imagine she'd be okay with me helping her put a fresh pair on. So, I would do it when she wasn't able to object. I stripped her bed and just threw the sheets away. I wasn't sure if we could even remove the stains, but I didn't care. I'd rather just discard them and purchase new ones. I went into her closet and specifically picked the beige to offer a sense of warmth and comfort. I hadn't dressed a bed before, usually Audra took care of that, but I did my best. I had even gone so far as to fluff her pillows like I'd seen Audra do to ours on multiple occasions to give the bed a fuller and cozier appearance.

"You don't need to thank me," I stroked her hair and kissed her head before I helped her get into bed and pulled the freshly dressed sheets over her. I smiled, as she rested on the pillows partially sitting up so that she wouldn't need to adjust herself when Nathan came in.

I could tell she was going to pass out any minute as she struggled to keep her eyes open. I felt the same way, if my head were on a pillow I'd be out like a light. She managed to stay awake long enough to have a few sips of tea but was too wearied to eat. Nathan and I sat on the edge of the bed, lightly talking about whatever came to mind just to keep her company. It didn't take long before her exhaustion took over. I watched as her eyes gently closed and she peacefully drifted off. I took the cup of tea that was resting between her hands and placed it on her side table. I silently stood with Nathan and left her room, closing the door behind us. I yawned, wanting to follow Vivian's lead and get some sleep ourselves.

After I had fixed up her room last night, I'd immediately gone back to the hospital to see how she and Nathan were doing. She was still pale but was resting peacefully. Nathan, on the other hand, was awake and fading quickly. I could tell he was a mess. The circles under his eyes were darkening by the hour, and his eyes becoming bloodshot from the lack of sleep. He was nauseous from drinking that evening and, although he was just sober enough that he could control his actions and words, he still had a bit of a hangover. Still, despite his discomfort, he insisted on staying awake all night and I couldn't help but join him.

As we went downstairs to grab a bite to eat, I rubbed my face trying to wake myself up.

"I need to call the school and tell them she won't be in for a few days," Nathan said as he took a sip of tea before having a bite of the toast he'd made.

"We need to try and get ahold of Audra too," I added as I leaned against the counter. I had continuously called the apartment last night, but no one answered. By the time Nathan finally arrived, I'd given up calling and decided to try again in the morning; it was possible she wasn't even staying there last night.

"Audra?" he asked, confused, "you know where she is?"

"She's... uh... she's been staying at my apartment," I admitted. I'd chosen to keep her whereabouts a secret, wanting to give her some privacy while she processed everything. I knew I should've told Nathan or Vivian, but the last thing Audra wanted was for one of them to come banging on the door begging for forgiveness. When, or if, she was ever ready, she'd come to them. Regardless of what her decision ended up being, it was hers to make alone. I waited for Nathan to say something, but he just stared at me. I couldn't tell if he was upset or not. Given his poor state, it was hard to read his face. "I tried to get ahold of her last night, but she didn't answer. I guess she was out."

"Yeah, she was," he said. I stared at him for a moment, unsure why he was speaking so matter-of-factly. He shook his head as he continued, "she showed up here."

"She did?"

"Mhmm, but I sent her home."

"What? Why?" I asked, almost agitated.

"Look, I didn't know about Vivian, and Audra was drunk."

"What was she doing here?"

"I don't know. She wanted to talk to Vivian, but I told her it wasn't a good idea," he tried to defend himself as I stood up straight and crossed my arms, waiting for an explanation. "Come on Will, it was the middle of the night and she reeked of alcohol. I just told her to come back when she was sober; it wasn't fair to wake Vivian to that."

"That wasn't your call."

"Seriously? With all the stress Vivian's been under, I doubt she needed an inebriated confrontation with Audra to top it all off."

"That should've been a decision for her to make," I shook my head, furiously. "You had no right to send Audra away, drunk or not."

"No right? Are you kidding me? After everything that's gone on?" Nathan did his best to keep his voice low as he began getting upset. Nathan didn't often raise his voice, but he was starting to get angry. Luckily, it wasn't anything I couldn't handle. "Vivian was a mess when she stormed out. She hasn't even called *once*. She acted immaturely, and then when she shows up drunk out of nowhere, *I'm* the bad guy for telling her to sober up before she tries to walk back into Vivian's life?"

"You just don't get it, do you? Maybe she was impulsive and maybe she was a bit spiteful, but she deserved to be. Do you any idea what she's even going through? How much you both hurt her?" I shook my head. "Not only did she find out that the love of her life slept with someone else, but that she ended up *pregnant* as a result. Audra has always felt threatened and jealous of the relationship that you and Vivian share, regardless of whether it's real or not. The fact that you can go out together as a couple, so to speak, and that you have the beautiful luxury of calling her your wife. It's something Audra will never be able to do. Your relationship may be a lie to all of us, but it's real to everyone else. It took her a long time to come to terms with that, and to learn how to cope with her feelings when she saw you two going out in public together. She was able to live with it because she knew that she and Vivian shared a *real* love, like you and I do. The thing is, Nathan, having a baby creates a very real bond that is hard to match – one that she'll never be able to compete with."

"Yeah but–"

"Let me finish," I cut him off, I wanted him to hear

what I was saying. "One of the main reasons you and Vivian were against the idea was because of Audra. You knew exactly how she would react, and yet you slept together anyways. You knew she would get upset, but now you're angry that she can't just accept it and move on. It's as though after you two slept together your brains just stopped working."

"That's not fair."

"Isn't it? You came to me before you even really considered it and I was there for you, yet you didn't tell me you'd actually gone through with it. I had to find out by accident. Do you have any idea how terrible that made me feel?" I sighed as my eyes began to get teary. "I don't think you realize how incredibly lucky you are, Nathan. I understood your reasons, and I was able to wrap my head around the idea because that's the kind of person I am. Maybe it's because I'm more of a free spirit, or maybe it's my supportive nature, or maybe it's because I've had a lot of meaningless sex with people. I don't know. The point is that I wasn't happy about it, but I understood your reasons. To me, sex is just sex, but if the roles were reversed and I had slept with Audra – I'd bet you any money that your reaction would be similar to hers."

He stood there silently because he couldn't deny that I was right. I knew for a fact Nathan wouldn't be able to wrap his mind around the idea of me sleeping with someone else. When we first started dating, he was taken aback by the number of people I'd slept with, as he'd only been with a few. However, despite the number of men or women I'd been with in the past, I'd never once cheated on a partner. For a while, he was worried that my more promiscuous past might make me more inclined to end up in bed with someone else, but his concerns were misplaced. The number of partners that someone's had has pays no bearing on their whether they will be faithful or not. After all, when it came down to it, he was the one who ended up sleeping with someone outside of our relationship. I sighed, as he stared at the ground, feeling embarrassed and upset. I felt bad for what I said. I knew if they could turn back the hands of time, they would. They had never intended to hurt anyone, themselves included.

"I know you love Vivian, I do too, but Audra - she loves her more and she loves her differently. She loves her the way you love me. You can be there for Vivian all you want as her friend, but you can't step in and dictate what's right or wrong for her. I understand that on a piece of paper Vivian is your wife, but as far as we're concerned, she's Audra's."

"She cried for her," Nathan said quietly, I took a step closer to him, getting him to repeat what he said so that I could hear him clearly. "At the hospital in her sleep, Vivian kept calling Audra's name... I shouldn't have sent her away."

"Like you said, you didn't know. All we can do now is try to reconcile the situation."

As Nathan announced that he was going to the apartment to talk to her, I stopped him. It was better I went. At this point, I had a better relationship with Audra, and I could relate to what she was going through. It was hard to tell what her reaction was going to be but no matter what it was, it would be okay.

Nathan stayed home to keep an eye on Vivian in case she needed anything while I drove over to the apartment. It was only a few blocks away, but I was too tired to walk the whole way.

Once I reached the building, I anxiously headed upstairs with my spare key in case Audra wasn't there. On my way out the door, Nathan told me that Audra had been out by herself late last night which immediately put me on edge. Worse-case scenarios began running through my mind, and the fact that she hadn't answered a single phone call I'd placed to the apartment last night didn't help my nerves. The streets were no place for a lady to be alone after dark. Had I known, I would've gone by the apartment sooner to ensure she was safe.

I stood outside the large grey door and knocked on it loudly a few times. I waited before trying again. It wasn't until the third round that I heard the lock click and chain unhook. I barely caught a glimpse of Audra as she swung the door open and turned, walking away from me towards the couch. I sighed as I closed the door; relieved she was home, but suddenly feeling my worry start back up for different reasons. The curtains were drawn and the apartment dark. I observed the almost finished liquor bottles on the coffee table before my eyes wandered over to her as she lay on the couch with her hand over her head.

I went and grabbed her a glass of ice water before coming back to the living room. She groggily thanked me as

I sat on the chair across from the couch and watched her.

"I guess Nathan told you 'bout last night," she said as she groaned, adjusting herself to get more comfortable.

"A little."

"So, what're you here for? To gimme a warnin'?" she replied sharply.

I tried not to take it personally; she was hungover and bitter about last night. It was understandable. I stared at her for a moment, she looked worse than any of us. I began to contemplate if I should even tell her about Vivian, but quickly pushed the thoughts out of my mind. I'd just given Nathan a speech about not interfering in their lives, and I would be a hypocrite if I kept the secret. However, I suddenly couldn't resist finding out the real reason for her appearance. For all I knew she showed up to end their relationship, and if so, should I even tell her? If she did intend to leave Vivian, I didn't want this to change her mind, it wasn't fair to either of them.

"Why did you come to the house last night?" I asked. I watched as she turned to me, looking at me with only one eye open. There was very little light in the room, but it was still enough to make her squint.

"I just wanted to talk to Vivian."

"I guess that means you made a decision," I tried to fish. I apologized as she raised an eyebrow at me, knowing exactly what I was doing. "I'm sorry Nathan told you to go home. That wasn't his call to make."

"No, it wasn't... but what's done is done, right?" she replied. I couldn't help but sense a partial double meaning in her question. "I'm not feelin' well, Will. Do you need somethin' from me?"

"I do, actually," I was surprised by what came out of my mouth, but I was unable to stop myself. "I need to know what you were going to say to Vivian last night."

"That's between me and her."

"I know, and I don't normally like to pry but it's important."

"Why?" she struggled, but slowly sat up. I wasn't sure if it was my tone or if she was feeding off of my tension, but I kept a straight face.

"She misses you."

"I miss her, too," she replied sadly as she took a sip of the water and sighed. She sat there for a moment with a perplexed face; I could tell she was contemplating on sharing what was on the edge of her lips. I stayed silent; I didn't want to push anything. "I, um, I almost slept with someone last night."

"Oh?" I was surprised, it wasn't what I had expected to hear come out of her mouth. "Almost?"

"Yeah, we were cork-high and bottle deep. She walked me home, and then one thing led to another..." she shook her head. "Before it was too late, I realized how much of a mistake that would've been. I just couldn't do it. You know, I can't for the life of me figure out what sparked Nathan and Vivian to roll into bed together after all these years. Vivian never *once* had a curiosity; she never had a thought that crossed her mind. She explicitly expressed her distain and yet-"

"She wanted to have a baby," I unintentionally cut her off, unable to control my mouth. "I don't know when she started thinking about it, or when she started feeling that way, but I do know that it was something on her mind."

"What? How do you-"

"She accidentally told Nathan and he panicked, so he told me," I said.

"She wanted to... but..."

"I don't think it's what you think. She didn't want to sleep with Nathan, but she did want to have a baby. She was stuck between a rock and a hard place," I told her, watching her expression. Her eyes shifted back and forth as she tried to wrap her head around the information she was receiving. "She realized that she wouldn't be able to mentally go through with it and Nathan was uncomfortable with the whole idea, so they decided against it. However, when we were in Georgia, they got drunk and practically blacked out. At some point in the evening, I guess they idiotically and impulsively... well..."

"Lord have mercy."

"Nathan told me that Vivian was so distraught about what happened that she had to go and stay with her friend," I went on. "I think they didn't tell us because it was so hard on them that they just wanted to forget the whole thing. I don't think they ever expected to end up pregnant like that."

I watched Audra's face, waiting for some kind of reaction or response, but her expression stayed blank. I sat back and waited while she attempted to process everything.

"Why didn't she tell me?" she questioned. I wasn't sure if she was asking me or herself as she tried to run through the series of events. "Maybe if she'd just told me-"

"What? That she wanted to get pregnant?" I retorted. "What would you have even said, Audra? It was difficult for her to comprehend, let alone you. What matters is it happened, and it won't happen again."

"How do you know?"

"Trust me, I know. If Nathan was that worked up about it, I couldn't only imagine how upset Vivian was, and she was the one who had to leave the house afterwards."

"It's just- I spent so long thinkin' I was crazy for worryin' 'bout somethin' like this and it turns out I was right to be nervous."

"I'm sorry. I just, I thought you should know the reason behind their impulse. It wasn't a curiosity thing, or a bored thing. They decided against it, and the alcohol made them question that decision," I replied as I got up to leave. I'd come to tell Audra what happened, but I found myself unable to. I had just unloaded a lot of information on her, and it wasn't fair to share my real reason for showing up if the truth was going to alter her decision. "Whatever decision you make about your relationship with Vivian, I still love you... but you need to make one."

"I already made my decision."

"You have?" I asked as I turned and looked at her.

"I hate this situation, but I can't live without her," she answered as she dropped her head and stared at the floor. "I want to come home. I can't say it's goin' be easy or that I'm goin' come 'round to forgivin' 'em anytime soon, but I'm goin' try because that's what family does."

"I'm glad," I replied, sadly. She looked at me confused by the tone in my response. She had expected me to be happy and excited, and yet my disposition was hindered by a heavy weight. As much as I was relieved that she'd decided to come home and try to mend her relationship with Vivian, her decision also gave me no choice but to tell her the truth.

"I thought you'd be pleased 'bout my decision."

"I am, I just... um... well, it's just..." I rubbed my neck, finding the truth harder to say than I had anticipated.

"Will, what's goin' on?" she looked up at me with wide eyes and a worried expression as she began to stand up. As I stared at her with teary eyes, struggling to speak. Before I could utter a single word, she knew what was about to escape my lips. A devastated expression crossed her face as she shook her head, collapsing back onto the couch as if the wind was knocked right out of her. "No... no..."

"Yes," I choked back tears, confirming exactly what she thought I was going to say, "Vivian lost the baby last night."

CHAPTER TWENTY-NINE

VIVIAN

I slowly woke to the feeling of a soft hand against my cheek, stroking my face. I stirred as I tried to open my eyes, but I was so exhausted, they felt as though they were glued shut. I groaned as I tried once again to wake from my slumber.

"Shhh, it's all right. You sleep," I heard a gentle voice say. In my daze I could've sworn it was Audra. I was comforted by the thought of her there with me. When I was at the hospital, I kept dreaming she was there, but each time I opened my eyes and found my subconscious had tricked me. It did give me comfort to see Nathan sitting in the chair next to the bed; I felt better having someone with me. I loathed hospitals; they always felt so cold.

Before Nathan arrived, Will was allowed into the room to see me. I had already been given my diagnosis privately by the time he entered the room, but I could tell he had a feeling. It was a safe assumption. All I had to do was look at him and shake my head and he understood. I was told that normally they would send me home, but I had a bit of a fever, so they insisted I stay the evening as a precaution. Before I even had a second to object, Will agreed it was the right call. I was too exhausted to argue. I just kept thinking if I closed my eyes and slept, morning would come quickly, and I could be discharged. I just wanted to go home.

As I lay in my own bed, I thought I'd only kept my eyes closed for a few minutes, but when I was finally able to open them, I saw the clock showed the time to be nearly six. I'd been sleeping most of the day. I placed my hand to my head and rubbed my eyes as I stared at the ceiling.

"You're awake," I heard a gentle Southern voice come from the doorway. I thought I was dreaming when I saw Audra leaning on the doorframe. She gave me a soft smile, "I brought you some tea."

I didn't say anything as I stared at her for a moment in disbelief. As I slowly sat up, she walked towards me and handed me the cup before taking a seat on the edge of the bed. She reached over and placed a hand on my cheek, stroking it. I leaned into her palm, missing her soft comfort. I looked into her piercing dark eyes and sighed; I didn't need to ask.

"Will told me," she said, sadly. "Vivi, I'm so sorry, I should've been there."

"How could you have known?" I replied as I took her hand. What mattered was that she was here now. I took a sip of the freshly prepared tea and welcomed its warmth. I heaved a heavy sigh, still slightly exhausted, but I wondered if I had just overslept.

"I wanted to come home," she said quietly as she stroked my hand that rested on her thigh. "But ev'ry time I tried, I just froze. When you told me the truth, it just hurt so badly I didn't know how to cope."

"You don't have to explain. You had every right to leave."

"Just the thought of him with you like that tore me apart. So, when you told me what happened, I just couldn't handle it," she wiped the tear that fell from her cheek. "I'm still learnin' how to let it go."

"I know," I replied. "Still now, I have nightmares about what happened."

"What're you talkin' 'bout, Vivi?"

"It sounds foolish, I know, but it was a mistake on so many levels. I never realized how much it'd affect me. Since that night with Nathan, I've had so many nightmares. I'd have these images of what we did, how I felt… the image of his hands on me…" I began to say as I bit my lips holding back my tears. I looked into her eyes; she was doing her best to hold herself together with what I was saying but I could tell she was a mess on the inside. "I felt sick. I didn't expect a great reaction, but I didn't expect to feel like that. I didn't anticipate the evening to play on repeat in my mind to the point of nausea. Nathan's my best friend and I could barely look at him… I could barely look at myself. I had to do everything in my power to separate my emotions from what happened, or I was going to drive myself crazy."

"You were still havin' 'em when I got back from Georgia, weren't you?"

"I still have them."

"Why're you just tellin' me this now?" she sighed and rubbed her shoulders. "Vivi, you should've told me as soon as I got back."

"I didn't want to risk losing you over a mistake, and I guess I figured the nightmares were my punishment for what I did," I replied, before I took a sip of tea. I stared into the cup and took a deep breath. I hadn't told anyone that. Not Nathan, not Will, not even Elaine. When I stayed at her house for those few days, I had shared with her my feelings about the situations but at the time, I didn't have many memories of the evening. I was mostly consumed by the fear of losing Audra, and by the horror I experienced when I realized Nathan and I had slept together. It wasn't until I got home that the memories resurfaced and once they'd returned it was as though they were playing on repeat. Almost every night I woke in a cold sweat to my heart pounding. It felt as though I was vividly reliving the event and it killed me. I didn't say anything because I felt humiliated. It didn't make any sense to me; I couldn't understand why I was so traumatized by something like that. The kinds of reactions I was experiencing would be something I'd expect someone to go through if they'd been robbed, or assaulted, or something else just as horrid. None of those things happened to me. I was just reckless. I was drunk and did something I regretted. Maybe I could begin to understand my emotions if I had met someone in a bar who I didn't know, but that wasn't the case. I slept with Nathan. *Nathan.* One of the most kind-hearted, beautiful, protective people I'd ever met. He was my best friend, and yet, there I was – feeling as though it was the worst thing that I'd ever gone through next to… well, next to last night.

"Vivi…" she didn't know what to say, and understandably so. As she looked at me, I think it occurred to her that my actions hurt me just as much as they did her. I placed my tea down on my side table and took her hand. I realized I didn't know what else to say either. Finally, to my relief she leaned forward and placed a kiss on my lips. I didn't realize how much I missed the taste of her until now. She slid closer and wrapped her arms around me as I took her in the same embrace. I inhaled the smell of her hair and buried myself in her neck. It wasn't until she spoke again that I slowly released my grip on her. "Let's move to San Francisco."

"What?" I moved my head back and stared into her eyes, I wasn't sure if she was being serious or not.

"When you're feelin' better," she continued. "I want to take you away from all of this. I think it'll be good for you – for us. I know it's a heck lot to ask but you said yourself that you wanted to go before."

"I know but-"

"But what, Vivi? All I want to do is be with you, just you, without this masquerade. It's not doin' either of us any good. This whole ordeal with my family made me see how what we're doin', how we're livin', is hurtin' me so much inside and now I can see it's hurtin' you too. Besides, if Faith could accept the idea of us, wouldn't others?"

I shifted my position uncomfortably as I registered what she just said. When she got back from Georgia, she had told me about Faith and Taye's plans to move to California, but she had neglected to share the part where she confided private information with her like that, "Faith knows?"

"Yeah. So?"

"Audra, my privacy is not for you to share. How dare you spill my secrets like that," I said distressed. I was incredibly selective on who I confided my private life to, and

I was not in the slightest bit comfortable with her family knowing. Besides Elaine, and some of the friends I'd met at lesbian bars, no one else knew and I wanted to keep it that way. I understood Audra's desire to be outspoken and free, but she never listened to me. Didn't she understand the risks that came with making something like that public knowledge? Those risks were the exact reason I married Nathan in the first place.

"They're my secrets too!" she replied. "Besides it doesn't matter because-"

"But it does! Don't you see that? Don't you see that we are in different places? Exposing me, my life, is not only dangerous for us Audra, but could be the end of so much I've worked to maintain. It could mean the end of my career, my relationship with my family. I mean my mother would-"

"Forget 'bout your mother, Vivian."

"That's easy for you to say."

"It should be easy for you too! How did she react when you told her you were pregnant? Did she ask how you were doin' or was she more interested in her gossipy little circle?" she asked. She nodded as I remained silent, she wasn't wrong in her accusations. "I see."

"I hope you realize how incredibly selfish you're being," I snipped without fully meaning to. I was upset with her. After everything we'd been through, after what *I* just endured, she thought now was an appropriate time to bring up San Francisco? I wasn't sure why I was reacting this way, but I found myself unable to let my defensive guard down.

"Selfish? How the heck am I bein' selfish?"

"You're asking, not even asking, *expecting* me to just drop everything and move. Move to a place where we know nothing and no one, and you won't even consider my reasoning, my answer to why I'm upset and startled."

"I know your reasonin'."

"Then acknowledge it. Try to understand because from where I'm sitting, everything I'm saying seems to be going in one ear and out the other."

"Change is good, Vivian."

"Maybe it is, but not something as drastic as this."

"If that's how you feel," she said as she sat back, creating some space.

I shook my head at her response, "Audra, really?"

"I'm goin' to San Francisco. I want you to come," she said firmly.

"Audra, I just-"

"I know you just gave me an answer but I- but I want you to come. I don't want to go without you."

"Then don't. Stay here with me," I tried to reach for her as she stood up.

"I don't know if I can," she responded, shaking her head. "I want to be with you more than anythin' but I realized I don't know if I can truly be here anymore if this is the life we're to have. We're both hurtin' so bad, and only livin' half-lives. I need to grow, and I think in order to do that I need to leave. I was up all night talkin' to Faith and havin' some time to think. I came to New York to learn things 'bout myself, to be free from my old restraints, and most importantly, to no longer hide who I am."

I watched silently as she sat back on the edge of the bed and took my hands in her, squeezing them. She looked deep into my eyes, trying to make me see her point of view. I understood why she wanted to go, why she wanted to run, but it was easier for her than it was for me. She'd already packed up and left before. New York was my home; I'd never lived anywhere else. I moved from my parents' residence to my home with Nathan. I stayed in the same school district and could still drive to my favorite bookstore. The idea of leaving New York petrified me. With everything that had gone on and all that I'd been through recently, picking up and leaving just seemed like running away.

"I've come to realize that I have nothin' left to learn here. I got so close to makin' a permanent commitment to hide for the rest of my life, and I just couldn't do that. I love you more than anythin' in this world but this whole setup is hurtin' me. When you told me that you were havin' a baby, a small part of me was happy for you, but mostly, I was jealous. It killed me that you and Nathan were sharin' somethin' like that, and it made me realize for the first time, despite what y'all said, that I really did have to share you with him," she said sadly. "Even though you two are technically married, I've never had to share that intimate side of you with him, and then suddenly out of nowhere I did. It felt like my heart was bein' ripped out of my chest. I didn't think I could feel any worse until Will showed up at the apartment and told me that you lost the baby. I can see it in your eyes how broken you are, how that hurt ain't goin' nowhere for a long time, and that pains me to see. You need a fresh start just as much as I do, Vivi. I want you to come with me; I *need* you to come with me. I want it to be just us. Vivi, please, I love you and I don't want to leave here without you."

She leaned forward and kissed my lips before she stood up again. I watched as she walked towards the doorway, and I found myself at a loss for words. All I could do was utter her name, "Audra…"

She stopped and turned to me with a small but hopeful smile, "I'm gonna to buy two tickets for Saturday. I pray by then you can make a decision."

"Audra? Audra!" I called as she left down the hallway. I sat there in shock for a moment before burying my head in my hands. I wasn't sure what happened. I suddenly found myself faced with the choice to either follow the love of my life across the country and leave everything I knew, or I keep my life, home, and comfort intact but lose her forever. I threw my head back into my pillow, not knowing what to do. It was an unimaginable decision, but one I was being forced to make… in less than a week.

CHAPTER THIRTY

NATHAN

Who are the flowers from?" I glanced up as Vivian came into the living room to see two bouquets sitting on the table. I watched as she opened the card to the first one, which was a beautifully pink arrangement of daisies, chrysanthemums, and carnations. "*Vivian, sorry for your loss. Elaine.*"

"She didn't believe the lie when I called the school and told them you had the flu again," I replied when she looked at me. "I figured you'd be okay with me telling her."

"I am, thank you," she answered before taking the card from the second set of flowers, which consisted of white roses, red Gerber daisies, and some kind of purple flower I didn't know the name of. "*To Vivian. Feel better soon. Gregory Miller.*"

Before she had the chance to attack me in a panic I stopped her train of thought, "he doesn't know, he *did* believe the flu story."

She exhaled a sigh of relief before putting the card

down and walking towards me. She took a piece of toast from my plate and had a bite before she sat down. I was glad she was feeling better - for the most part. Although she was recuperating well, she'd decided not to return to work early. I had told them she'd be off for the week and felt thankful she was taking the time. The last thing she needed was to go back too soon and suffer a setback in her recovery, both physically and mentally. I think we were both barely starting to wrap our minds around what happened. I know for me, it felt very surreal. It was as though it were one giant dream. Everything from our awkward encounter, to finding out she was pregnant, to the news that she'd lost it after all. It didn't seem fair. After everything we'd been through, especially Vivian, to lose the baby - it made me wonder how or why we ever got pregnant in the first place. It seemed like a cruel joke.

I watched as she sat at the table, staring into the distance. I reached out and took her hand, "did you end up making a decision?"

I studied her face as she looked at me. I could tell she had, but she didn't seem happy with the choice she made. However, I didn't think either option would make her completely happy. I didn't know what I would choose if Will had left me with an ultimatum. I'd like to say I'd go with him but, truthfully, I wasn't sure I could. Like Vivian, my whole life was in New York. My job was here. My mother was here. My property, my investments, everything, was right where I was. As much as I loved Will and couldn't imagine my life without him, I had to stop and consider what we'd do if something ever happened to one of us? What if one of us got sick, or if we split up? I'd have given everything up and would be left with nothing. Right now, Vivian had stability and a promising future. If she left for San Francisco she'd be starting from scratch and that was not an easy thing for a man to do, let alone a woman. Personally, I thought what Audra was asking Vivian to do was completely unfair and unjust, but like Will said, it was not my choice to make.

That night at dinner, after Audra left the house, Vivian told us what she said. We were as dumbfounded as she was. It was an impossible decision to make. Throughout the week, we'd been too shy to ask if she was leaning towards one option or the other, but she gave no indication of coming close to an answer. She avoided the conversation all together. In fact, she was quieter than usual, but it was to be expected.

I was dying to intervene and say something, but Will convinced me not to. It had been pointed out multiple times now that I had a tendency to insert myself into things that had nothing to do with me. As much as Will wanted them to make amends, it wasn't his place to say anything either. For the last several nights we'd sat in bed talking about the possible outcomes. Although the situation was between the girls, I made Will realize that Vivian's decision affected me too. If she chose to leave, I would be the one dealing with the repercussions and questions about my wife. We'd either have to get a divorce or figure out a way to explain her whereabouts.

If it were up to me, I'd have her stay. She worked so hard to get to where she was, and Professor Miller seemed to be the only one at the university to care about her. Originally, I'd been a bit suspicious of his kindheartedness, but Vivian assured me it was harmless. If his intentions were as innocent as she claimed and she continued working with him for the next year or so, for all we knew she could get the promotion she'd been aiming for. She'd also be losing her relations. As much as her family could be a pain, she still felt a close connection to them, and she'd also struggle to lose her friends like Elaine. The selfish part of me didn't want her to go because I wasn't sure I could handle losing my best friend. There were so many moments I wanted to beg her not to leave, but held my tongue, knowing that despite everything in me telling her to stay, if she really wanted to go, she would go. Plus, I wasn't sure if she decided to leave, and I said something to change her mind if she'd later resent me.

"Vivian?" I tried to catch her attention when she didn't reply. "It's Saturday."

I watched as she turned her attention to the clock. It was nearly eight in the morning. Normally on the weekends we'd still be in bed, but it seemed we all had trouble sleeping last night. I wasn't sure what time Audra would be coming over to get Vivian's answer, but I was certain it would be before noon. I had taken the liberty of checking the schedule for any trains heading from New York to San Francisco, and the only one departing today was at four in the afternoon.

"I know," she replied before she got up, excusing herself to go and get dressed. I sighed as I watched her head upstairs, still left without an answer. I was beginning to wonder if she even had one.

"Is Vivian awake?" I heard Will ask as he came through the front door with a basket of fruit. He'd taken the day off from the market, but still took the early trip down to the pier for some groceries.

"She just went upstairs to change."

"Did she say anything?"

I shook my head in response to him. For the remainder of the morning, she stayed fairly quiet and reserved. Her lack of interaction or emotion made me begin to worry. I anticipated that she'd be upset, maybe cry, or even lash out. I didn't expect her to be straight-faced and silent. I watched her glance at the clock every fifteen minutes or so, not knowing when Audra planned to appear. As each hour passed, her anxiety started to rear its ugly head.

It wasn't until the clock struck half past eleven that we heard a knock at the door. In unison, our attention snapped in its direction before Vivian finally stood and straightened out her skirt before walking over to answer it. It was unusual for Audra to knock but, given the circumstances, she probably thought it was appropriate.

"Hi," Audra said, quietly. She stood in the doorway for a moment before Vivian stepped aside and gestured for her to come in.

Will and I nodded before heading upstairs after they asked for a moment alone. We knew we should've given them the complete privacy they wanted, but we couldn't help but sit at the top of the staircase and eavesdrop. Truthfully, we had no idea what to expect.

"What'd you decide?" Audra asked her. I couldn't see her face, but I could hear the nervousness in her voice as she spoke.

"Audra..."

"Please don't make me go without you."

"But you will," Vivian said, drawing attention to Audra's words. "If I don't say yes, in this very moment, you'll choose to go without me. You'll choose a risky adventure over me."

"How do you think I feel when you're constantly choosin' your fake marriage over me?"

"I do not."

"You do, Vivi," she said matter of fact. "And for what? People's approval? You seem to care more 'bout what other people think than you do 'bout yourself."

"That's not true."

"But it is!" Audra exclaimed, frustrated. "You're always goin' on about how deaf I am, that ev'rythin' I hear goes in one ear and out the other. Well, maybe that's because I choose not to listen to the negativity, to all the bullshit people say, and that works for me. But you, you're blind. You're blind to the issues that are right in front of your face, you're blind to how idiotic this whole ordeal is, and you're blind to how horribly your mother treats you, yet you *still* try to please her."

"Audra-"

"I want you to see, Vivi. Don't you get it? I want you to see ev'rythin' you could see if you just opened your eyes, but I know that sure as hell won't happen here," Audra said, her voice shaking. I could hear her pace back and forth while Vivian remained silent. "I love you, and I will always love you no matter what decision you make. I just hope you make the decision to put yourself first. This is the last time I can ask before I go, Vivi, are you comin' with me?"

I hung on her words, waiting for Vivian's response. This was it, the moment I was waiting for, that we were all waiting for. The moment I was going to find out if my best friend was leaving, or if I'd get to keep her in my life just as it always has been.

"Audra, I don't-"

As if on cue, the telephone rang. I looked at Will who walked down the hall to pick the receiver up, but by the time he got there, it had stopped ringing. He glanced at me when we realized that Vivian had paused her conversation with Audra to answer it downstairs. I turned my attention from Will back to the girls, sitting as close to the edge of the stairs as possible while still staying out of sight.

"Hello? Oh, hello Mother," Vivian's voice echoed. I wasn't sure what happened, but I think Audra took Vivian's decision to answer the call as her verdict. She'd made her choice. I suddenly heard Vivian's voice as she cried out, "Audra! Audra! Come back! Please!"

As the door slammed shut, I sighed and stood up. I shook my head as I listened to Vivian remain on the line with her mother. I could only assume she had covered the receiver with her hand when she yelled out to Audra, for she drew no attention to what happened, and her voice immediately resumed its passiveness.

"Mother, I have to - yes, oh, sure... I'm fine, really, but I have-" she struggled to get a word in as per usual whenever she spoke to Mrs. Montgomery.

As I listened to Vivian on the phone, I felt a wave of relief pass over me. As bad as I felt about the way they were ending things, I had an overwhelming sense of happiness that she would be staying. From the tone of her voice, I think it was always her choice to stay. I didn't think she could will herself to just give everything up in a heartbeat and leave. Perhaps that was why Audra left, because deep down she knew what I suspected: it just wasn't in Vivian to leave everything and everyone she knew and loved.

As I was about to walk down the stairs I stopped when Will grabbed my shoulder. I turned and looked at him, worried when I saw the concern written all over his face. My eyes traveled from his and down to the suitcase he held in his hand.

"What?"

"I found it on Vivian's bed."

"She was planning to go?"

"She may not have been able to go through with it, but it looks like she wanted to," Will replied, staring at me.

I turned my attention to the staircase as I heard Vivian's docile voice carry as she spoke, "yes... I'm sure we'll be trying for another baby... soon... yes, I know, I'm not getting any younger but- yes, I know I said I was fine but I-"

It was in that moment that I understood exactly what Audra was trying to say. Vivian would never be free. There she was, giving the person she loved up to make everyone else happy. Her mother just found out that we lost the baby and the first thing she was asking was when we were going to try again. The truth was, she wouldn't ever be free, and for some reason, Vivian was accepting that burden. As she continued to talk to her mother, her voice was becoming so defeated it sounded lifeless.

Without thinking, I took the suitcase from Will and rushed down the stairs with it. Before Vivian could utter another word, I took the phone from her and placed it on the receiver, hanging up on her mother.

"Nathan!"

"Go."

"What?"

"Audra's right. You need this, you need change, and frankly... you need her."

"What about work? What about my mother? What about *you*?"

"I'll handle your work and your mother, and don't worry about me. I'll be fine. I just expect you to call me and keep me up to date on what's going on in your life, and to come visit at Christmas."

"Nathan..."

"If things don't go well in San Francisco, you'll always have a home here. You both will," I pulled her into a tight embrace and hugged her harder than I'd ever hugged anyone. I held her like I was going to lose her, but I knew that wasn't the case. I couldn't believe what I was saying or doing, and although my heart was breaking at the thought of her leaving, I felt a warmth inside knowing she might finally find a piece of happiness – a real piece. "I love you, Vivi. Now go and catch up to her. You can drive the car to the station; we'll go pick it up later."

She nodded as she broke from my embrace. She ran over to Will and wrapped her arms around him as he took her in a large bear hug, kissing her cheek. "Be safe, Vivi."

"I love you both," she cried as I handed her a set of keys for the Buick. She picked up her suitcase and headed for the front door. We watched as she took one last glance before catching my eye, "Nathan?"

"Yes?"

"Thank you," she said as she gave me the biggest smile I'd seen on her face in years.

Once she closed the door behind her, I felt myself become overwhelmed with emotion and began to wipe away the tears that streamed down my face. I took the handkerchief I had out of my pocket and wiped my eyes.

"I'm proud of you," Will said as he came over and wrapped his arms around me before he kissed me on the cheek.

"I'm going to miss her."

"So will I, but this was the right decision."

"I know. She wouldn't have been happy here. Now she has the chance to really be free... well, as free as she can be," I replied. They may still not be able to walk down the street holding hands, or kiss in public, or get married, but they'd be liberated in their own way. No fake husbands, no overbearing parents, no more lying. They were leaving to be rid of the stress their lives here brought, and I couldn't be more thrilled for them. I just prayed they stayed safe. I had solace knowing that if things didn't go quite as they expected, and they needed to come home for any reason, Vivian knew our door was always open. After all, they're family no matter what.

"Did I ever tell you how much I love you?" Will asked, still holding me in his embrace. "Now, what are we to do with the girls gone? We've got the whole house to ourselves."

I turned to him and smiled coyly. As I slid my hands around his waist, I placed a kiss on his lips, "I think I have a few ideas."

ABOUT THE AUTHOR

Cheyenne Isles holds her BFA in Theatrical Production with a Minor in Acting/Dance Studies. She discovered her passion for storytelling at a young age and has been putting pen to paper ever since. She currently resides in Ontario with her wife and two little boys. You can visit her online at www.cheyenneisles.ca.

9 781738 060405